FLY AWAY TO ZION

PETER RIZZOLO

Create Space, a division of Amazon Publishing

Cover design by Phil Daquila

First Edition August 2017

Also by PETER RIZZOLO
Novels
THIS THING CALLED LOVE

FORBIDDEN HARVEST

JUDGING LAURA

To the many dedicated and outstanding teachers in the fields of medicine and liberal studies, who through their skills and commitment to excellence have enriched my life and work.

ACKNOWLEDGEMENTS

I want to thank John Kessel, Professor of creative writing in the English department at North Carolina State University, in whose writing class I began this work. He and my classmates were extremely helpful.

I also want to thank the members of my writing group, who helped me work through my story from first drafts to its completion: Beverly Lemons, Carol Mann, Frank Stallone,
Charlotte Hoffman, Hal Glickman, Chuck Hauser, and Tom Shetley.

Chapter One

Smithfield Hospital

July 1992

The Emergency Department staff lounge was cluttered with disabled medical equipment, stacks of disposable paper supplies, a cabinet crammed with drug samples left by pharmaceutical reps, a fridge, a rumpled couch and, along one wall, a row of metal lockers. A halogen floor lamp in a far corner, dimmed to medium intensity, was the room's only source of light.

Steven Johnson, one of Smithfield Hospital's spanking new interns, a steaming cup of black coffee in one hand, sat at a table studying a dog-eared Merck Manual. He had hurriedly donned a fresh scrub suit. Normally curly and unruly, his sand-colored hair, still wet from a quick shower, was brushed straight back. His prominent cheekbones, jaw-line and fair skin revealed a hint of Viking ancestry.

He struggled with the urge to close his eyes. Fatigue and nagging anxiety about the second month of his two-month emergency room rotation made it nearly impossible to concentrate.

He chose a rotating internship rather than going directly into a residency program after medical school. He had not decided which specialty he wanted. Family medicine and pediatrics were the specialties that most interested Steven. Smithfield Hospital was a good choice; it was noted for excellent programs in both Family Medicine and Pediatrics.

Steven was going to need outstanding evaluations to beat the stiff competition from his fellow interns and applicants from other hospitals. Every word in his evaluations would be scrutinized by the residency admissions committee for hidden messages that this particular young man might *not* be destined for greatness.

The night before, he had admitted a middle-aged man with chest pain, a thirty-year-old woman with a hot gallbladder, an eighty-year-old gentleman who couldn't urinate, and a truck driver with shortness of breath and coughing up blood.

He had learned from his initial encounters with attending physicians that unless patients admitted during the night were not likely to live to see the day, their personal physicians were usually content to defer seeing them until morning. In those instances, they relied on the intern's clinical assessment and the supervising resident's expertise. Often, however, one or another of the attendings, would call him after making rounds, taking issue with something he had or had not done regarding his handling of the admission, or pointing out some obscure finding he had missed.

To Steven it seemed preposterous that he was required to cover the medical service when he hadn't yet rotated through internal medicine and wasn't familiar with the quirks of the some attending physicians or the rigidity of the nursing routines.

He jumped when a nurse walked behind him and placed her hand on his shoulder. His coffee cup slipped from his hand, drenched a box of day-old doughnuts and floated the soggy Merck Manual onto his lap.

He stood, pulling his soaked scrubs from his thighs.

"Sorry, Dr. Johnson."

Miss Knight, the charge nurse, dumped the doughnut box into a wastebasket and blotted the coffee with a wad of paper towels.

He walked gingerly toward his locker to retrieve a clean set of scrubs.

She started toward the door and turned. "You've got a forearm laceration in exam room two. Omar's irrigating the wound. You might want an X-ray," she suggested. "And there's a preacher at the reception desk in the waiting area. He's demanding to see you immediately. You saw him a couple of weeks ago. I ordered his chart."

Steven stepped into the dazzling fluorescent-lighted ER. At a cluttered central work area bordered on three sides by a waist-high counter, the doctors and nurses did their charting, collected their mail, and hunkered over computers lined up along the countertop.

Along a far wall, several small curtained-off patient exam areas were arranged in tandem. Opposite the nurses' station were four large rooms used for trauma or patients requiring extensive care. Behind the work area were floor-to-ceiling cabinets, boxes of supplies, several wheeled stretchers and crash carts painted fire-engine red.

As Steven approached the nurses' station, Martha Knight looked up from her charting, handed him the patient's record, flashed her dimpled smile and pointed in the direction of exam room one. He resented her smile, her energy, and her damn certainty about everything. She had given him a dismal evaluation after the first month of his ER rotation. "Always runs behind, does not project professional image, and is often hesitant to make decisions." She could just as easily have said, "Thorough, meticulous, does not talk down to his patients, realizes his inexperience, and appropriately seeks the opinion of others." Fortunately, as a mid-course evaluation it wouldn't be part of his permanent record. He was confident he could pick up his efficiency as he became more accustomed to ER routines and procedures.

The chief surgery resident assigned to the ER for July and August was Dr. David Beck, who the interns referred to as, 'Beck-n-forth,' because of the way he paced when he was mulling over a clinical problem or dressing down an intern. Steven recalled his meeting with Beck in the staff lounge the first day of his ER rotation. Beck wore a freshly starched white coat, dress shirt and tie. He paced with his hands clasped behind his back, when he wasn't checking his watch.

"For the next two months, I'm assigned to the ER," Beck said. "Most ER encounters are a waste of my time. If you beep me, have your ducks in a row. Complete history and physical, all relevant labs and diagnostic studies. I have no tolerance for screw-ups. I am not a hand-holder. I'm not your big brother. I focus primarily on the negative." He forced a smiled.

Is he putting me on? Does he have a sense of humor? George C. Scott's rendition of General Patton...of course. Steven stood erect. “Yes, Dave,” Steven said. “I can’t wait to encounter the enemy.”

Beck stopped pacing. He jabbed his index finger in Steven’s direction. “Don’t be a wiseass, Johnson. I’m talking about incompetence. And you will address me as ‘Dr. Beck.’”

Also making Steven’s short list of *personae non-grata,* was his ER attending for the month of July, Dr. Parton, who put in twelve-hour shifts and wasn’t very interested in teaching. He had such infrequent contact with Steven that in his evaluation of Stevens’ performance, he had relied almost entirely on input from the charge nurse.

Still, there was much he liked about those early weeks of his internship. He loved his present ER attending, Dr. Murphy. She was medically sharp, enjoyed teaching and had a great sense of humor. Definitely fun to work with. If she weren’t his boss, he’d probably have already asked her out for a beer or two, maybe take in a show in Princeton.

At Smithfield, the opportunities to connect with the type of woman he’d like to hang out with were not good. The staff nurses were either married or too old, the student nurses too young, and most of the female attending physicians more than a little austere. Dr. Murphy fell into the older, single, but definitely interesting category.

Steven entered an exam room where a burly man wearing a hardhat sat at a table, a tray of instruments nearby. Omar Diack, an emergency room nurse, was using a bulb syringe to irrigate the wound with sterile saline.

The patient asked Omar, "You from Jamaica?

"Yes, man. How could you tell?" Omar said, pretending surprise.

"I work with a guy who talks just like you."

Steven sat at the man's side. He introduced himself as he slipped on safety glasses and sterile gloves. He examined the wound. The edges of the four-inch laceration were jagged and grayish blue. He would have to cut away the crushed margins before closing the wound, but first he would have to rule out nerve or tendon damage.

"How'd it happen?" He sponged the wound, exposing subcutaneous tissue and muscle. As he probed, a shaft of blood splattered onto Steven's glasses. Omar tried unsuccessfully to conceal a smile, as he covered the arterial bleeder with a sponge. Steven went to the sink to wash his glasses.

What happened?" Steven asked again, as he slipped on a clean pair of gloves.

"Some idiot was hoisting an I-beam. It swung round. Caught me in the arm. This is nothing. I was lucky it didn't take off my head. You should a seen the blood shoot out. I thought the guy working the crane was gonna have a heart attack."

Steven recalled a summer job during college when he had worked in a lumberyard assembling shipping crates. By quitting time, he was exhausted, but it had been satisfying to look at the massive pile of crates he had assembled through the day.

"You enjoy working outside?" Steven asked.

"Spring and fall's great. But it's boiling hot in summer, and I freeze my ass off in winter."

Miss Knight leaned into the room. Steven was hunched over the man's arm, a scalpel in one hand and forceps in the other as he cut away dead tissue. Omar had left.

"That preacher I told you about. His name's Jones, Reverend Jones. You saw him two weeks ago. You thought he was depressed. You gave him a prescription for Prozac."

Steven, himself six feet tall, had felt small next to the preacher. “Yes. I remember him. A gentle giant." Steven recalled him vividly. The preacher’s wife had died after a long struggle with breast cancer. It was the first anniversary of her death. The man couldn’t concentrate, couldn’t sleep or muster the energy to prepare his sermons. His face was mask-like. Although he denied being suicidal, he presented a classic picture of clinical depression. Steven had considered admitting him.

“I called Psych,” Steven said. “The resident suggested I start him on an antidepressant and have him come to the psych clinic in a week.”

Several people were seated in the waiting room. A receptionist sat at a counter next to double doors that led to the patient treatment area. She filed her nails as she cradled a phone in the crook of her neck. A tall, elderly black man in a dark suit, white shirt and a black tie stood before her. His three-hundred angry pounds seemed not to impress her. She recalled his previous visit to the ER. She covered the mouthpiece.

“Reverend Jones, like I said already, you have to wait your turn.”

The preacher’s face was covered with perspiration. He turned and looked frantically from person to person.

“You see him? You see him settin’ there in the corner?” the preacher asked.

People turned to look where he pointed. In the corner was a small table with a lamp and magazines.

“He’s trying to get me! You watch out, folks. He’s got lots of tricks...lots of friends...you can’t tell them from the rest!” The preacher turned from side to side, looking frantically about the room, then back at the far corner. "Oh, Lord, he's gone. Where'd he go? Lord, where did he go?"

A mother, startled by his bizarre behavior, gathered up her child, clutching the toddler to her breast. Other patients sat wide-eyed, silent.

The receptionist picked up the phone. She said with her hand cupped over the mouthpiece, "Miss Knight, you'd better call security. The preacher's ready to flip."

Reverend Jones headed toward the treatment area.

"Hey! You can't go back there!" the receptionist shouted, as he barged through the doors.

He collided with Dr. Murphy, sending her sprawling. He scanned the area, spotted Steven through the open exam room door, and rushed toward the room. Omar helped Dr. Murphy to her feet, and then took off after the preacher, who turned, grasped a wheelchair and pushed it into Omar's path. Miss Knight saw the preacher headed toward the exam room. She ran ahead of him and entered the room, but before she could close the door behind her, Preacher Jones grabbed her from behind. He wrapped his forearm around her neck, and pushed her toward the exam table. Omar and a male attendant entered the room behind them.

"Back off, you hear!" He tightened his arm around her neck, lifting her off her feet. Miss Knight struggled to pull his arm from her throat. She gasped for air.

"My God, you're choking her. Let go!" Steven snapped.

Reverend Jones released his hold on the nurse. She slumped to the floor, clutching her neck.

With a sweep of his arm, the preacher knocked the startled construction worker from the stool.

"What the hell?" the man shouted. He lay on the floor grimacing in pain, as he clutched his injured arm.

A surgical tray was situated between the preacher and Steven. Reverend Jones grabbed a pair of scissors. "You're the devil himself. You gave me poison. I know what to do to blue-eyed devils!"

Steven stared at the scissors. The man's pupils were widely dilated. He must be on drugs: speed, maybe crack, Steven thought. He wanted to place the scalpel he held in his right hand on the surgical tray, but he didn't dare move. He must remain calm. Where the hell was security?

"Reverend Jones, please put that down. I want to help you!"

The preacher's eyes narrowed. He moved forward. The construction worker, sprawled on the floor behind the preacher, got to his knees and lunged, sending the preacher over the surgical tray and into Steven. They fell to the floor, Reverend Jones landing on top of Steven, who struggled to get out from under him. Two guards rushed into the room and grabbed the preacher from behind. They were able to roll him onto his back, pinning his arms and shoulders to the floor. The construction worker sat on Jones' legs. Wild-eyed, the preacher tried desperately to free himself. Suddenly he stopped struggling and closed his eyes.

The scalpel Steven had been holding was lodged in Reverend Jones' neck. He must have fallen onto the blade as he collided with Steven. The blade handle pulsated with each heartbeat. An expanding pool of blood formed a crimson halo about the preacher's head.

Steven knelt at the preacher's side. He raised his hand as though about to remove the scalpel. He hesitated. He turned as

Murphy rushed into the room. She approached the preacher. Dr. Beck entered and nudged Steven aside.

"The scalpel probably penetrated his jugular," Murphy said. "We don't dare touch it. We don't want to risk severing the jugular or damaging the carotid."

The doctors hoisted him onto the table. The nurses quickly bared his chest and attached EKG electrodes. They applied a blood pressure cuff and an oxygen monitor.

"Start an IV with an 18-gauge needle, and type and cross-match for eight units!" Dr. Beck shouted. "Rapid infuse o-neg for now."

Dr. Murphy gowned and gloved as Omar broke out a surgical tray. She picked up a scalpel and forceps. Dr. Beck applied sterile towels to the man's neck and chest.

"I've got to clamp the jugular or he's going to bleed out," Murphy said. Steven was amazed how calm she remained. His insides churned like boiling water.

The construction worker pressed against Dr. Murphy, looking over her shoulder as she made a vertical incision in the man's neck, close to and parallel to the stab wound. Blood welled up from the site.

"Geez How can you see what you're doin'?" the construction worker asked.

"I can't get a blood pressure, and the pulse is too rapid to count," a nurse reported.

"Hey," the construction worker shouted, "what about me?" A length of suture with an attached needle hung from his forearm. Blood oozed from the partially closed laceration.

"Someone please take this man to another exam room," Dr. Murphy snapped.

An attendant led him from the room.

Dr. Murphy glanced at the heart monitor. "Ventricular tachycardia. Charge the defibrillator to 200."

Beck reached for the paddles and applied them to the man's chest. "Stand back!" The shock didn't change the abnormal heart rhythm. "Charge to 300." After the second shock, the Preacher's heart beat reverted to normal.

"O_2 sat's down to 81!" Omar shouted.

"Beck, intubate him. Johnson, you assist me."

My God, the man's going to die, Steven thought. Why was this happening? What have I done? He removed his soiled gloves and reached for a sterile pair.

"Dr. Johnson, hurry for Godsakes. I need suction!"

Steven moved alongside the attending and began suctioning. He noticed tiny bubbles in the wound. Could the blade have damaged the man's trachea? He was about to say something when Dr. Murphy spoke up.

"Air bubbles," she said in almost a whisper. "The scalpel must've nicked the lung."

Steven strained to recall the complicated anatomy of the neck. Yes, of course, the apex of the lung extended above the level of the first rib. The tip of the blade could have punctured the lung; it is only protected by soft tissue.

Dr. Beck had quickly and skillfully inserted an endotracheal tube. A nurse hooked it to oxygen. Beck grabbed a stethoscope and listened to the preacher's chest.

"No breath sounds on the right. He needs a chest tube!"

"Alert the OR and thoracic surgery," Dr. Murphy said. "I can't control the bleeding from the neck."

It took just moments for Beck to make an incision in the side of the man's chest and insert a tube. A nurse connected the tube to water bottles and suction.

Steven watched as they wheeled the preacher toward the doors of the exam room. The man hadn't been overtly psychotic when Steven first saw him. He wasn't delusional, paranoid or hallucinating. What had happened in the interim? Had Steven missed something?

Dr. Beck turned to face Steven. "Nice work, Johnson. Stab a patient in the neck. Puncture his lung. Better call risk management. They're gonna love this."

Chapter Two

At the emergency room workstation, Mrs. Cantor, a middle-aged, attractive black woman with a no-nonsense look about her, spoke on the phone. Seated next to her, Steven Johnson studied volume I of the preacher's hospital chart. Dr. Murphy was alongside Steven, looking through volume II, the more recent part of the preacher's record. Volume II was all that had been available at the time Steven had seen the man two weeks prior to that.

"There's no flag here indicating he had a separate outpatient psych record," Johnson said.

"Ditto for volume II," Murphy said. "I see he's been to the medicine clinic. Any mention of his psychiatric history in the old record? There's none here."

Steven's face flushed. He had been poring over pages of old progress-notes, handwritten, before the hospital had begun to employ transcriptionists. He had found only one, barely legible, cryptic entry by a medicine resident, who stated he was referring Reverend Jones to the psych clinic. Johnson opened the chart to the entry. He pointed to the reference. Dr. Murphey leaned over and studied the note.

Mrs. Cantor cupped the phone mouthpiece. "Dr. Murphy, the medical director's secretary is on the phone. Dr. Ewing wants you and Dr. Johnson to meet with him in his office at six sharp. Said it was urgent."

"Did she say what it's about?"

"No."

"Tell her we'll be there." Dr. Murphy rolled over a stool and sat next to Steven. "Damnit, Steven, you should have documented your conversation with the psych resident. See if he'll add a note to the chart saying you conferred with him."

"I've already paged him."

The squawk box announced a motor vehicle accident was on the way. Three injured; one dead. A child thrown from one of the cars had incurred severe head and possible neck trauma.

Omar entered the work area.

"Omar," Dr. Murphy said, "Make sure we have enough rooms ready." She turned to the secretary. "Page surgery. Call pedes and anesthesia." She asked Omar, "How's Martha doing?"

"Still pretty shook. But other than a bruised neck, she's okay. Can I give her ten of Valium?" Omar asked.

Dr. Murphy shook her head. "Steven, let's you and I and Dr. Beck meet in my office at five. We need to talk." She stood. "I'm going to check on Martha."

The secretary handed Johnson the phone. "It's the psych resident, Dr. Costello. He said you paged him." She handed the phone to Steven.

"Hi Mark. Remember the preacher I called you about a couple of weeks ago?"

"Sure. I told you to set him up with an outpatient appointment in the psych clinic. You never told me he'd been seen in psych before."

"I didn't know at the time. All I had was a new folder that only covered the past year. They couldn't locate his old record. You suggested I start him on Prozac."

"We discussed medication. But I would never suggest you start him on anything. Not without seeing him first."

"What?" Steven asked in disbelief.

"Listen, Johnson, you never told me you didn't have his complete medical record. You goofed. Don't try to pass the buck to me."

Steven was stunned. He was certain he told Mark he only had volume II of the preacher's record. He had never experienced such a flagrant lie from a medical colleague. He didn't know what to say. "Mark, I'm not trying to shift blame. I just want to establish that I sought the advice of a psychiatrist."

"I didn't tell you to start him on Prozac! End of discussion." He hung up.

Steven replaced the handset in its cradle. Mark Costello had come to the ER to consult on several of Steven's patients. He was always helpful. A decent guy. Damnit, it didn't make any sense. It was a mistake to have talked with him over the phone. And how had Mark learned so soon about what had happened to Reverend Jones?

Omar handed Steven a chart. "There's a twelve-year-old girl in two. Belly pain for twenty-four hours. Nausea, vomiting, low-grade fever...looks like the same old intestinal virus we've been seeing all week. Mother's ticked about the wait."

As Steven walked to exam room two, he wondered how Reverend Jones was doing in surgery. Maybe no news was good news. Was Costello right? Had he goofed? Was he trying to pass the blame onto someone else?

Just weeks into his internship, he was already being called to the principal's office. What else could Ewing want to see him about other than the debacle with Reverend Jones? The muscles along Steven's spine tightened. Beads of perspiration gathered on his brow. He felt guilty worrying about his own backside as Reverend Jones struggled for his life. He prayed.... dear God, don't let the man die.

Exam room two was pretty much like any other. A wheeled stretcher in the center of the room, a small sink, excessively bright fluorescent lighting, the smell of disinfectant.

The girl, eyes red-rimmed, lay supine, both hands covering her abdomen, as though to protect it from anyone threatening to examine her. The girl's mother glared at Steven as he approached the gurney. He guessed her to be in her early forties, tailored suit, pale blue eyes, blondish-brown hair pulled back in a bun, no makeup.

"Hello. I'm Dr. Johnson. Sorry for the wait."

"I'm sure you are," she said, her eyebrows raised, her lips a straight line.

He smiled at the girl, who looked nothing like her mother. Olive complexion, black hair, brown eyes, frightened.

"Hello, Maria. Can you tell me when you first felt sick?"

"For Godsakes, I just gave the nurse all that information," her mother said.

"It's okay, Mother," Maria said. "It started yesterday morning. Crampy---not like a real pain. I thought that maybe my period was coming. It's due around now."

"Where did it hurt?" Steven asked.

"Right here," she pointed to her mid-abdomen. "My stomach was queasy. I threw up. That never happens with my period."

"I thought it was a virus," her mother added. "She said a bunch of kids at school were out sick. Her temp was only 99.6. I called her pediatrician. He said to give her clear liquids, to call if her temperature went any higher or the pain got worse."

"What happened then?" Steven asked.

"The cramps eased off," Maria said.

"This morning she was hungry. Ate a good breakfast, but then the pain and vomiting started up again."

"What was that like?" Steven asked the girl.

"It wasn't crampy like the day before. More like a toothache. It won't let up."

Her brow was knitted, her lips trembled. Her eyes glistened. She glanced at her mother, who did not make a move to comfort her daughter. There was an undercurrent of tension between mother and daughter that Steven did not yet understand. The girl placed her hand over her mother's as though to soothe her. Was there a man in the home, he wondered?

"Anyone else in the household been sick? You or your husband?" Steven asked.

"She's my only child. I've been fine. Her father and I are divorced."

Maria looked at her mother as though about to speak. Her mother's eyes narrowed. The girl remained silent.

So much for just another intestinal virus. He studied Maria's chart, trying to determine where to go next. Could she be pregnant? She was only twelve, but she was already having her period. He'd never done a pelvic on a twelve-year-old.

"My daughter's in pain. Can't you give her something?"

"I don't want any shots!" Maria said.

"For now, I have to determine what's causing her pain. If we mask the pain with medication, it will only complicate matters. I'm sorry, Maria..."

"It's okay. It's not so bad that I can't stand it."

Steven warmed his stethoscope by rubbing it against his palm. He lowered the abdominal drape to her lower abdomen. He placed his stethoscope on Maria's abdomen, listened for a few seconds then asked her to draw up her knees and to imagine her belly was a giant marshmallow. She smiled. Her mother watched intently, as he gently probed her abdomen. The girl tensed her muscles in response to pressure. He would most likely have to do a pelvic exam. He could repeat the abdominal exam at that time. He would have to probe deeper to rule out the presence of a mass, localized or rebound tenderness.

"Tell me where it hurts when I press," he said as he palpated. "Does it hurt here?" He applied pressure to the right side of her lower abdomen.

"Sort of hurts all over. A little more right here." She pointed to her mid-lower abdomen. Her mother removed a cell phone from her purse and went across the room. She talked into the phone with her back to Steven.

"Do you have a boyfriend, Maria?" Steven asked quietly.

Maria blushed. "I have lunch sometimes with Timmy O'Connor. He's just a friend-friend. Not like a real boyfriend."

Her mother tucked the phone into her purse. She walked across the room and stood alongside her daughter.

"Mrs. Goodman, would you mind stepping out for a few moments? I'd like to talk privately with Maria."

"I certainly do mind! You can ask anything you like. My daughter and I have no secrets."

Steven recalled a line from Macbeth. Or was it Hamlet? *The lady doth protest too much, methinks.* "I'm glad to hear that." He looked at Maria. She rolled her eyes.

"For now, Maria, you can't have anything to eat or drink. I'm going to start you on intravenous fluids."

"I don't like needles," Maria said.

"You'll hardly feel it. I promise." He picked up her chart. "Excuse me. I'll be back in a few minutes."

Omar Diack was at the desk at the nurses' station. He looked up as Steven approached.

"What do you think? Omar asked.

"Could end up being viral but there's more serious stuff we have to rule our first. Keep her NPO. Start an IV of Ringers lactate and send off a complete blood count, electrolytes, and a clean-catch urine. And get a urine pregnancy test."

"Whoa. What did her mother say about that?"

"I didn't tell her."

Steven was surprised to see Dr. Beck approach the nurses' station. He was still wearing an OR cap and shoe covers. He was on the phone. Dr. Beck placed his hand over the mouthpiece.

"Hey, Johnson, I just got a call from recovery. Bad news. Reverend Jones crashed soon after he arrived there."

Steven was barely able to speak. "What do you suppose happened? A post-operative bleed?"

"He was stable when he left the OR. They believe he had a massive myocardial infarction. Nothing they could do to save him." Steven sank onto a chair, his head lowered, staring at the floor. He could see Reverend Jones towering over him with a pair of surgical scissors raised high over his head. But what happened next was a blur. Could he have instinctively lunged the scalpel blade into the man's neck? When he looked up, Dr. Beck had hung up the phone and was reviewing Maria's chart. Steven really wasn't ready to present the patient to him. Her labs were pending, his exam incomplete.

"Any luck contacting Jones' family?" Beck asked.

"Wife's dead," Omar said. "I found his son's business card in Jones' wallet. Name's Nathan Jones---lives in New Haven. He's flying in tonight...should arrive around eight."

"I know you're off tonight," Beck said to Steven, "but you'd better hang around. Should have an attending there, too."

"Of course," Steven said. He hoped Murphy would agree to be present, not one of the evening shift attendings, who would know nothing of what had happened.

"How about this girl? You think she has viral gastroenteritis?"

"Well, that's in the differential. The pain hasn't localized; maybe slightly more prominent in the midline. Appendicitis obviously. Urinary tract infection's a possibility; an ovarian problem or maybe even pregnancy. Then again the fever may be a red herring."

"You do a rectal?" Beck asked.

"I thought I might have to do a pelvic exam, so I decided to hold off on the rectal."

"She sexually active?"

"I didn't ask her directly. Her mother was there."

"I'd better take a quick look at her now, before I get tied up in surgery."

"I haven't presented her to my medical attending."

Steven never called for a surgical consult before checking with his ER attending unless it was an urgent situation or an obvious surgical problem. But Beck was already headed for the exam room. Steven rushed to catch up with him.

They entered the girl's room. A nurse's aide was holding an emesis basin against Maria's cheek, supporting Maria with her arm.

"Hello, Mrs. Goodman, I'm Dr. Beck, surgical resident. Dr. Johnson's filled me in on the history. I'd like to examine Maria."

Mrs. Goodman looked startled. Steven hadn't told her he was asking a surgeon to see Maria; he hadn't made up his mind what was going on. Actually, he might have decided to consult with a gynecologist rather than a general surgeon.

"It's her appendix, isn't it?" her mother said.

Maria was wide-eyed. "Am I going to need an operation?"

Without bothering to answer her question, Dr. Beck removed the abdominal drape and began to examine her. He kept pressure on her belly and pressed more deeply each time she exhaled. She winced no matter where he probed, but jumped when he probed the lower mid-abdomen.

Steven was startled at how deeply Beck was probing. What if it's an ectopic pregnancy? Or an ovarian cyst? It might rupture!

When Beck released the pressure on her abdomen, she again reacted. He turned to Steven.

"You didn't mention there was rebound tenderness?"

Steven didn't know what to say. He had examined her more gently than Beck. He had intended to re-examine her after her labs were back; especially the pregnancy test. But he didn't want to mention the pregnancy test since he hadn't discussed it with Maria or Mrs. Goodman.

"I did notice more tenderness in the midline," Steven said. "That's why I was concerned about a bladder infection or some other pelvic problem."

Beck walked to a wall-mounted glove dispenser. He slipped a glove onto his right hand. "I need to do a rectal exam, Mrs. Goodman."

Maria raised her head. She looked from Dr. Beck to her mother. Her mother grasped her hand.

"Is this absolutely necessary, Dr. Beck?"

"Yes," he said. "It may be her appendix. The information we gain from a rectal exam is very helpful."

He asked Maria to turn onto her side and draw one knee to her chest.

Steven grasped Maria's other hand. "Concentrate on your breathing," Steven said. "In and out, in and out."

When Dr. Beck probed deeply she cried out in pain.

After completing the rectal exam, Dr. Beck headed for the exam room door, stopped and turned. "One more question Mrs. Goodman. Is your daughter sexually active?"

"What kind of question is that? My God, she's only twelve."

"No! I'm not," Maria said in a tremulous voice.

"Good. In that case, you don't have to worry about the pregnancy test being positive," Dr. Beck said as he left the room.

"Maria, I'm sorry," Steven said. "I didn't want to ask in front of your mother."

Maria had rolled onto her back. She drew her knees to her chest.

"I don't want him to operate on me. He's too rough."

"Let's not jump the gun. We're not certain you need an operation." He adjusted her IV. "I'll stop back as soon as the lab tests are back."

Mrs. Goodman's attitude changed from anger to fear. She said in a tremulous voice, "Let me know about the pregnancy test as soon as you hear."

"Mother!" Maria pleaded.

"Steven," Dr. Murphy said, "Dr. Beck, you and I and Omar have to huddle sometime this afternoon. I just came from the Medical Director's office. Ewing was going over the Reverend's chart. He was furious about you treating him without consulting the complete medical record. He said legally we don't have a leg to stand on."

"But we do it all the time."

"God almighty!" Dr. Murphy said. "You say that and he'll go into orbit."

Steven noticed the smug expression on Beck's face. Beck's actually enjoying this, Steven thought. Why? Why wasn't he supportive?

"It's not Dr. Johnson's day," Dr. Beck said. "He was just about to send a young girl with acute appendicitis home. Thought it was a virus."

"That's not true! Besides, you insisted on seeing her before I'd completed my workup."

"Her labs are back." Beck handed a computer printout to Steven. "What do you think now?"

Steven read the reports aloud for Dr. Murphy's benefit. "White count's up. It's 12K. Left shift. The urine's concentrated; heavy ketones, a few white cells, but otherwise okay. The pregnancy test was negative."

Dr. Murphy joined in. "What else might it be?"

"It's a pretty big differential," Steven said. "But the high white count, left shift and rebound tenderness, narrow it down to an inflammatory process. Probably bacterial. Acute appendicitis is the biggest concern. But the midline tenderness isn't typical."

"And if she's sexually active?" Murphy asked.

"Inflammation of the uterus from venereal disease could cause this picture," Steven said. "That would explain her midline tenderness. But she denies being sexually active. And she hasn't had a vaginal discharge."

"You can't depend on that," Murphy said.

"Her rectal exam wasn't helpful," Beck said. "She was diffusely tender. I noticed the hymen was intact when I did the exam. That makes pelvic infection from venereal disease pretty unlikely."

"Could be a twisted ovarian cyst," Murphy said. "Let's get a pelvic ultrasound."

"Only if we can get it done stat," Beck said. "Because either way, she has a surgical belly. And I'm still betting it's her appendix." He opened a file drawer and removed an operative permit.

"I'll get her mother to sign this." He headed for the girl's room.

"I'd like to scrub," Steven said to Dr. Murphy.

"No, we need you here. You'll be on your surgical rotation soon enough." She handed him a chart. "There's an eleven-year-old boy in the cast room with a knee injury. Give me a call after you've seen him."

Steven's head was in a swirl. First Reverend Jones and now Maria. He still wasn't convinced it was her appendix, but the consequences of having the appendix rupture were too grave to justify taking too long to make the diagnosis. And he knew it was better in some instances to operate on a normal appendix than to delay surgery and have an inflamed appendix rupture. Pus escaping from a ruptured appendix could cause a pelvic abscess, and in a young girl, could even lead to problems with childbearing. God almighty, he thought, how easy it is to mess up even as you're trying to do your very best.

He stared at the boy's chart. He had injured his knee in gym class. That shouldn't be too tough. His thoughts drifted back to

Reverend Jones. How was he going to explain to the preacher's son what had happened?

Steven entered the cast room. A young man in a green sweatshirt and gray gym pants was standing beside a chubby black boy in a wheelchair. Across the man's chest were the words: Lincoln Middle School.

"Hi, I'm Dr. Johnson. You must be Jason."

"Hi," the boy said.

Steven turned to the man standing beside Jason. He extended his hand.

"I'm his gym teacher," the man said. He shook Steven's hand. "We were playing a game of murder-ball. Jason, in trying to avoid the ball, lost his balance and fell. He grabbed his left knee. He couldn't get up. I helped him to his feet, but he couldn't put any weight on it. I had to carry him to my car." He winked. "That was no easy job."

"Is it hurting now?" Steven asked the boy.

"Just when I move my leg."

Steven examined the boy's knee. There was no swelling or discoloration. He probed the joint for tenderness. He gently moved the knee through a range of motion, and then carefully drew the lower leg toward him to check for internal ligament damage. The boy winced, but the ligament appeared to be intact. He grasped the boy's lower thigh just above the knee.

"Please, don't . . ."

"Sorry, Jason," Steven said. "We're going to X-ray your knee. I'll be back as soon as the films are ready. In the meantime, I'll have the nurse put some ice on that."

At the nurses' workstation Dr. Murphy and Steven stood before a lighted view box looking at X-rays of the boy's knee. The knee had been X-rayed from front-to-back, and also a side view.

"Any signs of ligament or cartilage injury on your physical exam?" Murphy asked.

"Went through the usual maneuvers. No abnormal motion or locking. But he did experience pain when I stressed the anterior cruciate," Steven said.

She leaned in closer to the view box. "Nothing unusual here."

"So, should I send him out with pain meds, crutches and follow-up with rehab?"

"Chances are that's all Jason'll need. But I wouldn't send him home, not just yet."

The last thing Steven needed was to have anything else go wrong. Maybe there was some subtle change on the films. He picked up a magnifying glass and held it to the X-ray images. He couldn't detect any abnormalities.

"Referred pain," she said. "You are familiar with the phenomenon of referred pain?"

"Sure, when there are common sensory pathways the brain can be tricked."

"So?"

"Hip pain can be referred to the knee," Steven said. "But the pain started when he twisted his knee, and he definitely experienced pain when I stressed his cruciate ligament."

"If you pulled hard enough you could have stressed his hip. Anyway, let's assume the pain is coming from his hip. What's in your differential?"

Steven was almost certain he hadn't pulled that hard on Jason's knee, but she was right; he had to consider hip pathology.

“Rheumatoid arthritis is seen in children. But there was no previous episode or family history."

“And the onset with rheumatoid isn’t usually this dramatic. What else?” she asked.

Steven could picture his anatomy text description of the epiphysis, a cap-like ledge of bone that covers the end of the femur. It was where bone growth occurs. He knew that until maturity, it was a weak spot. A forceful shearing motion could displace it.

“He’s the right sex and age for slipped femoral epiphysis,” Steven said. “But it wasn’t much of a trauma.”

Dr. Murphy smiled and nodded, as though in agreement, but added, “The trauma can be minimal. And he’s obese, another risk factor. We need to X-ray both hips.”

Steven knew that there was a possibility of cutting off the blood supply to the end of the hipbone when the epiphysis dislocated. God, how much had they moved his hip when they did the knee films? If it were a hip problem, it would be essential to totally immobilize the hip until they were sure of the diagnosis. He’d better accompany Jason to X-ray.

Referred pain had crossed his mind. But the pain on stressing the cruciate ligament had caused him to dismiss the thought. Had the news of the preacher’s death, and all the uncertainty around Maria’s diagnosis, primed him to minimize the boy’s knee injury? As a medical student, he was at times criticized for missing the obvious in his effort to come up with some exotic explanation of symptoms. One of his professors often said, “If something looks like a horse and smells like a horse, and acts like a horse, it’s probably a horse.” That was good advice. But still, there are zebras out there, and today he had seen his share.

Steven was busy repairing a chin laceration when Dr. Murphy came into the exam room. She looked over his shoulder as he placed the last stitch.

"Nice job, Dr. Johnson. You check his immunization status?"

"He's fine. He had a DT booster nine months ago."

"Good. Jason's hip films should be ready. Let's check them as soon as you're finished."

Dr. Murphy and Steven carefully compared the X-ray films of Jason's left and right hip. They were relieved to find that there was no evidence of dislocation of the left hip epiphysis.

Steven was impressed by Murphy's quiet competence. She was the youngest ER attending, having joined the hospital staff right out of residency. She couldn't be more than three or four years older than Steven. Brainy, a sense of humor, the girl-next-door kind of good looks. He was definitely interested.

"Based on these films," she said, "it's probably just a sprained knee. Be sure to explain carefully in your note why you ordered the hip films. Otherwise the insurance company won't pay for them."

Steven was relieved. He was eager to tell Jason that his hip was okay, but he was still concerned about the possibility of a partial tear of the cruciate ligament. He asked Murphy if he should refer the boy to orthopedics for endoscopic examination of the knee.

"I agree. Nice job managing the boy, Steven."

Thank God for Jason. At least something went well today, Steven thought.

Chapter Three

Steven and Dr. Murphy were seated on a couch in Dr. Ewing's office on the fifth floor of the hospital's administrative wing. Ewing's knitted brow and grim expression conveyed the unspoken message, *I don't have time for this nonsense.* Behind him two oversized windows admitted the mellow light of a lowering sun, a sharp contrast to the unsettling tension Steven felt as he glanced about the room. He was a lesser, dispensable part of a hospital constellation of powerful people, who could easily redirect Steven's career down paths he did not want to contemplate.

Off by himself in a corner of the room, Clyde Gordon, a young hospital attorney, sat at the edge of his seat. He looked at Steven with a blend of amusement and contempt. His bushy mustache, meant to give him a mature look, was actually comic. All he lacked, Steven observed, was a pair of oversized horn-rimmed glasses and a cigar to pass for a reincarnation of Groucho Marx. As frightened and concerned as Steven was about the events of the day, he had to fight a smile as he pictured a duck on a string dropping from the ceiling above Gordon's head.

Gordon had been one of an army of hospital administrative types who had spoken to the interns at orientation for new housestaff. He had talked about the hospital's growing number of malpractice suits. Steven couldn't recall much of what he had said except that he kept repeating the importance of documentation. If it's not in the record, you didn't do it. By the end of his talk he had the interns chant, doc-cu-ment...doc-cu-ment...doc-cu-ment!

By the way Clyde Gordon was looking at him, Steven was sure he was recalling that mantra and wondering how this supposedly bright intern could be so stupid. Ewing was the first to break the awkward silence.

"This meeting is strictly off the record. No notes and not a word of it to leave this room." He looked from person to person. "We may be facing a major malpractice suit. Clyde has reviewed the record and talked discreetly to a number of individuals. He's not only concerned about medical care that clearly did not meet hospital or community standards, but the more serious charge of deliberate patient abuse."

"That resulted in a man's death," Clyde added in somber tones.

"Abuse? Nonsense!" Dr. Murphy said. "Dr. Ewing, the man fell on the scalpel. He was threatening Dr. Johnson with a pair of surgical scissors."

"I was debriding a wound," Steven said, "when he forced his way into the exam room. Reverend Jones was out of control. He was about to attack me. I tried to calm him."

"Or was a paranoid patient protecting himself from someone brandishing a lethal weapon?" the attorney asked as he raked his mustache with the tips of his fingers.

Steven did not believe the attorney could possibly be serious.

"For Godsakes, Gordon, the man knocked me down," Dr. Murphy said. "Then he grabbed Miss Knight and practically choked her to death. He was out of control long before he saw Dr. Johnson."

"Admittedly the preacher was psychotic. He was hallucinating, probably delusional. But that was the direct result of Dr. Johnson's inept care," Gordon said.

The word "inept" was a barbed dart that struck Steven's chest so violently he gasped. The preacher had met all the usual criteria for clinical depression with the exception of suicidal intent. He had been sleepless for days, tearful, and unable to muster the energy to dress or prepare meals. In the absence of any other psychiatric history, starting an antidepressant would immediately help his sleep problem and, in a matter of a few days, reverse most of his other symptoms. He had administered the usual standard of medical care, based on the information available.

Perhaps Gordon was just playing devil's advocate, anticipating that the dead man's family would certainly be asking hard questions. Did he really expect anyone could construe the stabbing of Reverend Jones as anything but a tragic accident?

"It seems to me," Ewing said, "you're taking a rather extreme position, Gordon. You interviewed other persons who witnessed the event. What was their perspective?"

Gordon looked from person to person before responding. "I've spoken with Miss Knight, an ER supervising nurse, Omar Diack, a physician's assistant, the two security guards and Mr. Garcia, the patient in the exam room at that time. Their perspective is part of our predicament. Let me demonstrate." He stood and went behind Ewing's high-back chair. "Tell me what part of me you can see from where you're sitting."

They said in unison, "Your head."

"Exactly. The chair's the preacher, I'm Dr. Johnson. That was all the witnesses could see. No one could say they saw Dr. Johnson's hands, or the actual stabbing. We have only Steven's word that the man fell onto the scalpel."

"My God!" Steven shouted. "Do you believe I purposefully stabbed him?"

"No. I'm saying there's no way to verify your account," Gordon said. He returned to his seat.

"Okay, Gordon," Ewing said, "your point is well taken. But I'd like to move the discussion in another direction." Staring over their heads, he leaned back in his swivel chair. "Tell me, Dr. Johnson, you do realize that the Prozac you gave the preacher could trigger a manic psychosis in someone with bipolar disorder?"

"Yes, I was aware of that. But he denied a history of psychiatric problems, or symptoms consistent with bipolar disorder."

"But there was enough in the record to have alerted you," Gordon said.

"Yes, his full medical record would have, but it wasn't available," Steven said. "I waited two hours for the record room to locate his old chart, before consulting with the psychiatric resident."

"Never, never treat without the record," Gordon said.

"I had a record that covered the past year. It was marked volume two," Steven said. "Volume one was lost. And his psychiatric record was in a locked file in the psych OPD."

"Speaking of his psych record," Gordon said, "this afternoon I had his psychiatric medical record reviewed. It indicates that two years ago, he had had an adverse reaction to Prozac."

Steven looked at Dr. Murphy. She threw up her hands. His sentiments, exactly!

"Dr. Ewing," Dr. Murphy said, "the problem with psych outpatient records has come up before. We must change the policy of separate psych records."

"It's not a systems problem, damnit!" Ewing shouted. "It's a people problem. Someone misfiled volume one; someone failed to place a flag on volume two indicating the existence of a separate psych record." Ewing turned to Steven. "And you, young man, could still have prevented a disaster if you had paid attention at orientation!"

"Steven ran this by me," Dr. Murphy said. "I suggested he call the psych consulting resident."

"The psych resident suggested I start him on Prozac and set him up with a psych outpatient appointment," Steven said.

"You didn't put that in your note. Besides, you failed to tell the resident the man had already been seen in the psych OPD," Gordon said.

"I didn't know that at the time," Steven said.

"It was part of his medical record," Gordon shot back.

Steven was exasperated. The patient's psychiatric history was the part of the missing medical record. They had already covered that ground.

"In addition," Gordon said, "The psych resident denied he told you to start the Prozac. He said that you and he spoke in general terms about drug therapy."

"He's lying," Steven shot back without hesitation.

"Someone is. Discrepancies like that alone can trigger a malpractice suit," the attorney said.

"Listen, Clyde," Dr. Murphy said, her voice tense with emotion, "I've never met a more honest, unpretentious intern than Dr. Johnson. He has a superior fund of knowledge. He's a careful, thoughtful intern."

"Hold on, Dr. Murphy," Ewing said, "I've seen the evaluation of Johnson's first month in the ER. Not exactly an honors performance."

Steven felt the muscles of his neck and jaw tighten. The hospital Medical Director had been privy to that dismal assessment! Steven had graduated in the top ten percent of his medical school class at the University of Pennsylvania Medical School. He had scored in the ninety-fifth percentile in his national medical board examination. He was not accustomed to poor evaluations. He had the urge to tell Ewing that the evaluation was unfair, and that the quality of his supervision during his first month in the ER had been dismal. But he knew that a defensive posture would only make matters worse. The room was silent. Dr. Ewing stood and turned to face the window behind his desk. A light rain had begun to fall. The sky was a blanket of gray. It could be any time of day, Steven thought. Dr. Ewing glanced at his watch, turned and sat on the edge of his desk.

"Clyde, tell them what you discovered concerning the medical record," Ewing said.

"I asked another psychiatry resident to go through Reverend Jones' record this afternoon. He found that volume I contained what, in my opinion, was enough information to indicate the patient had a history of serious mental illness--probably bipolar disorder. There were lab slips from several years ago, showing that lithium levels had been drawn when he was in for a hernia repair."

"I had checked all the computerized lab data," Steven said.

"But computerized data only go back five years," Gordon countered.

"The record I had summarized his past medical history. There was no mention . . ."

"You can't rely on that," Ewing said. "Why in hell do we keep complete records if you rely on summaries? You can be sure the patient's lawyers will sift through them as though they're panning for gold." He turned to Dr. Murphy. "July and August are especially critical months regarding supervision of the interns." He raised his eyebrows. "As you know, it's hospital policy the interns present all their patients to their supervising attending."

"I'm not denying my responsibility in missing those lithium levels," Dr. Murphy said. "But the record of those lab tests was only on the old chart that we did not have available. And the record we did have should have had a flag indicating he had a separate psychiatric record."

"You're absolutely correct, Dr. Murphy. The hospital also has exposure here," Gordon said. "If a suit is brought, they'll go after Dr. Johnson, and you as the supervising attending, and the hospital. In my opinion, it would be in our best interest to settle this disaster out of court."

Steven's actions had exposed Dr. Murphy to censure and a possible lawsuit for having depended on incomplete information he had given to her. She couldn't possibly spend hours sifting through the patient records, repeating everything he supposedly had done. She had trusted him. He knew an out-of-court settlement would be seen as an admission of guilt. It would be on his and her record for life, impeding their careers at every turn.

"I don't believe we should settle," Dr. Murphy said. Her face reddened, her expression solemn. "Yes...there were some problems in the management of this patient. But in my opinion the errors did not contribute to the patient's death and do not rise to the level of malpractice."

Steven was deeply moved by her support, by her belief in him. He wanted to make eye contact with her. To silently mouth "thank you." He dreaded leaving his emergency department rotation, to face a new cast of senior residents and attendings. It made his flesh crawl to think they too might look on him as inept.

Dr. Ewing broke the awkward silence that followed the emotional intensity of Dr. Murphy's remarks. "Let's not rush into rigid positions," he said. "I'm more worried about some green-eyed malpractice lawyer claiming criminal negligence."

Chapter Four

Dr. Murphy, Steven, Omar Diack and Dr. Beck sat at a table in the hospital cafeteria. They had gathered to prepare for the encounter with the preacher's son, Nathan Jones, who was due to arrive at the hospital later that evening.

The cafeteria smelled of corned beef and cabbage. Steven pushed his plate aside. He felt too much empathy for the cow, to eat what he would normally have consumed with gusto.

Beck, freshly shaven and dressed for an evening out, hadn't taken any food. He drummed his fingers; checked his watch frequently. Omar, who appeared to be enjoying his corned-beef, rolled his eyes in response to Beck's display of impatience. Dr. Murphy didn't seem in a hurry to start the discussion.

It would have been a reasonably good day in the ER for Steven. He had seen twenty patients. He was becoming accustomed to the rapid-fire pace and the variety of pathology. It was so unlike being assigned to a particular service, such as pediatrics or general surgery. In those departments, there was an established philosophy of patient care, routines in management and predictability in types of problems encountered. But the ER was a potpourri of persons of all ages, with afflictions ranging from benign sprains and strains to severe trauma, acute surgical emergencies, or the complicated multi-system problems of the elderly.

He had found Dr. Murphy to be knowledgeable, patient-centered, and not only willing but eager to teach. Her Socratic style allowed him to work through the maze of history, physical findings and laboratory data, all of which had to be assessed in order to arrive at a diagnosis and treatment plan.

He should never have allowed Beck to see the girl with abdominal pain before he had completed his workup. He would not make that mistake again. The boy with the knee injury had also taught him an important lesson. Never rule out referred pain because of a physical finding at the site of injury.

He and Dr. Murphy discussed several examples of referred pain patterns. Cardiac pain referred to the left arm and jaw; sciatic pain to the leg and foot; diaphragmatic pain to the shoulder; nerve root pain referred to the nerve's peripheral distribution; gallbladder pain often felt in the back; and the pain of dissecting aneurysm also referred to the back.

"Steven, I appreciate you sticking around on your night off," Dr. Murphy said. "The meeting with Nathan Jones must be handled delicately. He's grieving. His ability to absorb information will be limited."

"Just what do I tell him?" Steven asked.

Beck didn't wait for Murphy to respond. "No more than you have to," Beck said. "You referred him to psych. He didn't keep his appointment, showed up in the ER a week later, came at you with a pair of scissors."

"It was all so fast," Steven said. He wished he could rewind the events that preceded the actual stabbing. Replay it in slow motion. Had he thrust the scalpel blade in the man's direction or had he stood frozen as the man became impaled upon it? If pressed, could he swear with certainty to one or the other scenario?

"If you're vague, his son's going to suspect you're hiding something," Omar said.

"He's right. Patients can smell guilt," Beck added. "You have to project confidence, no maybes or could-haves."

"My instinct," Steven said, "is to come clean, to tell the preacher's son that I'd made a mistake in prescribing a medicine that could potentially have brought on an acute psychosis."

"No way," Dr. Murphy interrupted. "As soon as you say 'mistake' people see dollar signs."

"I'm not so sure of that," Omar said. "People know doctors make mistakes. What they resent is being patronized or lied to. They respect honesty."

"But right now, his son's going to be shocked and angry about what's happened," Dr. Murphy said. "The word *mistake* will be like a red flag to a bull. Steven, tell him you made a judgment call based on the facts as you saw them."

"No matter how you slice it, it's still baloney," Omar said. "Suppose a student tells his teacher after he flunks a test, that he didn't make any mistakes. He just made judgment calls based on the facts as he saw them. She's going to say, nice try, Jack. Then give him an F."

"That's not a valid comparison," Dr. Murphy said. "Medicine's not about facts. It's about making educated choices. We rely heavily on patient history, which is subjective and often inaccurate. Physical findings can be ambiguous. Lab data can be falsely positive or falsely negative. X-rays, CTs, MRIs are all open to interpretation. The published medical literature is rife with controversy. We're constantly forced to make judgments about what to believe and what to reject."

Omar shook his head, stood, and gathered his meal tray. "I'm sorry, Dr. Murphy, I have to go or I'll miss my ride. You already know how I feel."

Before leaving, Beck repeated his admonition that Steven project a confident image, say as little as possible and not be pulled into a discussion of hypotheticals.

Steven was more confused than ever. He didn't want to face this man alone, but he was glad Beck would not be around.

"Doctor Murphy," Steven asked, "would you have time...?"

"Of course, I'll be there," she said, anticipating his question. "And let me do the talking."

After Steven received word that Nathan Jones was on his way from the airport, he called Dr. Murphy. They met in Dr. Ewing's office. She stood at the window, her back to Steven, who paced and fidgeted with his stethoscope.

"For Godsakes, sit. You're making *me* nervous," Murphy said.

There was a knock at the door. A tall, black man, impeccably dressed in a charcoal-gray business suit, entered. After introductions, Dr. Murphy sat at Ewing's desk, Steven and Nathan sat in chairs alongside the desk. Steven estimated Nathan to be in his early thirties, a handsome, slimmed-down version of his father. Steven wondered how he would feel in that situation. When his own father had died suddenly at age sixty of a heart attack, Steven was shocked, deeply saddened. His dad had appeared to be in robust health, then without warning he was gone. He had never told his dad how much he meant to him. How proud and fortunate he was to have had him as a father.

"Your father was taken to the operating room to repair a neck injury," Dr. Murphy said. "He tolerated the surgery well. But soon after arriving in the recovery room, his heart went into an abnormal rhythm that couldn't be reversed. He suffered a massive heart attack. They did everything possible."

"I'm sure they did," Nathan said. No one spoke. He stared at his hands for a few moments. "He'd been pretty down since my mother died. I called him two weeks ago. I hadn't heard from him in a while. I wondered how he was doing. He said he had stopped taking his medication. He cried. He said he wasn't sleeping. I called one of his parishioners and asked him to take my father to the emergency room."

"The man did bring your father in, but he knew nothing of your dad's history," Dr. Murphy said. "Dr. Johnson saw him initially."

Steven wondered why the man who brought the Reverend to the ER hadn't told Steven that he had spoken with the Reverend's son.

Nathan looked at Steven and nodded. "Yes, I called my father a couple of days later. He told me he saw a nice young doctor. I was concerned he might become manic, losing all that sleep. He's had bipolar disorder as long as I can remember. Of course, you were aware of that. He's been seen many times in the psychiatric clinic. I assume you restarted his medication?"

"When I initially saw him, he denied a psychiatric history. I didn't know he had a diagnosis of bipolar disorder."

Nathan looked confused. "I don't understand. He's been coming here for his care for years. It's part of his medical record."

"For confidentiality reasons," Dr. Murphy said, "psychiatry maintains a separate file."

Jones looked from person to person. He shook his head in disbelief "He was referred to psychiatry from his doctor in the medical clinic. How could you not know that?"

"In the part of his medical record we had available at the time," Dr. Murphey said, "there was no history of mental illness. Your father denied any previous psychiatric care."

"You only had part of his medical record? Why was that?" Nathan snapped."

"I waited over two hours for the old record to be retrieved," Steven said. Your father threatened to leave. I felt compelled to treat his depression."

Nathan was silent for a few moments. "Why was he taken to the operating room?"

"When he returned to the ER early this morning he was in an extremely agitated, psychotic state," Dr. Murphy said.

"My God," Jones said.

"He almost choked a nurse to death, then grabbed surgical scissors and attacked Dr. Johnson. In our efforts to subdue him, he accidentally incurred a neck laceration."

"From the scissors?" Nathan asked.

"No," Steven said. "I was with a patient at the time. I had a scalpel in my hand. He lunged for me. I fell over backwards. He landed on top of me. He was injured by the scalpel I was holding."

"There was massive bleeding," Dr. Murphy said. "We did all we could in the ER, then sent him to the operating room. His condition was stable by the time he left the OR."

Nathan Jones looked from Dr. Murphy to Steven. His eyes glistened. Dr. Murphy came and sat beside him.

"We're so sorry, Mr. Jones. The autopsy showed your father had severe coronary artery disease. There was nothing we could have done to save him."

Steven wanted to say, oh yes there was. If I had known his previous psych history I wouldn't have given him the damn Prozac.

The heart attack was no coincidence. The massive bleeding probably brought it on.

Nathan locked his stare on Steven, as if inviting him to say what he was thinking. He turned to face Dr. Murphy. His expression had hardened.

"Did you also see my father when he initially came to the emergency room?"

"Dr. Johnson presented his findings to me. I suggested he call Psychiatry."

"A psychiatrist examined my father?"

"No, he didn't feel it was necessary to see him. He discussed management with Dr. Johnson."

"He didn't see my father, either. Why is that? Is that how you treat all your patients?" He jumped to his feet. Walked toward the door, turned and walked to Dr. Murphy. "A black man can't sleep," Nathan said, "he's mourning his dead wife, simple enough. Give him a few pills; get him the hell out of your busy ER. Don't bother to check his record!"

"It wasn't like that," Steven said. "I took a lot of time with your father. I was concerned about him. I believed the medicine I gave him would help."

He fixed Steven in a withering stare. "My father was a good, gentle man. Now he's dead. He became manic because you gave him the wrong medicine. And you're supposed to restrain a disturbed patient, not attack him!"

"The wound was an unfortunate accident. We successfully repaired it," Dr. Murphy said in a calm soothing voice. "I totally understand how you feel, but I assure you that our mission in the emergency department is to save lives. Unfortunately, we're not always successful. We do our best."

"If this is your best, I pity---I feel for your patients." He stood. "Lord! I don't believe this."

"I know how you must feel." Dr. Murphy said, "I'm sorry."

"If you think you're sorry now---damnit!" He slammed his fist against the arm of the chair.

No one spoke. Steven had little experience with a patient this angry. "It's okay . . ."

"Nothing's okay," Nathan snapped. Tears filled his eyes. "My father was a simple man. A holy man. He's dead---my children's only living grandparent. How can you possibly understand how I feel?" He stood. "Have you done an autopsy?"

"We need your permission to perform an autopsy," Dr. Murphy said.

"Yes---yes, I do want you to do an autopsy. I want to know what caused his death. Something's rotten here. I am going to find out exactly why this happened to my father. You can be certain of that."

Chapter Five

"You want to go for something to eat or drink?" Dr. Murphy asked Steven, as they headed for the elevator in the hospital administrative wing.

Steven wasn't looking forward to his empty apartment but didn't want to spend any more time rehashing the day's events. "I was on last night. I'm bushed."

"I promise...no doctor talk. Get your mind off things."

He wished he'd had her as his attending his first month on the ER service. Things probably would have gone a lot better. At orientation, he'd been told that he would have to choose an adviser no later than three months into his internship. He had the option of choosing either a hospital-based attending or a community-based staff physician. He was leaning toward asking Dr. Murphy.

"Sure," Steven said. "I'd like that, Dr. Murphy."

"Just Chris after hours. Okay?"

He nodded. Chris Murphy, as Irish as Patty's pig...delicate features, reddish hair, fair complexion with a freckle here and there. An easy face to be with.

"I'll drive," Chris said. "Meet you out front in ten minutes."

The Silver Bullet Express, a diner located just a few blocks from Smithfield Hospital, was a refurbished 1920s train. The interior fixtures were reproductions of art deco pieces, the booths, a rich mahogany, were upholstered with a deeply tufted burgundy fabric. Steven could imagine a row of flappers dressed in slinky silk, bouncy-bobbed hairdos, and dainty high-heeled shoes, doing the Charleston on the stainless-steel countertop, their admiring beaux dressed in skin-tight single-breasted suits and bowler hats, cheering them on.

"A dime for your thoughts," Chris said. She was seated alongside him at the counter. She added a third pack of artificial sweetener to her black coffee.

"I was trying to escape from the present, I guess, thinking about this train when it was a dining car. The exuberant twenties. I have a fascination with that era." He sipped his Coke. "Do you believe in reincarnation?"

"I've never really thought about it. It's pure speculation."

"So were radio, television and computers."

The waitress arrived with their food. Apple pie with a scoop of vanilla ice cream for Steven and a slice of pecan pie topped with whipped cream for Chris.

"So, who does the transplant? God?" Chris asked.

"Whoever's pulling the strings."

"It sounds like you're talking about God."

"You see rules, you look for rulers," Steven said. He hadn't talked about the big picture in a long time. He figured she was probably Catholic. He came from a long line of Lutherans.

"I had a roommate in premed who was a Buddhist," Steven said. "He got me interested in Buddhist philosophy. I ended up with a minor in religious studies."

"I know nothing of Buddhism. Enlighten me."

Steven sipped his coffee. The entire diner seemed to grow expectantly quiet. He didn't want to sound preachy. "It's like the difference between the Sermon on the Mount and the Ten Commandments. More about what you should do, than what you shouldn't do."

"As a Catholic," Chris said, "I got a heavy dose of both. Maybe eighty-to-twenty on the don't side."

Steven nodded. They quietly ate their pies. Chris pushed her dish toward him. "You want to swap? The pecan's delicious."

"Sure," he said. It was obvious she wanted to change the subject. "How come you're so different from the other ER attendings?"

"All sorts of people go into medicine. It's a long, tough haul. People change along the way."

She stared into her coffee cup as though to find there the words she was seeking.

"Shift work suits some," she said. "It's not as demanding as private practice; you don't have to buy equipment or set up an office. Or go through two or three lean years, waiting for the practice to build."

"I've grown accustomed to lean," he said. "Besides, I can't stand not knowing what happens to patients after they leave the ER. The next day, the next month, the next year."

"I felt the same way at one time," she said. She sipped her coffee. Neither spoke for several moments. "Working in the ER is like reading a short story," she said quietly. "It's an episode in someone's life, important to them. I find it satisfying to be a part of the story."

"I wasn't questioning your commitment."

"It's okay," she said. She wiped her mouth with a napkin and pushed her half-finished pie toward him. "As a senior medical student, I elected to spend a month with a community-based general internist. I loved the medical part. He was a great teacher. Good with his patients. But he wasn't happy. He complained bitterly that he wasn't prepared for the business end of his practice. The hiring and firing, the HMOs, the tons of paper work."

He hadn't meant to put her on the defense. He liked her, respected her skills and the way she related to patients. ER Medicine seemed to him a doc-in-the-box kind of option, but she was his supervisor, and he could do without another disastrous evaluation. He busied himself finishing her dessert.

"For many patients," Chris said, "the ER's the only face of medicine they get to see. I'd rather see fewer Becks and more Johnsons in my ER."

He looked up. She was waiting for a response. It was the nicest thing anyone had said to him since he started his internship.

"Thanks. I needed that," he said. But her kindness couldn't erase the fact that he, and she, and the hospital were probably going to be sued because of him. He felt a riptide of emotions: fear, self-doubt, remorse, and not least of all, anger. He dreaded going to work the next day. He could imagine the jokes going around, the sideways glances, and Martha Knight's patronizing smile.

Chris looked at her watch. "I'd better be going." She picked up the tab. "Jimmy will be worried to death."

"Jimmy?" He'd heard she lived alone.

"A stray I picked up at the homeless shelter."

Steven cocked one eyebrow.

She laughed. "He's got four legs. He likes milk and catnip."

On the drive to his tiny housestaff apartment, Steven thought of the pint-sized terracotta Buddha perched on his bedroom dresser, patiently waiting for him to return. Cats are Buddha-like, he thought. Dignified, calm, inscrutable.

He studied her profile as she drove. Her lips were a little too thin, her nose a little too sharp. But the intensity of her hazel eyes and the warmth of her smile were more than enough to make her appealing. He would have to ask her out after he completed his ER rotation. For now, she's his boss.

The housestaff quarters, a cluster of one and two-bedroom garden apartments, were located on a wooded acre two-hundred yards from the hospital's emergency entrance. A gleaming Honda motorcycle was parked on a concrete slab at the back door to his apartment. It was covered with a clear plastic tarp. A silver helmet hung from one of the handlebars.

As Chris pulled to his back door, she glanced at his motorcycle. "About time you graduated to a four-wheeler?"

"Not on my salary. Besides, I find riding a bike relaxing. Take you for a ride sometime."

He exited the car and walked around to the driver's side.

"It looks powerful. What kind is it?"

"A Honda Shadow. 1099cc liquid-cooled engine," he said.

"Sounds impressive, but no thanks. I've seen too many two-wheelers-versus-four encounters. They ain't pretty."

"I've been riding for six years. No broken bones yet."

He leaned onto the edge of the open window of the driver's side. "Thanks for everything."

"That's my job. Besides, I believe you're going to make a hell of a good doctor. See you in the morning."

Steven watched her drive off. The problem is, I'm already a doctor, he thought. But he understood what she meant. As an intern, his learning curve would be steep. That was how the hospital justified the eighty-plus-hour-work weeks---to pack in as much as they could in that important formative first year. How had his dad done it? In his father's day, they worked even longer hours.

His father had been a loved and respected general practitioner in Zion, a small town in central Kansas. Steven had spent the summer before his third year of medical school shirt-tailing his dad as he saw office patients, made house calls and visited hospitalized patients. He was able to take patients' histories, examine the patients, and discuss diagnosis and treatment with his father. After years of intense study with virtually no patient contact, the experience with his dad was exciting. He couldn't wait to start his third year. He'd finally be applying what he'd learned in the classroom.

One of his dad's patients, a nine-year-old boy, had terminal leukemia. Steven and his father made a house call after the mother phoned and said her son vomited a basin-full of blood. By the time they arrived, the boy was dead. Steven's father held the mother as she cried. Neither spoke. Steven telephoned the woman's husband. He and his father remained with the child's mother until her husband arrived.

Steven's dad was quiet on the drive back to the office. "Son, medicine's not about you and other doctors. It may seem that way during medical school and residency. It's about you and your patients. Never forget that. Your professors can teach you the book learning and the clinical skills, but not the caring. That's got to come from you. If you don't have that, you'd best choose some other way to earn a living."

Steven pulled his keys from his pocket and inserted one into the door lock, hesitated, then withdrew it. He went to his bike, uncovered it, put on the helmet and slipped a key into the ignition. He was too revved to sleep.

Soon the roar of the motor, the cool evening wind on his face, the tapered ribbon of light stretching before him, allowed him to leave in his wake the troubling, tragic events of the day.

Steven showered, put on a clean pair of briefs and inspected the refrigerator. He removed a milk carton, sniffed, and then poured a glass. He ate peanut butter from the jar, using his index finger as a spoon. He checked his watch. Ten-fifteen. Only nine-fifteen in Kansas. Not too late to call his mother. He went to the phone in his bedroom.

The phone rang several times. He was about ready to replace the handset when his mother picked up.

"Hi, mom."

"Steven!" his mother said. "I was beginning to think you lost my number. It's been weeks..."

"Sorry, mom. It's been pretty hectic these past few weeks."

"Wish you were closer. Plenty of good hospitals in Kansas."

He sat on the edge of his bed. She knew why he had chosen Smithfield Community. He hoped to get into their strong pediatric program. She was really saying she was lonely.

"How are *you* doing, mom?"

"Okay. I guess."

Steven waited. She didn't sound okay. He didn't want to burden her with his problems. But he recalled how his father would occasionally turn to her on the rare occasions he felt overwhelmed. Like the time a patient of his went into premature labor and delivered in the breach position minutes after arriving at the hospital. He was able to deliver the baby's torso, but the head remained trapped behind an insufficiently dilated cervix. He tried everything he knew to do, but the tight cervix refused to allow the after-coming head to deliver. Thirty frantic minutes later he held a stillborn premature infant in his arms.

That night young Steven, whose bedroom was next to his parents, heard them talking as they lay in bed. He had never heard his father cry. Was it possible his dad was crying? Their voices were muffled. He pressed his ear to the wall.

"She was a perfectly healthy young woman...no reason to deliver so prematurely. I must have missed something. It was my fault. Things like this don't happen for no reason."

"You did everything possible, Michael."

"A caesarian section might have saved the baby."

"But everything happened so fast. There was no way the surgeon could have gotten there in time. Sometimes a premature delivery is nature's way of preventing the birth of a fetus with a severe defect." She whispered something Steven couldn't make out. He felt guilty eavesdropping on his parents.

"I miss your dad something awful. I wasn't ready to have him go so suddenly." She paused. "And you and your sister so far away."

"I miss him too. You hear from Claire lately?"

"She's busy with her two little ones. Calls once a week though. Not like her big brother. Will you be home for Thanksgiving?"

"I'm on call. I will be home for Christmas."

"You sound a little down, Steven. Something wrong?"

Should he tell her about all the mean-spirited people he had to work with? Or the disastrous Reverend Jones incident?

"Mom, I'm not sure I have what it takes to practice medicine."

"Your father always said you'd make a fine doctor. His dream was for you to practice with him here in Zion."

Was that why he'd gone into medicine? To fulfill his dad's dream? He had never even considered any other field. What would he do other than medicine? How he wished he could talk it over with his dad.

"You still there, Steven?"

"Dad practiced thirty-five years and was never once sued. I've been at it only six weeks...something bad happened today."

"Oh, Steven. What? What happened?"

He wanted to spare her the details, but once he started, everything flooded out. He told her of the meeting with the Reverend's son.

"It's a pity the man died, but it wasn't your fault they couldn't find his record. You didn't do anything wrong. That psychiatrist person should be ashamed, lying like that."

"If I *am* sued, I might as well forget about getting into a competitive residency."

He explained to her that if he quit, he'd have to break his contract with the hospital. That would ruin his chances of finding a decent internship anywhere else.

"You're a lot like your father, Steven. Always wanting to be perfect. It's not possible. Bad things happen."

"I don't know how much bad I can stand..."

"You've gotta deal with the bad, one thing at a time, in the best way you know how. Don't beat yourself up for things you have no control over."

He had never thought of his mother as the starch in his dad's spine. There were probably more of those bedtime consultations than he had been aware of.

"Thanks, mom. I needed that."

Steven sat on the floor in the lotus position. He extended his arms, his palms resting on his knees, the index finger and thumb of each hand opposed. He closed his eyes. Soon he was transported to his private place of tranquility.

He is underwater, yet able to breathe normally. Below him in the warm blue-green water a school of rainbow trout glides by. He is dazzled by their vivid colors. He swims among them. Slowly, gills begin to form. His arms become fins and his legs are fused. Iridescent scales cover his body. He glides effortlessly among the smaller fish. His mind is slowly cleansed. He is filled with a sense of calm, peace, and serenity.

Following his meditation, he went to bed where he picked up a journal from a pile at his bedside. He read an article titled, “Failure to Thrive.” He didn’t quite make it through the article when his eyes closed and the journal slipped from his hands. In the moments before he dropped off to sleep, he struggled unsuccessfully to purge the recurring image of Reverend Jones on the floor of the ER, the scalpel protruding from his neck pulsating with each beat of the man’s heart.

Chapter Six

Because of the threat of a malpractice suit, the hospital medical director, Dr. Ewing, ordered that the ER attending closely supervise Steven's patient care. All of the patients seen by Steven had to be evaluated and examined by Dr. Murphy. The nursing staff could not implement his orders unless they were countersigned by Dr. Murphy. These restrictions were to be maintained throughout the final two weeks of his ER rotation.

Since Dr. Murphy was often busy seeing her own patients, Steven experienced a great deal of down time. He began to help the nurses triage patients, check out equipment, draw blood and start intravenous fluids. It became obvious to him that the smooth operation of the ER depended as much or more on the nurses, as it did on the physicians. He was gaining a better appreciation of Martha Knight's obsession with efficiency.

As a student, Steven had looked forward to the day when he could write orders on the patient's chart. He had never given much thought to how much was involved in implementing those orders. Nurses had to anticipate the patient's needs, make sure necessary supplies and drugs were on hand, draw blood, start IVs. The list was endless. He told Martha Knight that it was obvious to him that she needed more nursing staff.

"Nursing's going to be even more understaffed after you move on, Dr. Steve," Martha had said, as she and Steven helped an elderly patient to the bathroom.

The patient, a frail woman in her mid-eighties, leaned heavily on Steven's shoulder. She turned to face him, looking at him intently. "Have we met before? I believe I know you."

Martha had told Steven that the woman lived in a nearby nursing home. She was being evaluated for frequent falls and memory loss. A fall a year ago, had resulted in several fractured ribs.

He wished he could better read the topography of her wrinkled face. Hills and valleys that, like grooves on a vinyl record, had recorded the experiences of a lifetime.

"Yes," Steven said, staring into the woman's eyes, "perhaps we have."

Ms. Knight looked at Steven with a puzzled expression. He had never discussed his fascination with reincarnation. She probably thought he was patronizing the woman.

Steven learned from Martha that the nurses believed he was being treated unfairly, that the problem of delayed retrieval of patient records was a common occurrence, and that the ER staff had to do the best they could with what information they had available. Ewing was making him the scapegoat for a hospital-wide problem.

Chris Murphy also expressed the opinion that Dr. Ewing's decision was unjustified. Steven appreciated her patience and her willingness to let him work through patient evaluations, when he knew she could have arrived at the same endpoint in half the time.

On the morning of the last day of his ER rotation Steven entered the staff lounge. Nurses, nursing assistants, other staff, and Chris Murphy were crowded into the small room. The work table had been cleared and in the center a chocolate cake was adorned with the words, “Gonna miss ya, Dr. Steve.”

He was stunned. He had never dreamed his rotation would end this way.

Martha quieted the group by banging the diaphragm of her stethoscope against the metal cart that held the cake.

“I speak for the entire ER staff,” Martha said, “in saying how much we’ve enjoyed having you with us these past two months. And if you have any elective time available later in the year, we would welcome you with open arms.”

Martha hugged Steven as the rest of the staff clapped, then descended on the chocolate cake and other goodies. Chris Murphy moved toward Steven. As she reached to grab his hand a spark of static electricity passed between their fingertips. They both started, and then laughed. Their eyes met as she pumped his hand.

Later that day, Chris collared Steven and led him to an unoccupied exam room. “We have to talk,” she said.

She sat on a stool. “Ewing’s heard from an attorney representing Nathan Jones. He requested permission to review all hospital records pertaining to the care of Reverend Jones.”

Steven felt light-headed. He leaned against the exam table. Until then the talk of malpractice had been pure speculation. “What happens next?” Steven asked, trying to keep a tremor from his voice. He hoisted himself onto the table.

“His lawyer will ask for statements from the people involved. The hospital attorney will help us with our statements.”

“When?” Steven asked.

"I don't know. It may not be for weeks," Chris said. "Maybe months."

Months! He stared at the floor. It was spotless. Polished. No trace of blood. "My God," he whispered.

She stood and walked toward him. She placed a hand on his knee. With her other hand, she turned his face toward her. "Hey, don't look so glum."

"Have you ever been through anything like this?" he asked.

"Once. The case was eventually dropped. Malpractice lawyers work on a contingency basis. If they aren't convinced they can win, they move on to greener pastures."

"I don't mean the legal stuff. The feeling that you screwed up. Somebody died."

"You'll get over the guilt. We all do. We have to get past the lawyers for now."

"You saw how angry the preacher's son was. I can't see him dropping the charges."

"Hopefully time will temper Nathan's fury." She turned and again sat on the stool. She crossed her legs. "And speaking of time, you start on pediatrics tomorrow, right?"

"Right. And after eight tomorrow morning you'll no longer be my supervisor," Steven said.

Chris blushed. "Was I that bad?"

"You're a tough taskmaster. I still haven't gotten through all the articles you've given me."

"Don't worry; I've already submitted your final evaluation. We should go over it sometime today."

"I'm not sure I want to," Steven said.

She smiled. "A few points off for a pending malpractice suit," Chris said. "Knocked you all the way down to *superior*."

He should have felt relieved, but didn't. Hardly a day had passed since the preacher incident that he hadn't thought about what he might have done differently. Why had Reverend Jones denied any previous psych problems? Was there something in the man's body language that should have told Steven he was concealing important information? If Steven had suspected that, he might have asked for permission to call his son.

"I don't deserve a superior grade," Steven said.

"For Godsakes, Charlie Brown! Stop beating up on yourself. You made a mistake because the system failed you. You've got to move on!"

He was stung by the analogy. He didn't see himself as a Charlie Brown.

"And if I can't move on?" Steven said. "Maybe there is life after medicine."

"Sure. Discard eight years of intense study. Maybe teach anatomy to freshmen medical students. Now there's a way to avoid patients."

"But I love interacting with patients," he protested. "Each time I pick up a chart before entering an exam room, I know that beyond that door is a unique individual. Most often a total stranger...their well-being in my hands."

"We can ask questions even their closest friends would be reluctant to pursue," Chris said. "That MD after your name gives you license not simply to look and listen, but even to touch. It is pretty awesome."

"I'm not sure anyone deserves that much," he said.

"I really believe you're enjoying feeling sorry for yourself. Hey, you're not perfect," Chris said. She did a complete revolution on the stool, throwing up her hands in mock exasperation. She stood, walked to Steven and tugged on his lapels. "Superior isn't so bad," she whispered. Their faces were inches apart. As they were about to kiss, an aide poked her head in the doorway.

"Oops! Sorry, but I need to get this room ready. An MVA's on the way in."

"We'll be done here in a minute," Chris said. After the aide left she said to Steven, "You need a hobby."

"I meditate."

"If that's all you do, pretty soon you'll look like Buddha!"

Steven patted his belly. "That's not how I want to emulate him," he said. He stood. They walked toward the door.

"You need to get physical!"

"What do you have in mind?"

She blushed. "I mean like jogging, tennis. That sort of physical."

Steven was charmed by the way she became embarrassed every time he made a not-too-subtle pass. Why did she blush? Did the pass bring to mind fantasies she harbored concerning him? That was wishful thinking. Or was it a signal for him to stop, that she had undergone trauma in a previous relationship and wasn't ready for intimacy? He had heard she had been engaged, a wedding date already set, but for some reason aborted.

"Do you play tennis?" he asked.

"A little."

"Like to play sometime? You know, for the sake of my physical and mental well-being."

"When you put it that way, how can I refuse?"

As Chris opened the door someone shouted, "Dr. Murphy, you'd better check the board. The natives are getting restless."

Chris sighed. "Sedentary isn't all bad either. Give me a call if you want to cry over a beer sometime."

****

The transition from the emergency department to the pediatric inpatient service was like going from the floor of the New York Stock Exchange to a candle-lit dinner at a country inn.

The housestaff on pediatrics was divided into two teams. His team consisted of a third-year medical student, himself, a second-year resident, and an attending physician. Steven's team was responsible for fifteen to twenty children. He would be responsible for six to eight. The teams admitted patients on alternate days.

Steven and the intern on the second team, Jerry Russo, were about as alike as a tortoise and a Jack Russell terrier. Steven had seen Jerry at the intern orientation. Medium sized, and more than a bit over-nourished. Jerry had moved about the reception area, pumping hands and flashing a broad smile. He's only an intern, and already running for chief resident, Steven thought. Their paths had crossed infrequently since orientation. Yet Steven liked him.

"Hey, Steve," Jerry said, as he clasped his hand. "Been looking forward to working with you. We married guys envy you. Tooling around on that monster bike."

It was six in the morning, the first day of their rotation. Steven and Jerry had come in early to look over patient charts before the beginning of teaching rounds. They were seated at a counter in the chart room next to the nurses' station. The work surface was covered with stacks of charts, a couple of computer terminals, a scattering of partially empty coffee mugs, day-old fries and a bowl of unopened packets of soy sauce and catsup. A coffee maker in one corner gurgled gently. Steven's caffeine habit totaled six mugs a day. The fresh brewed aroma beckoned him.

Steven had taken some ribbing about where he went on those late-night bike rides. Most of the housestaff were married, and some already had children. They looked back nostalgically to bachelor days.

"How are Gloria and your little girl doing?" Steven asked. He'd heard Jerry's wife and two-year-old daughter were in a car accident.

"It was just a fender-bender. They're fine. So is the little Russo in the oven."

"Oh? How far along is she?"

"Four months," Jerry said. "She had an ultrasound last week. It's a boy. No doubt about it. Hung like a goat."

Steven cringed. "I'm glad she's doing well."

Steven walked to the coffeemaker and poured himself a mug full. "You want a cup?" he asked.

"No. I'm already wired tight as a drum. Now shut up," he said with a smile, "and let me get through these charts."

Steven welcomed the silence, but it lasted only moments.

"You're lucky, Johnson. You drew the best pedes attending. Guess you could use a break after what happened in the ER."

Steven began gathering his charts. "My second month in the ER wasn't bad. Had Murphy as my attending. She's great."

Jerry raised his eyebrows. "Heard you and she got kind of cozy."

"The rumor's not true. Not yet." Steven headed for the door. "See you later." He hurried down the hall, a stack of charts under his arm. A young black woman in the uniform of a student nurse approached him. She asked if she could make rounds with him. It was her first day.

"Sure." He read her nametag. *Ms. Jacqueline Martin* "Hello, Ms. Martin. I'm Steve Johnson, one of the new interns."

"I know," she said. "Omar's my cousin. He said he liked working with you."

Her accent, he realized, was similar to Omar's. Not exactly the same. Her skin was the color of milk chocolate, her eyes dark and almond-shaped. She wore a powder blue, pinstriped uniform. Around twenty, he guessed.

"Sure. I'd be glad to have you tag along. But I've only got thirty minutes to see eight patients. I won't be able to discuss the patients with you. Maybe later today we can get together to talk about them."

She nodded. "I will be a lizard on the wall. I promise."

Steven liked the analogy. A lizard could remain virtually motionless. It could change color to blend with its surroundings. At the far end of the hall a group of white coats were huddled around a cart piled high with patient charts. They were probably discussing an admission from the night before.

He checked his list of patients. He stopped at room 302, flipped open the patient's chart. Penny Miller, a five-year-old girl admitted for evaluation of enlarged glands on the right side of her neck. Her blood smear showed increased numbers of lymphocytes, many of which were abnormal. When her mononucleosis test proved to be normal, her doctor's concern about possible lymphoma increased. A needle-aspiration biopsy of a neck gland had not been diagnostic. A bone marrow biopsy was scheduled for that afternoon.

When Steven and Jacqueline entered the room, the child was asleep. The window blinds were drawn, the room was dark. The only light came from the bathroom, where the door was slightly ajar. Someone was showering. Steam drifted through the door and spilled into the room. He was about to leave when the little girl sat up in bed, rubbing her eyes with the fist of one hand as her other hand pressed a limp stuffed animal of unrecognizable species, to the side of her face.

Steven smiled. "Hi. I bet your name is Penny."

She nodded. She looked past him to where Jacqueline was standing by the door. She began to cry for her mother. The shower stopped.

"I'll be right there, sweetheart," a female voice shouted from the bathroom.

Penny continued to cry. A young woman, a bath towel wrapped around her body, came into the room. She went to her daughter and gathered her into her arms.

"Oh, God. Look at me. I didn't know anyone was here."

"I'm sorry," Steven said. "I'm Dr. Johnson. I'll come back later."

"No. Don't go. I want to know about the tests," the woman said. "Let me throw on some clothes." She hurried into the bathroom, the little girl still in her arms.

Steven would have to ask the mother to sign an operative permit for the bone marrow biopsy. But it seemed to him premature to be doing such an invasive procedure. If he was going to challenge the attending's decision to go ahead with a bone marrow biopsy he had better give Penny a thorough going over. He checked his watch. That would be all he'd have time to get done before rounds. He should have come in earlier. Now he'd have to sit back and have the resident present the patients and field questions. *So much for making a good impression on the first morning of his rotation.*

Chapter Seven

This, his first day on the pediatric service, had been especially stressful following his tumultuous ER experience. The preacher's death and potential malpractice suit had signaled him out as someone to watch. But all in all, it had been a good day; no screw-ups and even tepid praise from his attending. His was looking forward to the evening off. To escape the hospital and feel the lazy night-time air against his skin; to cruise the winding road that hugged the Raritan River; to glimpse couples in canoes and rowboats, drifting in the river's gentle currents, unconcerned and perhaps unaware of the rapids.

He sat at the workstation reviewing notes, handwritten on three-by-five index cards, each headed by an imprint of the patient's name, hospital room number, and date. His team wasn't admitting new patients that day, so he had time to become familiar with the children assigned to him.

He looked around for Jacqueline. He had glimpsed her through the day, huddled with her nursing supervisor, sitting in the rear of the room at noon conference, and walking hand in hand with a child in knee braces. He'd caught her once or twice looking at him.

He spotted her nearby, studying a patient's chart. A colorful knit cap covered what appeared to be a considerable up-cropping of hair. He went to where she was sitting. He tapped her shoulder.

"I've a little time before evening rounds."

She smiled, flashing a set of world-class teeth. "I too have time."

"I could use a cup of coffee. How about the snack bar?"

She nodded. Two cords of braided hair were visible beneath her nursing cap. Is she Rastafarian, he wondered? He and his college roommate had made a trip to Jamaica the summer of their junior year. He thought it a strange religion. How could they believe Hailie Selassie was their messiah? He had read somewhere that Selassie had squirreled away billions in Swiss banks, as his people struggled to survive in a poor country plagued by recurring drought and famine.

The cigar-sized Jamaican joints had impressed him. He'd tried one at the urging of his friend. He remembered little after the first few drags. But heard all about how he had danced with abandon, laughed, cried, and as they watched the sun rise gloriously from the Caribbean, he toppled into the tepid surf.

He awoke the next morning with a blockbuster headache and no recollection of the events of the night before. He never tried another stogie, but did become addicted to Bob Marley. As they walked to the snack bar the *Rasta man* chant played in his head:

One bright morning when my work is over
Man will fly away to Zion

They went through the self-serve line at the snack bar. Steven grabbed a coffee, Jacqueline a Coke. They settled into a booth.

"You have no records. You carry everything in your head?"

Steven withdrew the index cards from his breast pocket. He fanned them. "Pick one."

"You want to play cards?" she asked. Only the slightest hint of a smile indicated she was joking. "Tell me about the little girl, Penny. Why did you cancel the biopsy? And what did you see in her eyes?"

"Her doctor was concerned about lymphoma."

"I do not know much about lymphoma."

"It's cancer of the lymph nodes. But I believe she has an infection. I wanted to order further blood tests and an ophthalmology consult. My resident and attending agreed."

"In my country children get big glands from tuberculosis," Jacqueline said.

"That's from drinking milk from tubercular cows. But her mother said Penny has never drunk raw milk."

"You asked her what her kitten's name was. How did you know she has a cat?" Jacqueline asked.

"She had scratches on her hands. It was a guess. When she said that cleaning out the cat's litter pan was her job, I had a hunch that my ophthalmoscope might find the answer to her problem."

"What was so interesting?"

"A few patches that looked like blobs of cotton."

"What does that mean?"

"This afternoon the ophthalmologist saw her. He said the eye lesions were typical of toxoplasmosis."

"Don't persons with HIV get that?" Jacqueline asked.

"Yes. But she has no risk factors. I did order an HIV test."

"So, you are Penny's hero?" She smiled.

"My attending said, 'nice pickup Johnson,' then moved on to the next patient. But I must admit it did make my day." He couldn't hold back a broad grin. "If you care to round with me tomorrow morning, meet me at the nurses' station at six. We can talk about my patients as we round. No more lizard on the wall."

"I cannot come. I have a class. Maybe the next day?"

"Sure, anytime."

He was eager to get to know her better. He was confused. "Your cousin, Omar, is from Senegal. Were you originally from there?" Steven asked.

"No. My father came from Senegal. I have many relatives still there. I came to Smithfield because Omar is here."

Chris Murphy, coffee mug in hand, approached their booth. "Hi, Steven, care if I join you?" She slipped into the booth beside him.

He introduced Jacqueline to Chris. Jacqueline stood. She looked embarrassed. Steven wondered if Omar might have shared with Jacqueline the rumors about him and Chris. Jacqueline looked at her watch.

"I must go to nursing rounds, I am already late," Jacqueline said. "It is my pleasure to meet you, Dr. Murphy." She nodded to Steven and hurried off.

"You don't waste time, Steven."

"We were talking shop."

"I had assumed your taste ran toward older women."

"Absolutely." He pressed closer to her. He felt the warmth of her thigh against his.

"You've been off my service for almost twenty-four hours and not a word from you." She sipped her coffee. "She has a British accent--and so formal. Where's she from?"

"Jamaica. Omar Diack is her cousin."

"He's one of our best nurses. He's Muslim, is she?"

"I don't believe so. But I don't really want to talk about her. I'm off Friday night."

"Pick you up at eight?" Chris asked.

"Great, but I'll drive this time. Better wear long pants and a wind-breaker."

In addition to covering the pediatric ward, Steven and his resident were responsible for newborns assigned to the pediatric service. They attended deliveries where they were responsible for checking the newborn's breathing, heartbeat, color, muscle tone, and reflexes. Depending on those findings they assigned the baby a score, called the Apgar score, with ten being a screaming, pink, vigorous baby with normal breathing, heart rate and brisk reflexes. But all too often the babies came out limp and pale, their respiratory effort either labored or absent. It was always a thrill when one of the low Apgar score babies began to cry and pink-up. The mother, moments before paralyzed with fear, now ecstatic, reaching out as the baby was brought to her.

His studies had stressed all the bad things that can happen. Medical texts are filled with pictures of infants with immense hydrocephalic heads, spinal cords splayed open, or grotesque facial defects. Fear of possible disaster hangs over the birthing suite, an invisible presence dissipated only by the emergence of a healthy, vigorous infant. Steven hoped he would never grow so accustomed to this miracle of creation that it would not continue to fill him with awe and humility.

Later in the nursery he would do a thorough general physical examination, with special attention directed toward the presence of heart murmurs, possible hip dislocation, or enlargement of the kidneys---findings infrequently encountered but of grave consequence if missed.

It was late morning of the second day of Steven's pediatric rotation. He and the senior pediatric resident stood in the corridor at the entrance to the newborn nursery. The resident, Dr. Scully, on call the night before, had assisted with three deliveries and two caesarian sections. He wore rumpled scrubs under his starched white coat. Steven guessed him to be six-feet-four, maybe taller. He hadn't had time to shave before morning rounds, and his dark hair, still wet from a hasty shower, was slicked straight back. He had a long narrow face, a razor-sharp nose and close-set eyes that reminded Steven of the crows he tried to hit with his homemade slingshot as a boy. One day he actually made a direct hit and injured a crow's wing. He took the crow home and kept it in the garage until it was able to fly again. After that he shot at tin cans.

Without notes or charts, Scully ran through a detailed recounting of the mothers' pregnancy histories and highlights of the deliveries.

Dr. Scully peered through the glass window that ran the full length of the nursery. He pointed to one of the babies. "That noisy little fellow over there needs a circumcision. You ever do one?"

"A few, as a fourth-year student. But it's been a while."

They walked to a large stainless-steel sink where they put on shoe covers and surgical caps. They scrubbed, then donned disposable paper gowns. As they entered the nursery, Scully asked Steven to describe the technique he had used.

Steven quickly ran through the steps of the procedure.

"Good," Scully said. "But I like to leave the clamp in place exactly ten minutes by the clock. The biggest problem besides taking off too much skin is removing the clamp too soon. I'll watch you do this one. After that you're on your own."

Steven wasn't keen on circumcisions and was convinced that someday medical historians would consider it a cruel and primitive procedure. Still, studies had shown it reduces infections and might even limit the risk of cancer. He checked the chart to make sure the infant's mother had signed an operative permit. She had. Her signature was child-like in its exaggerated non-fluent strokes. The name on the consent form was Anna Amin.

Some of the newborns slept quietly while others screeched at decibel levels astonishing for such small persons. Nurses in caps and gowns scurried about preparing babies to bring to their mothers, some of whom hovered anxiously in the corridor. Steven noticed a woman wearing a traditional Muslim hijab that covered her head and forehead, the lower part drawn up tightly under her chin. She stared intently through the glass at the infant Steven was preparing to circumcise. Her dark eyes brimmed with tears.

Scully nudged Steven. "That's the baby's mother. She and her husband had a hell of fight about the circ. He insisted he would not have an unclean son in his home. She insisted he not be circumcised until he was much older."

The woman struck her fist repeatedly against the glass as she watched the nurse restrain her baby's arms and legs on a cross-like board. She turned from the window and hurried down the corridor.

"I want to talk to the mother," Steven said.

"Why? She signed permission."

Steven removed his gloves. "I'm sorry. I can't do this without first talking with her."

"We've held the baby's feeding," the nurse said. "Mrs. Amin is scheduled to go home this afternoon; there won't be time to do it later."

"If she agreed under duress, the permit's not valid."

"Hell, I'll do it," Scully said. "There's nothing to be gained talking to her."

"Don't do anything until I check with her."

"Damnit, Johnson," Scully shouted. "You're the one taking orders around here. Come back!"

Chapter Eight

As far as Steven knew, circumcision was as much a custom among Muslims as it was among Jews. So why was Mrs. Amin so terrified? He picked up Anna Amin's chart at the nurses' station.

He knocked on her door. There was no response. Perhaps she was in the bathroom. He poked his head in the room. She was standing at her bedside hurriedly packing a suitcase.

"Excuse me, Mrs. Amin. I'm Doctor Johnson. I was supposed to do the circumcision on your baby."

She closed the suitcase and slipped it under the bed before turning toward him. She stared at the floor. Steven pulled up a chair and sat, indicating that she too should sit.

"I examined your baby earlier today. He's a beautiful, healthy boy."

Her dark eyes met his for an instant then she lowered her gaze, staring at her hands folded in her lap.

"You have already done the operation?" she asked quietly.

"No. That's why I came to talk with you. I know you signed for it. But I saw you at the nursery window. You were obviously very angry. Have you changed your mind?"

She looked up. Her large dark eyes, unadorned with makeup, conveyed desperation and fear.

“This is not the proper time or place to do this. He must always have his way. I cannot bear to be with him any longer. I must leave before he gets here.”

“Why?”

“He said if I did not allow the circumcision he would repudiate me. That he would keep my baby.”

Steven knew that repudiation in the Muslim world was tantamount to divorce. It carried with it a stigma so heinous that even her own family might refuse to take her in.

It didn’t make sense. If hers was a good marriage, would she risk repudiation for the sake of preventing a circumcision?

“Would you like me to speak with him?"

"Anwar will not listen to you. He was raised to believe in the old ways."

The “old ways” Steven knew was that a married woman was a virtual prisoner in her home. No man other than her husband could gaze upon her body. He opened her chart. Still, physical abuse was not consistent with Muslim teachings that admonished husbands to love and protect their wives.

He saw from the chart that she was only sixteen. "Have you been married long?"

"My father promised me in marriage when I was twelve. We married when I was fifteen.” She leaned over the bed, resting her head on her arm. She cried like the child she was.

Her obstetrician, not surprisingly, was a woman. There was a note indicating that physical examination was limited because of the patient’s religious beliefs. The doctor noted that Mrs. Amin’s husband was present at all visits. Steven read that Mr. Amin, an exchange student from Algeria, was enrolled in a graduate program at Princeton University.

Anna raised the portion of her shawl that covered her forehead. There was a purplish jagged scar, three inches long. It looked as though it had never been properly repaired. Scar tissue was heaped up in irregular mounds along the margins of the wound. She lowered her shawl to cover the scar.

“Did he do this to you?” Steven asked, his voice shaking with suppressed anger.

She nodded. She averted her eyes. “He beats me if supper is not ready when he comes home. Or if I dare to question what he says or where he goes. I cannot leave the apartment unless he is with me. He pretended to be a devout Muslim in order to win my hand and receive a large dowry. He is ashamed of how I dress. He does not obey the prohibition against alcohol and certain foods. He beats me with his fists when he is drunk. He is a hypocrite.”

“Why do you remain with him?”

“He says he will kill me if I do anything to shame him.”

“Are there any relatives or friends you can go to?”

She removed her suitcase from under the bed. “I have no one here. I am alone. Alone.” She went to a closet, hastily removing her things and tossing them on the bed.

“We have places where he can’t hurt you," Steven said. "Do you want me to have someone talk with you?”

“He said he would be here at ten.”

Steven checked his watch. It was nine-fifty-five.

“He will be furious when he finds the baby has not been circumcised.” She added in almost a whisper, “He will never allow me to leave with his son.”

A nurse poked her head in the doorway. “Dr. Johnson, the nursery called. They’re waiting to hear what to do about the circumcision.”

“She changed her mind. Bring her baby to her.”

The nurse looked at Anna for confirmation. She nodded. “I must feed my baby.”

The nurse shrugged. She hurried down the hall.

Steven couldn’t let her run off with a newborn baby. Where would she go? Did she have any money? There was no time to contact a shelter and make the necessary arrangements before Anna’s husband arrived. If he allowed her to leave with her husband, perhaps he could get her and her child to a shelter at a later time. But what if something should happen to her before then? He had no idea what laws applied to non-citizens who were being physically abused. Could an American court give her custody of the child? He doubted the police would be willing to intervene. He must get her to some safe place until arrangements could be made to transfer her to a shelter.

“Mrs. Amin, have you heard of shelters for women who want to get away from husbands who abuse them?”

She nodded.

“Do you want to go to such a place—you and your baby?”

She nodded.

“It will take time to make arrangements. Let us do the circumcision. Go home with your child and husband. When he is away at school, someone from the shelter can take you and your baby away.”

“He hired a woman to stay with me and the baby. Once I go to that apartment I can never get away. I must go when they bring my baby. Do not stop me. I beg you.”

There was no time to consult Anna's attending physician.

"Let me take you to a safe place, until I can find out what to do."

Her eyes met his for a moment. She then averted her gaze. Her hands trembled. "I do not know who to trust."

"I understand," Steven said softly. "I have a younger sister. I cannot imagine her going through what you have experienced. Please let me help you."

"I must. I must trust you. I will come with you. But we must hurry."

Steven went to the door and looked down the corridor. The nurse was coming toward him rolling a bassinet in which the screeching Amin baby lay. Steven went to the crib and gathered the baby in his arms. He handed the nurse Anna's chart. "I'll take him to her."

"Dr. Johnson, I want to warn you, Dr. Scully's pissed."

After giving Anna her baby, Steven went in search of a wheelchair. He knew there was one at the nurses' station but he didn't want to run into Scully or have to explain to the charge nurse where he was taking Mrs. Amin.

At the far end of the corridor was a room used for storage of supplies and medical equipment. He hurried down the hall. He was in luck. A folded wheelchair lay atop a stack of boxes of disposable diapers.

When he entered Anna's room, her baby was at her breast, all but the infant's face covered with her shawl. She got into the wheelchair. Steven carried her bag as he wheeled her toward the elevator. He didn't dare look in the direction of the nurses' station. He pressed the *down* button several times. As the door opened, he heard someone call his name. He pretended not to hear. He rolled Anna into the elevator, where there were already several people. Anna covered her baby's head.

Once at ground level, Steven went to the emergency department reception area. No one would bother her there. They would assume she was waiting to be seen. He parked her as far removed from the receptionist as possible.

“You can stay here. If someone questions you, say you’re waiting for a ride.”

“When will they come?” she asked.

“I’m not sure how soon someone can get here from the shelter. An hour or two. Maybe longer.”

Steven hurried to Chris’ office located along a corridor between the emergency department and the X-ray suite. On the way, his beeper began to vibrate. He read the digital display: “211 stat.” That was the nurses’ station on the obstetrical floor. He decided to ignore the message.

He was relieved to see Chris sitting at her desk in the cramped office. A desk lamp and a greenish luminescence coming from a computer screen dimly lighted her windowless room.

“You got a minute?” he asked as he sank into a chair alongside her desk.

“Sure. What’s up?” She spun her chair around to face him.

Steven hurriedly described what had happened.

“Are you totally insane? Why didn’t you check with her obstetrician?”

“Anna was terrified. Her husband was due to arrive any minute. And that ugly scar on her sweet young face. She was about to run away with a newborn. How soon can we get her into a shelter?”

“All sorts of arrangements have to be made. It could take days!”

“Damnit! Why so much red tape?”

“They’re secretive, they have to be. Once a shelter location is exposed, it’s useless, even dangerous,” Chris explained. “Your call could be bogus—a husband trying to find his wife." Her beeper went off. She glanced at the display.

He nodded. Of course, they couldn't rush into a situation on a moment's notice. Now what was he to do? They were bound to discover her if too much time went by, or if the hospital security guards began to search for her.

"The police at times can be asked to help if there's evidence of imminent danger," Chris said. "If they can't or won't, I'll take her."

"You know where the shelter's located?"

"I can take her to a place where someone from the shelter will meet me."

"You've done this before."

"Yes." She reached up and pulled a pamphlet from a bookshelf. She checked the index. She circled "woman's crisis hotline," then handed the pamphlet to Steven. "Get them involved immediately." She stood and placed both hands on his shoulders. "And call her obstetrician. This is not the Wild West, Steven. I know your heart's in the right place, but there are rules."

"You didn't see the terror in her eyes."

"I have. In other women," Chris said. "I know how you feel. But her doctor has legal responsibility. Suggest to her attending that Anna not be discharged until possible abuse can be documented."

"I believe Anna."

"That's not good enough. I'll check her into the ER. Get X-rays and photos."

"But the ER's probably the first place they'll think to look," he said.

"I'll check her in under different name. How about *Mrs. Farley*?"

Steven grabbed Chris, gave her a bear hug, lifting her off her feet.

She gently separated from him. "I'll take a raincheck on that. We need to hurry. Stall the OB attending. I'll need at least a half-hour to get things done." She left her office.

Steven dialed the nurses' station on the obstetrical floor. "You beeped me?"

"For the past half hour! Mr. Amin's here. He's going up and down the hall, barging into patient's rooms searching for his wife and baby. I've had to call security to restrain him. He's livid. Where are Mrs. Amin and her baby?"

"I took them to a safe place," Steven said.

"You can't just run off with a patient and her baby over a stupid circumcision."

"It's not about the circumcision. She's terrified of him."

"Dr. Smiley's here to discharge her," the nurse said. "I'll put her on."

Steven waited anxiously for the attending to come on the line. The nurse was probably filling her in on what he had said.

"Dr. Smiley, here. Is this the intern who ran off with my patient?"

"Yes. I..."

"Dr. Johnson, you get them back here immediately. How dare you usurp my authority?"

"She told me he beats her. That he's threatened to kill her. I'm concerned about her safety."

"He is a devout Muslim. You obviously don't understand the Muslim culture."

"This has nothing to do with the Muslim culture. Besides, his wife tells me he's Muslim only in name. He has been physically abusing her."

"Do you believe I cared for her for nine months and wasn't aware of physical abuse? My God, are you an idiot? Where have you taken them?"

"I can't tell you that." Steven hung up and dialed the shelter hotline number. He explained the situation to the woman who answered the phone.

"We're filled to capacity. We'll have to look around for a room elsewhere. It could take a day or two. But before I can do anything, I must talk to the woman."

"Yes, I'll have her call you. She's in imminent danger. Can't you take her at least until you can locate a place?"

Should he tell her Anna wasn't an American citizen--would they reject her?

"Hold on, doctor. I need to talk with my supervisor."

As Steven waited, he wondered what to do next. He believed he understood why the circumcision dispute had loomed so large for Anna. Her husband's cruel treatment of her had probably erased any love she might have felt for him. But the alternative of repudiation by her husband was worse than dealing with the physical cruelty. If he repudiated her, he would keep her child. She would have nothing. He had been told that repudiated women were often reduced to prostitution in order to survive.

Steven's beeper went off. It was Dr. Ewing's office. His pulse quickened. What could he possibly tell Ewing? That he took over responsibility for Dr. Smiley's patient because she had failed to recognize that Mrs. Amin was in grave danger? He felt he was in quicksand, reaching desperately for something, anything to hold onto.

The supervisor came on the line. "Doctor, would you give me your beeper number? I'll call the hospital operator and ask to speak with you."

"That's a waste of time."

"What you're asking bypasses our usual precautionary procedures. I need to be sure who you are."

He hung up then immediately dialed Ewing's number. "You beeped me, Dr. Ewing?"

Ewing spoke in the intense, precise cadence of barely controlled fury. "Mr. Anwar Amin is in Clyde Gordon's office. He is furious. He's threatening to call the Algerian Consulate unless we immediately return his wife and child to him. Dr. Smiley is sitting in my office. She just told me what happened. You must join us immediately."

Damnit! He shouldn't have answered Ewing's beep. They would insist he tell them where he had brought Mrs. Amin and her baby. His beeper went off again. It was the hospital operator. "A woman on the line asked me to beep you. We don't usually do that, but she said you were expecting her call."

"Yes, I'll take it." The operator transferred the call

"Hello, Dr. Johnson here."

"This is the supervisor at the shelter. Have your patient call this number."

"Will you send someone to pick her up?" Steven asked.

"I can't, at least for a couple hours."

"We can't wait that long," Steven said. "Dr. Murphy said she could transport her."

"Yes, I know her. Have her call me."

His beeper went off again. He glanced at the display. It was Ewing's number. Steven thanked her and hung up. He exited Dr. Murphy's office, and headed for the ER. Why hadn't he thought to ask Chris to be sure to get Anna out of her Muslim garb and into a hospital gown?

Chapter Nine

Steven pushed through the swinging doors to the rear area of the ER and went directly to the nurses' station.

"Is Mrs. Farley still here?"

"She's in room four. Dr. Murphy's with her."

Steven approached the exam room and knocked. "Dr. Murphy? It's me, Steven."

"Come on in."

Anna was seated in a wheelchair, her baby asleep over her shoulder. She didn't look up when he entered. She was wearing a tennis warm-up suit, and sneakers. Her hair was tucked into a baseball cap pulled down to cover the scar. Steven would not have recognized her except for the baby.

"Where'd you get the clothes?" Steven asked.

"Stuff I had in my locker. I've taken some Polaroids. I'm about to take her to X-ray."

"Ewing's been beeping me for the past fifteen minutes."

"I need more time. Stall him," Chris suggested.

The hospital public address system announced, "Dr. Steven Johnson, report immediately to Dr. Ewing's office."

“Tell him you took her to the cafeteria. By the time they send security, I should have her on her way.”

Steven’s heart pounded as he climbed the stairs two at a time to the fifth floor of the administrative wing. He paused in the anteroom of Ewing’s office, breathless. The secretary rolled her eyes and indicated with flicks of her wrist that he should proceed without delay. As he grasped the doorknob he had some appreciation of how the early Christians must have felt as they stepped onto center-stage of the Coliseum.

“Well, we meet again, Dr. Johnson.” Ewing leaned back in his desk chair, his arms folded, his mouth an angry line. “I assume you know Dr. Smiley?”

“We spoke on the phone,” Dr. Smiley said. She was sitting on a sofa opposite Ewing’s desk. She wore a navy-blue business suit. Her short dark hair was streaked with gray. “A conversation,” she said, “he rudely brought to an abrupt close. I have been a staff attending for over ten years and have never experienced such behavior.”

Steven stood awkwardly beside Ewing’s desk.

“Sit, Dr. Johnson,” Ewing said. “I want you explain to me what happened. Start with the circumcision; why you didn’t call Dr. Smiley, and where have you taken Mrs. Amin and her baby?”

Steven sat in a chair beside Ewing’s desk. “Mrs. Amin refused to have her baby circumcised.”

“Both she and her husband signed the operative permit,” Dr. Smiley snapped.

Steven went on to explain that the mother had been forced by her husband to okay the circumcision. How she had told him of physical abuse. He described her disfigured face.

"Mrs. Amin told me the scar was from an accident," Dr. Smiley said. "I did suspect, but she never told me that her husband physically abused her."

"How could she? You and she were never alone. She was frantic. She told me he'd threatened to kill her if she didn't allow the baby to be circumcised."

"And you believed her?" Dr. Smiley asked.

"When I went to her room she was packing her suitcase, preparing to run away."

"She was preparing to be discharged," Dr. Smiley said.

"No," Steven said. "She told me that she wanted to get away before her husband arrived."

"You should have called Dr. Smiley immediately," Ewing said. "Mrs. Amin has not been officially discharged, nor has she signed out against medical advice. Dr. Smiley and the hospital are responsible for her wellbeing."

"Precisely." Dr. Smiley stood and walked to where Steven was sitting. "Where have you taken her?" she shouted, her face inches from his.

"Sit down, Dr. Smiley!" Ewing said. "Let Dr. Johnson continue."

She started back toward the sofa, then turned and glared at Dr. Ewing. She stood defiantly facing him, her arms crossed.

Steven was stunned by the intensity of Dr. Smiley's anger. He had acted impulsively, yes, but he still believed he had no other choice. "I asked her if she wanted to go into a woman's shelter. She said she did," Steven said. "I believed she was in grave danger." He went on to recount his conversation with a woman at the shelter. He had taken her to a safe place expecting that someone from the shelter would pick her up.

"*Where* did you take her?" Dr. Smiley insisted.

Had he given Chris enough time to complete her workup? He looked at his watch. “I can’t tell you that.”

“Dr. Johnson,” Ewing said, “If you tell us, we will make sure she remains in the hospital until this matter can be sorted out. Dr. Smiley, you must get social services and children’s protective services involved immediately.”

“You’re suggesting to me how to manage my private patient?” she asked.

“That was not a suggestion, Dr. Smiley. I’m ultimately responsible for the quality of care of all patients, private or otherwise. You *must* initiate an investigative process before she is discharged.” He turned to Steven. “Dr. Johnson, she obviously trusts you. Go to her. I’ll make sure a security guard remains with her.”

“She’s terrified of her husband. She’ll deny he abused her if he’s there.” He paused. He checked his watch. “She may already be on her way to a shelter.”

Dr. Ewing and Dr. Smiley asked in unison, “What?”

“He’s lying. He could not possibly have gotten her to a shelter so quickly,” Dr. Smiley said. “Dr. Ewing, you must insist he tell us were he’s taken her.”

“You sent her to a shelter without real evidence of abuse other than what she said?” Ewing asked.

Steven couldn’t tell them that Dr. Murphy was documenting abuse—what if she hadn’t yet left the ER?

“Can I use your phone, Dr. Ewing?” Steven asked. Ewing shrugged. He pushed his phone toward Steven. He dialed the ER nurses’ station. “This is Dr. Johnson. Is Mrs. Farley still there?”

There was a pause at the other end of the line. “Excuse me.” Moments later she was back on the line. “She just now left with Dr. Murphy.”

Steven hung up. Inside he was shouting, yes, yes, way to go, Murphy! "She's already left for a shelter," he said, without expression.

"What in God's name am I going to tell Mr. Amin?" Dr. Smiley asked. She sank dejectedly onto the sofa.

"That his wife voluntarily checked herself into a woman's shelter. That it is out of our hands at this time," Ewing said. "Dr. Smiley, would you mind stepping out so I might speak with Dr. Johnson in private?"

She stood and beat her skirt into alignment with more vigor than seemed necessary. She headed for the door. She turned, her face the color of day-old grits. "Dr. Ewing, I intend to file a grievance with the hospital executive committee. According to our bylaws, insubordination on the part of housestaff is grounds for dismissal."

"That is your prerogative, Dr. Smiley," Ewing said. He pressed the intercom lever. "Mrs. Mack, call Gordon and tell him Dr. Smiley and I will join him and Mr. Amin in just a few minutes."

After Dr. Smiley left, Ewing stood and faced the windows behind his desk, his hands clasped behind his back. He said. "In the meantime, Dr. Johnson, I'll convene an emergency meeting of the housestaff committee to determine what disciplinary action should be taken. You must understand, Steven, whatever action they recommend does not reflect my personal feelings." Ewing turned and sat on the edge of his desk, next to where Steven was sitting.

"I would like to have an off the record, man-to-man talk with you."

Steven was speechless. Was he going to tell him to resign? That he wasn't cut out to be a physician?

"What you did, son, took a great deal of courage. Your commitment to the patient is admirable. Your heart is in the right place, Steven. Unfortunately, your head is not."

"I felt certain she was in imminent danger. I would do it again if I had to."

"And her baby?" Ewing asked. "Was he in imminent danger?

"A newborn needs its mother."

"It was not for you to have decided what was best for the baby. Theirs is a fiercely patriarchal society. Don't you realize Mr. Amin will move heaven and earth to get his son back?"

Ewing had touched on the injustice inherent in Steven's intervention on Anna's behalf without considering the father's rights. "I was looking at it from Mrs. Amin's perspective."

"In time, Steven, I hope and expect you'll learn to look at the big picture. Consider alternatives, policy issues, and other points of view. Think of all the patients you can potentially help in a lifetime. Yes, you may have to make some compromises at this stage."

"What would you have done, Dr. Ewing?"

Ewing sighed. "As an intern, I would not have had the gumption to do what you did. As children, my generation played *follow the leader*. We grew up with that same mindset. Today young people aren't in awe of authority. That's a good thing at times, but it does make for turmoil. You must temper the reformer in you. If not, the establishment will chew you up."

"Will I be fired?"

"I may have no other choice. I have no idea what kind of action Mr. Amin may choose to bring against the hospital. We have only her word against his that she had been abused."

"She was checked into the ER as Mrs. Farley. The ER took photographs and X-rays to look for evidence of abuse."

"Was that your doing?"

Steven didn't want to incriminate Chris. "I brought her to the ER."

"I see." Ewing stood. "Mr. Amin and Gordon are waiting to meet with me. I regret to do this, Steven, but as of this moment you are relieved of all hospital responsibilities pending a decision by the housestaff committee. As you probably know, I chair the committee and the members are the directors of the hospital's training programs. I will do what I can on your behalf. But I'm not optimistic."

Steven remained seated. He stared at Ewing's empty desk chair. A throne, really. A good man with a job to do, to hold together a staff of conservative, hard-working, fiercely independent professionals, who lived by the book.

Dr. Ewing had little time to ponder what to say when he encountered Anwar Amin. He hesitated at the door before entering Gordon's office. As Ewing stepped into the room, Mr. Amin shot to his feet. Gordon introduced Ewing as 'the head of the hospital's medical staff.' Amin, a medium-sized dark-skinned man, wore an expensive hand-stitched Italian suit and a white turban. His intense dark eyes bore into Ewing. He ignored Ewing's outstretched hand.

"I bring my wife to the hospital to have our child and you take them from me. This is an outrage. Where have you taken them?"

"I can understand your anger."

"You understand nothing. Nothing!" Anwar shouted. "What do you know of our culture?"

"Yes, you're right," Ewing said. "But domestic violence, unfortunately, is common in all cultures."

"Is it not domestic violence to take a man's son from him?"

"Mr. Amin," Gordon said, "the hospital did not take your son."

Anwar glared at Gordon. "You have said enough already. I do not want to hear from you." He turned to Ewing. "My wife has decadent

Western ideas. She watches your television; she reads your magazines. I have tried to teach her, but she is wretched, ignorant."

"Mr. Amin, your wife has voluntarily gone into a woman's shelter. Do you understand what that is?"

"She does not know her own mind. She shames me and her own family. She shames my people. I must cast her off like a dead animal." He sank dejectedly onto a chair. He stared at his hands. He clenched his fists and beat them against his temples. He looked up at Ewing. "I will not allow you to take my son from me. There is no price I will not pay to get him back."

Ewing felt empathy for this young man. Raised in a patriarchal culture, he believed he must protect his wife's honor and punish her for her sinfulness, as he had no doubt seen his father do before him. Ewing wondered if an American court would have the authority to make a custody decision when the disputing parties are not US citizens. "Mr. Amin, there are lawyers who specialize in custody disputes."

"You have kidnapped my son and now you talk of custody. I will go to the police, not a lawyer."

"I'm afraid they would not be able to help you." Ewing said.

"Is this a democracy? Is this a democracy?" Anwar shouted.

He stood and shook his fist at Ewing. "I will go to the Algerian Consulate. I will have justice!" He slammed the office door as he rushed from the room.

Ewing leaned back on the sofa and closed his eyes. "The baby is our Achilles heel, Gordon."

"An Algerian court would take the baby from the mother," Gordon said, "but our courts more often give the mother custody, especially a newborn."

"Does the hospital bear any liability?" Ewing asked.

"It does if we shipped her off without documenting abuse."

"I know that photographs and X-rays were taken in the ER," Ewing said. "I assume whomever saw her would have documented her account of physical abuse."

"Let's hope so," Gordon said.

"I wonder about Mrs. Amin's visa. If it's dependent on being the spouse of a student, what happens to that status if she leaves him?"

"I don't know,' Gordon admitted. "And what are we to do with our young rogue intern? This is strike two and he's been here just a few weeks. Will he survive another ten months?"

"Will the hospital?" Ewing asked.

Chapter Ten

On the floor of his bedroom, Steven sat in the lotus position. He closed his eyes, trying to clear his mind of the previous day's events. Jasmine-scented incense rose in slowly expanding spirals from a thimble-sized burner on a nearby dresser. He breathed deeply, concentrating on the rise and fall of his chest. When that didn't work, he began to concentrate on relaxing his muscles, starting with his toes and slowly progressing up his leg, his abdominals, back muscles, pectorals, then his diaphragm.

It still wasn't working, not this time. He checked his watch. He was to pick up Chris in less than a half-hour for their much-anticipated date. He slipped on a pair of clean jeans and a tee shirt.

He rummaged through a dresser drawer for a pair of matching socks. He looked through the front hall closet. It was too warm for his leather jacket. He grabbed a windbreaker.

Had Smithfield been a good match for him? If he'd chosen to train in a hospital in Kansas he would never have encountered the maniacal preacher, or the abused child-mother, nor would he have met the feisty girl-next-door Chris Murphy or the exotic Jacqueline Martin. Is there a pattern to life's events? Or is it a roll of the dice, a chaotic miasma of happenstance?

Stonybrook Estates, a fifteen-minute drive from the hospital, was located midway between Smithfield and Princeton. It consisted of a maze of oversized single-family homes, townhouses, condos and apartments. Winding about the complex in search of Chris's townhouse, Steven became totally disoriented. By the time he stumbled onto her place, he was fifteen minutes late.

He pulled from his windbreaker a small, somewhat compressed bouquet of roses he'd picked up at a supermarket on the way. He held the flowers behind his back as he rang the doorbell.

Chris was wearing black slacks, a white cotton tank top and a paisley scarf around her waist. He couldn't help staring at a tattoo of a butterfly, perched on her left shoulder.

She laughed. "An undergraduate indiscretion. I did <u>not</u> go out for the swim team. The Sisters of Charity at St. Mary's would not have approved."

Steven noticed a small crucifix on the wall behind her. She probably had a statue of the blessed virgin in the bedroom. He handed her the flowers. "Sorry I'm late."

"Actually, you're just in time. I got hung up in the ER. I just this minute slipped on my clothes."

An image of her stepping naked from the shower flashed through his mind. "A stiff price to pay for being late."

She led him into a miniature kitchen, removed the green paper wrap from the bouquet and searched through a couple of cabinets for something to put them in. She removed an empty milk bottle from the sink.

"This will have to do for now." She placed the flowers in the bottle. "Care for something to drink?" she asked, as she poured water into the bottle.

"What do you have?"

"Beer, wine, pop." She went to the fridge.

"Not used to hearing "pop' around here."

"You're from Kansas. I'm just trying to make you feel at home."

He leaned over her shoulder as she peered into the fridge. Her soft blond hair smelled of honeysuckle. "I'd just as soon get going while we have a bit of daylight," he said. "Maybe we can stop..."

"I already did." She removed an unopened bottle of wine from the fridge and placed it on the table. Steven inspected the label as she walked to the stove and removed an oil-stained bag from the oven. "Spicy fried chicken, extra crispy; biscuits and mashed potatoes. A week's quota of saturated fat."

"Beaujolais and Bojangles, a perfectly balanced meal. Would you like to picnic along the Raritan? I know a great spot. It reminds me of my favorite place back home."

"Should I bring a blanket?" she asked.

"I already have one in my bike saddle."

"A favorite tryst and all the accouterments." She went to the hall closet.

Steven laughed. "I like to camp out when I get a chance. There's this wooded area back home, just outside of Zion. A stony brook..."

"I thought Kansas was a prairie state. Tumbleweeds, tornadoes..."

"Our forests are as beautiful as you'll see anywhere. Mostly hardwoods. Lots of elm that somehow survived the blight. They're my favorite."

"What, no redwoods?" she asked as she reached into a drawer, removed some paper napkins and placed them in the bag of food.

"Afraid not," he said. "We'd better get going." Part of him would have preferred to stay in her cozy apartment, to share with her his disillusionment and humiliation at being on the verge of being fired from his internship, to be comforted, to be loved.

He picked up the wine bottle and followed her into the front hall.

Since his going-away-party in the ER, they had engaged in flirtatious banter. That millisecond when their fingertips met and a spark had passed between them seemed an omen. The scientist in him knew it was merely static electricity, but the romantic in him was convinced otherwise.

What did he really know of Chris? Of her aborted engagement? And why had she risked so much to help him? He wanted to tell her he'd been suspended by Dr. Ewing, that the hospital's housestaff committee held his fate in their hands. They could send him packing. That he had gotten word that his deposition in the malpractice suit would probably be sometime in the next week or two.

He stared at the crucifix that hung over a small telephone table. It brought to mind the image of Mrs. Amin's screaming baby strapped to the cross-like restraining board. Would her visa be voided? Would she and her baby be forced to return to Algeria?

"It belonged to my great-grandmother. The figure of Jesus is hand-carved out of ivory. How do you like my new jacket?"

Steven turned. She was wearing a brown leather flight jacket, World War II vintage.

"Picked it up in a thrift shop in Princeton," she said.

"I'm jealous; I've always wanted one of those."

"If you're not excessively vain, you'd be surprised what you can pick up at a thrift shop, especially in a town like Princeton."

They left Chris's apartment and walked to Steven's bike. It was a muggy, warm mid-August New Jersey evening. A swarm of mosquitoes in search of their evening meal buzzed about them. Two yellowjackets settled on the bag of food. He shook off the bees and placed the wine and food in his saddle storage compartment.

"Once we're on our way," he said, "I won't be able to hear a thing you say. Nudge me in the ribs once if you want me to slow down. Twice if you want to stop."

"Are those my only options?"

"That's it," he said as he handed her a helmet, then mounted the bike. She cinched the strap snugly under her chin, made a sign of the cross, straddled the rumble seat, put her arms around his waist and pressed against him. As the engine roared to life she gripped him so tightly, he could hardly breathe.

Soon they were on a winding country road, past the bustle of traffic. Her grip relaxed. She opened her jacket and put it around him. She pressed against him. He could feel the warmth of her body. He had the sudden urge to head west; to retrace the hundreds of miles he had driven his Honda Shadow from Kansas. The rushing wind and the roar of the engine began to fade until there was no sound but the mournful voice of Bob Marley, was it his father's voice, or perhaps his own? "Fly away home, mon, Fly away home to Zion."

Steven lay propped on one elbow, sipping wine from a paper cup. Chris sat cross-legged beside him. She poked around in the container of chicken and came out with a drumstick. The roar of the motorcycle had been replaced by the resonating love calls of thousands of crickets, the gurgle of the brook, the cry of an unseen owl, and countless other chirps and shrieks that Steven was unable to identify.

"What do you think?" he asked.

"It's lovely. How come no mosquitoes?"

"Be patient, they'll find us. If it gets too bad, I have some bug spray."

She poured herself a cup of wine. She raised it toward his. "To Anna...may she live happily ever after."

Steven tapped his cup to hers. "Thanks for all your help."

"When you barged into my office and told me about her, I thought you were crazy. But when I saw that scar, the bruises..."

"Did the X-rays show anything?" he asked.

"Old rib fractures. Two healing metatarsal fractures."

"Metatarsal?"

"He probably stomped on her foot."

"I'd love to show those films to Dr. Smiley," Steven said.

"She's already seen them. She came down to the ER after she left Ewing's office. I showed her Anna's chart."

"How did she react?"

"She read Anna's description of the abuse. She and I looked at the films. She left without saying a word."

"Was she still angry?"

"I believe she was crying."

Neither spoke. Steven lay back on the blanket. It was not quite dark. The tall trees obscured all but a small circle of sky. Some of the brighter stars were beginning to appear. Chris lay beside him. He rolled on his side, facing her. She stared at the sky.

"You suppose that bright one is Venus?"

"Yes, I believe it might be." He lightly touched her cheek with his fingertips. "I was half expecting sparks."

"We'll have to make our own, I guess." She pulled him toward her. "But don't think you're going to score because of your rugged good looks, charm, and lovely roses. It is our first date after all."

"I'd be content with a base-hit. Maybe steal second."

"Sounds reasonable. Where exactly is second?"

"Now that's a good question, teach."

They were oblivious of the forest sounds or the flashing of hundreds of fireflies or the smell of the sweet clover on which they lay. Venus, queen of the heavens, all seeing, all knowing, her radiant energy traversing millions of miles, shone gently upon them.

Chapter Eleven

On the fifth ring Steven picked up the phone, and rubbed his sleepy eyes. Dr. Ewing was on the line. He glanced at the bedside clock; it was ten in the morning. He sat on the edge of the bed.

"I wanted to let you know that Dr. Smiley just called me and said she wasn't going to go to the executive committee."

Steven was relieved. But other hurdles were yet to be jumped. "Does that change my chances with the house staff committee?"

"A charge of insubordination by a respected attending would have been impossible for them to ignore."

"Why did she change her mind?" Steven asked. He wasn't really surprised from what Chris had told him, but he wanted to hear it from Ewing.

"She said she'd spent a sleepless night thinking about it. Said she still believes you should have called her, but that she now understands why you felt compelled to act."

"How likely is it that I'll be fired?" Steven held the phone between his hunched shoulder and ear as he slipped on socks and a pair of jeans.

"More likely than not, I'm afraid."

There are plenty of second-rate hospitals with open positions, Steven thought. But would even those institutions be interested in him? "You have to make them understand that this wasn't something between me and Dr. Smiley. It was about me and a terrified woman who asked me to help her."

"Steven, their concerns will not center on your motives, no matter how pure they may have been. Their decision will be based on principle."

"What principle is that?"

"A hospital is much like the military. There's a chain of command. If they allow you to bypass the system and the bylaws that govern its function, they will be establishing a precedent that can only lead to chaos."

"It's beginning to sound like a foregone conclusion." The phone dropped to the floor as Steven attempted to slip on a tee shirt. He quickly retrieved it. "Sorry."

"As an isolated event, the Anwar Amin incident wouldn't be a fatal error. But on top of the malpractice suit it looms much larger. A secondary consideration is that this early in the year we're more likely to be able to fill your position. Some of the excellent candidates we had to turn away might still be interested."

"I can understand that principle," Steven said. "Thou shalt always have enough interns to cover thy days, nights and weekends."

"Damnit, Johnson. I'm trying to explain the system to you. Gordon may be right. He believes you're a loose cannon and a troublemaker."

Troublemaker! A loose cannon? It was outrageous Gordon concluded that. And why would Ewing's opinion of Steven be so influenced by Gordon? There's so little defense against summary judgments. It was cruel and unfair.

"Those are preposterous accusations," Steven said. "If you really believe that, you should send me packing."

"You must understand that, if you're fired, it will be virtually impossible for you to find a decent position anywhere else."

"Are you asking me to resign?"

"No. Not yet. But if they do decide to fire you, I'll insist they give you that option."

Steven struggled to remain calm. He breathed deeply. He thought of his tiny Buddha. "When do you meet?" he asked.

"We can't get a quorum together until Wednesday of next week. I want you to submit to me a detailed recounting of the entire incident. I want it on my desk by noon Monday. No speculation, Steven. Just what you personally observed and did."

What if Ewing had asked Chris to write up the incident? He'd better talk with her before writing his report.

"Yes, sir. I can do that."

Steven intended to leave out Chris's part in it. He had better make sure she just reported what she did after he had checked Anna into the ER.

"And don't use the hospital transcriptionist to type up your report. If you want to dictate it, drop off the tape at my office."

"How soon can I expect to hear what the committee decides?"

"I doubt they'll make a definitive decision without offering you a chance to come before them."

The thought of facing a roomful of angry program directors sent icy ripples coursing along Steven's spine. "If you believe it's necessary."

"You are aware that there is a protest procedure in the event you're fired," Dr. Ewing asked. "Is that a course you might take?"

"I wouldn't want to stay if the majority of the department heads decided to fire me."

"I'll do my best to prevent that. But I'll have a revolt on my hands if I overrule the will of the majority."

"I understand. Thank you, Dr. Ewing."

Steven spent the rest of the day catching up on things he hadn't had time to do while he was working. His bike inspection was overdue. He stuffed a Dick Francis paperback in his back pocket and headed for the Honda dealer in Smithfield. He flipped through several old issues of Field and Stream. The tune-up and inspection were taking longer than he'd expected. He was glad he'd brought something to read.

From there Steven went to a laundromat. He bought a doughnut and a cup of coffee. He sat at a table reading his book as the machines at the rear of the laundromat beat and tumbled his clothes. He was surprised to see Jerry Russo enter, a bulging laundry bag slung over his shoulder.

"Yo, Johnson," Jerry said.

He plunked the bag on the floor next to Steven. Judging by the odor, Steven was pretty sure what was in the bag.

"Our two-year old is allergic to disposable diapers, and Gloria has got to stay off her feet, so here I am." Jerry tore off a piece of Steven's doughnut. "You mind?"

Steven shook his head.

Jerry spoke as he chewed. "Scully had to re-work the whole rotation schedule. He's fuming. Wouldn't be surprised if he puts out a contract on you."

"I'm sorry about the extra work."

"Hey, don't worry about it. I'm already numb," Jerry said. "Dead is dead, right? Anyway, it's mainly the senior guys complaining about having to take primary call." He stood. "I'd better get started on these diapers before they throw me out of here. Talk to you later."

That afternoon Steven drove his bike to Princeton. As close as the University was to Smithfield, this was his first chance to go there. He walked aimlessly about the campus, where its ivy-covered buildings and stately trees stood in marked contrast to the baby-faced undergraduates milling about, playing Frisbee, sunning on the roof tops, scattered about the lawns reading, dozing, boy watching, girl watching. He imagined Albert Einstein ambling along that very path, picking up a wayward Frisbee, then sending it aloft. Watching as it wobbled toward outstretched arms, working out in his head a mathematical formula to explain its erratic flight.

He visited a bookstore in downtown Princeton. A middle-aged woman sitting at the information desk considered his inquiry about marriage in Muslim cultures.

She swung about to face her computer terminal.

"Muslim culture varies in different parts of the world."

"Algeria. Anything specifically about that?"

"Let's try a keyword search. We can use Algeria and marriage." She pulled a pencil from behind her ear and used the eraser end to peck at the computer keyboard.

"Here's one published this year---*Women of Algiers in Their Apartments*, by Assia Djebar."

Her name was vaguely familiar to Steven. He located the book and went to the espresso bar where he spent the next three hours reading. After his third espresso, he decided it would be cheaper to buy the book. It was dark by the time he arrived at his apartment. He finished the book at four in the morning. The stories Djebar told took place in the years after Algeria's long, bloody struggle for independence from France. Had conditions for women changed since then? For many, yes, but apparently not for Anna Amin.

He set his alarm for eleven-thirty. Before he dropped off to sleep, he thought of Anna. Free of her husband, but still in a way a prisoner. What was she feeling? Who would teach her to be a mother?

Steven was to meet Chris for lunch at the Silver Bullet Express in just thirty minutes. He hurriedly showered, shaved, slipped on a pair of khaki pants and a polo shirt. As he laced his sneakers, blood dripped onto his hands. He went to a mirror. He had nicked his chin while shaving. He retrieved a styptic pencil from his shaving kit and applied it to his bleeding chin. When it continued to ooze, he applied a small patch of toilet paper. He dashed out of the door to his apartment. Moments later he returned in search of his wallet.

He rode his Honda Shadow along the winding hospital drive. An ambulance, its siren wailing, its lights flashing, drove past him, heading for the emergency entrance. It was a beautiful summer day...the rolling hospital lawn a rich green, the sky a deep blue with scattered islands of clouds. The fragrance of Chris's perfume from the night before was as vivid as all that surrounded him. He should feel exhilarated to be free of the pressures of his internship, but instead he felt displaced, an exile. He was to have worked that weekend. Someone else had to fill in for him; someone who already had a burdensome schedule. Even if he were to be reinstated, there would be lingering resentment among the staff.

As Steven entered the diner, he spotted Chris seated at a booth. She was reading a newspaper and hadn't noticed him. She looked great. She had done something to her hair.

"Hi," he said as he slipped in next to her. "I hardly recognized you."

"You like it?" she asked as she turned her head from side to side.

"You look sensational." Her blond hair was done up in a million fluffy little curls. "How do you do that?"

"It was like this when I got up the morning after our tryst in the trees."

"Must have been the dampness. What are you reading so intently?"

"Look at this." She pointed to a front-page headline in the *Smithfield Currier.*

"Woman and newborn disappear."

Steven grabbed the paper.

> *A mother and her newborn son went missing from Smithfield Hospital yesterday, as reported by a hospital spokesperson. The woman, Mrs. Anna Amin, was last seen leaving the obstetrical floor in a wheelchair with a pediatric intern. Hospital sources said Anna Amin and her infant son were gone when her husband, an Algerian exchange student, arrived for then yesterday. Doctors had not discharged the patient or the baby.*
>
> *Mrs. Amin's obstetrician, Dr. Catherine Smiley, refused to discuss the case, on attorney's advice. Dr. Steven Johnson, a pediatric intern, was suspended soon after Mrs. Amin and the baby disappeared, hospital Medical Director, Dr. David Ewing, stated. He reported that Mrs. Amin had requested admission to a woman's shelter. Her husband, Mr. Anwar Amin, claimed charges of abuse were "nonsense." Mr. Amin will appeal to the Algerian Consulate for the return of his son.*

"Who do you suppose is Deep Throat?" Chris asked.

"Probably someone on the OB floor. Could be one of the nurses. I ran into Jerry Russo yesterday. He said Scully was furious. It could be him."

A waitress approached their table. Both ordered the same thing: oyster soup, a grilled cheese sandwich and coffee.

"Don't look so glum," Steven said. "I do have some good news. Dr. Smiley's decided not to submit a formal complaint to the Executive Committee."

"You know, I'm not surprised," Chris said. "She was pretty shocked when she saw those films and Polaroids."

"Ewing said the committee meeting is next Wednesday."

"Maybe this thing going public won't be all that bad."

"I don't understand," Steven said.

"People are bound to take sides. I can't see too many coming out on the side of a wife-beater. The hospital's going to look pretty bad if they come down too hard on you."

"And what if Deep Throat lets the paper know about a pending malpractice suit?"

Their soup and sandwiches arrived. They ate in silence. As he glanced out the window of the diner, a row of cars passed, giving Steven the sensation that the diner was moving. He wished it were the twenties; he and Chris lovers, headed for New York City to make the rounds of clubs and speakeasies.

"We'd better get our stories straight, in case Ewing or Gordon questions you," Steven said.

"I'll tell him what happened. That you came to me, not knowing exactly what to do."

"I already told Ewing no one else was involved," he interrupted. "I didn't want you sucked into this."

She placed her hand on his. "Hey, there you go again, Mr. Rescuer."

"Anna hadn't been officially discharged. They'll say you had no right to order those tests."

"Wrong!" Chris said. "Once Anna was checked into the ER it didn't matter if she came from the moon. She became my responsibility. And when she told me that she wanted to go to a woman's shelter, I was obligated to document the abuse."

Steven didn't know what to say. He munched on his grilled cheese sandwich. "What if I didn't tell you she hadn't already been discharged from the hospital?"

"That's just not believable," she said. "Where was I to assume you got her? Call Ewing, Steven. Tell him exactly what happened, that I suggested you check her into the ER. That I knew she hadn't been discharged by her obstetrician."

"Ewing suspended me. They'll maybe fire me. What will they do to you?"

"Interns they can replace, especially this time of year. A residency-trained ER specialist? No way. At least once a week I receive tempting offers from headhunters."

The waitress came by and refilled their coffee cups. "Ewing asked me to write my account of what happened. I'll print it up on my laptop and e-mail a copy to you. Would you mind?"

"Sure, I'd be glad to look it over," She jotted down her e-mail address on a paper napkin and handed it to him.

Steven glanced at the newspaper on the table beside him. Thank God for Chris, he thought. How would he get through this without her? Yet he knew so little about her. She never talked about her family. He wondered why. Maybe tomorrow they might take a lazy boat ride down the meandering Raritan. Plenty of time to talk. She was definitely someone he wanted to learn all about. He wondered what her family was like, what they meant to her. "You're famous," she said, tapping the newspaper.

"Infamous," Steven corrected.

"I hope Mr. Amin doesn't enlist the Algerian Mafia."

"They don't really have a Mafia, do they?" Steven asked.

"They probably call it something else," she said. "Hey, don't look so serious. I was kidding."

"What are you doing tomorrow?" he asked.

"Mass at eleven. Free after that."

"Can I come by?"

"Sure. Around two. Don't eat lunch. I'll fix something nutritious. All this stress is probably depleting your B-vitamins."

"How about a slow boat ride down the Raritan?"

Chapter Twelve

As Steven entered his apartment, he heard a familiar voice… "I'm unable to come to the phone right now. Please leave your name and number."

The display indicated he had fourteen messages. He took the phone to a small desk where he played them back. Dr. Ewing had called three times. Steven dialed his number first.

"Have you seen the paper?" Ewing asked brusquely.

"Yes."

"My phone's been ringing off the hook. Where the hell have you been? Never mind. I don't care. Have you talked with any reporters?"

"No, sir. I have no idea where they got their information. I do have phone messages from the Smithfield paper and a local TV news station."

"God almighty! Tell them nothing. The hospital has released an official response. Let me read it to you: 'A postpartum patient at Smithfield Hospital requested she and her newborn be sent to a woman's shelter. She was evaluated in our Emergency Department. We then arranged their safe transfer.'"

"Dr. Johnson," Ewing continued, "you must not tell anyone about the physical and X-ray findings in the emergency department. That is privileged information."

"What if they ask why I've been suspended?"

"Refer them to Clyde Gordon. He'll tell them your temporary suspension is related to procedural issues, not the part you played in Mrs. Amin's transfer."

"If the housestaff committee decides to reinstate me, how soon can I start back?"

"In a day or two. I'll need to notify pedes and other department heads."

Steven looked at a call schedule tacked to the wall above his desk. He would miss three call nights and one weekend. Scully wasn't going to make life easy for him. He'd certainly insist Steven make up the missed call.

"You might want to get away for a few days," Ewing suggested.

Chris was right. The hospital probably wouldn't want to make a martyr of him. His chances of being reinstated were looking better.

"Yes, I might do that."

"Let me know of your whereabouts, in case I need to get hold of you."

After speaking with Dr. Ewing, Steven looked through his other messages. He deleted calls from the media. There were calls from Martha Knight, Jacqueline and Jerry Russo. He called Martha. She said she'd heard what had happened and that she and the rest of the ER staff were concerned about him and wanted him to know they would help in any way they could. He thanked her. He called Jerry, who said Scully was still fuming but the other interns were cool. They didn't even complain about the extra call nights.

Steven saved the call from Jacqueline till last. He couldn't deny that he was attracted to her, but for now he was developing a warm, wonderful crush on Chris. He thought of Chris in his quiet inner moments. No, crush didn't describe the depth of his feeling toward her. How ironic that he had gone so long without a love interest. He'd been living the life of a monk since his college sweetheart ran off with one of her professors. Now, all of sudden, he found himself becoming involved with one woman while a second circled in a landing pattern, waiting for word from the control tower. Or was he being presumptuous? Was he misinterpreting those almond-eyed glances?

"Hi, Jacqueline. This is Steven. Thanks for calling."

"I have sadness for what has happened."

"Hey, I'm okay. How's my patient, Tommy?"

"He went to his home today. He asks for you."

"Good for him," Steven said."

"I haven't seen you in the cafeteria."

"Too many eyes. Too many questions."

"I am a good cook. Do you want me to bring you something?"

"I've got plenty of food in my apartment," he lied.

"I will cook you rice and chicken. You will like it."

"Don't bother, please."

There was a long silence from her end of the line. "I do not mean to bother you. Sharing food in my country is a sign of friendship. I will leave the food at your door."

"Jacqueline, that's not what I meant. I didn't want to put *you* to any trouble."

"The chicken will have trouble. I will be fine."

Steven laughed. "Okay. But only if you agree to stay and have dinner with me. As a sign of friendship."

They agreed on a time. He asked if she needed directions to his apartment, or if she needed to be picked up.

"I know where the housestaff apartments are. And Omar has agreed to lend me his car."

As soon as he hung up, the phone rang. He let the answering machine get it. It was a newspaper reporter from the Newark Star Ledger. He disconnected his phone.

How could he have refused without hurting her feelings? Would she still be wearing her student nurse's uniform? That would help to keep things on a professional plane. He hoped she wouldn't change into anything exotic. God knows she didn't need enhancing.

Maybe he could invite the Russos over for a potluck dinner. He dialed their number. Gloria answered the phone.

"Hi, Gloria, this is Steven. Is Jerry on call tonight?"

"No. He should be home by seven."

"A friend is coming over with some food. I wondered if you and Jerry might join us for dinner."

"We'd love to," Gloria said. "I have a ziti and sausage casserole in the oven. I can bring that."

"Great. My friend will be bringing chicken and rice."

"I'm not sure we can get a sitter."

"That's no problem. Bring little Mary along."

"I'll soak her in hot sudsy water for an hour," Gloria said. "That usually calms her down."

Steven again disconnected his phone. He rushed through his apartment childproofing it against a two-year-old with the destructive force and the physique of a tiny Sumo wrestler. The last time they had stopped by she tipped over an end table, sending a fake Tiffany lamp crashing to the floor.

After showering, he slipped on a clean pair of jeans and a tee shirt. On the front of his shirt was a black and white image of Bob Marley, his head surrounded by spoke-like dreadlocks, his guitar slung low across his thighs, his ever-present stogie in the corner of his mouth. In his bedroom, Steven lit some incense to mask the musty smell of the apartment's wall-to-wall shag carpeting. He heard a car pull onto his drive. Must be Jacqueline, he thought. He hurried to the door. He was shocked to see Chris's smiling face. She was holding a brown paper bag in the palm of her hand.

"Chris! Hey."

"I've been trying to get through to you for the past hour. Figured you probably disconnected your phone. I have to fill in tomorrow for one of the contract attendings." She handed him the bag.

"What's this?" he said stupidly.

"A tuna casserole. I picked it up at the Smart-Mart."

Oh God! "Ah..."

"You going to invite me in or what?" she said, as she edged past him into the room. "I like your shirt. What's that I smell? Jasmine?"

He stood in the open doorway, mute, unsure what to say.

"Shut the door and come in, Steven. And give that to me. I'll stick in the oven to keep it warm."

When she came back into the room she went up to him and put her arms around him.

"Hey, relax. It's just me. Is all this craziness getting to you?"

"I invited Jerry Russo and his wife over."

"That casserole won't be enough for four. Let's go out to eat."

"They're bringing food."

"Bet she's a good cook."

The doorbell rang. Steven didn't move. "Chris, I have to explain something..."

"It's probably the Russos," she said. The bell rang again. She hurried toward the door.

"No! Let me." He rushed after her. She opened the door. Jacqueline stood there, a picnic basket in her hand. She was wearing a burgundy-colored, ankle-length dress with a white form-fitting sleeveless high-collared top. Her hair was a mass of tight, spiral curls. She was wearing pendent earrings of interlocking gold rings. Not a lick of makeup. He was right, she didn't need enhancing.

Jacqueline looked from a flustered Steven to an astonished Chris. She smiled, with no trace of embarrassment. "Dr. Johnson, here is the food I promised to bring you."

There was an awkward silence.

"Chris, after I spoke with you, there was this message from Jacqueline..."

"Say no more. I understand perfectly," Chris said. She turned to Jacqueline. "Come in, Little Red Riding Hood. The big bad wolf is all yours." She stomped past Jacqueline toward her car.

"Chris, please," Steven said.

"I am sorry," Jacqueline said softly. "You did not tell me."

"It's okay. Come in, please." He hurried after Chris. "Chris, wait, I can explain." But by the time he reached her, she had already begun to back down the drive. He watched her spin her car about in a tight screech, then headed down the winding road that led past the hospital.

"I should go," Jacqueline said.

"No, of course not." He took the basket from her and led her into his apartment. "I invited Jerry Russo and his wife. They should be here any minute."

Jacqueline's chicken, brown rice with mushrooms and pine nuts, Gloria's baked ziti, and Chris's tuna casserole made for a sumptuous meal. Jerry ate with gusto, taking generous first and second helpings. Little Mary slammed cabinet doors for the sheer joy of the sound, pulled pots and pans from lower shelves. She beat on them with abandon, the lid of a pot in one hand, a small saucepan in the other. A poem fragment came to Steven: *they beat on their drums with the handle of a broom, boom lay boom lay boom lay boom!*

Jerry regaled them with a story about his dealings with the auto insurance company after Gloria's accident. Gloria mostly chased after Mary. Jacqueline, with prodding from Steven, talked of her family in Jamaica. She had two older sisters and a younger brother.

"You told me your father was from Senegal," Steven said. "What about your mother?"

Jacqueline smiled and looked about the table. "I do not know if everyone is interested in the story of my life."

Gloria said over her shoulder as she chased after her daughter, "Oh, please go on. I don't know a thing about Senegal or Jamaica, for that matter."

Jacqueline went on to tell them that her father had come to Jamaica as a young ship-hand. He decided to stay. He got a job at the Star Kist Foods plant. That's where he met her mother. He was of the Muslim faith.

"And your mother?" Steven asked.

"My mother was part Christian, part Rastafarian. When the children came, mother remained at home. She raised us as Christians, although she herself held to the Rastafarian faith. Mother and my two sisters baked bread and sweets. Many people came to our house, drawn by the smell of baking bread."

"Omar is also Muslim?" Steven asked.

“Yes. He came to live with us in Jamaica some years ago. He is like a brother to me."

"Was he already a nurse?” Steven asked.

"No. He studied nursing at a hospital in Jamaica. Later he got a job at Smithfield." She looked at Jerry, who was busy eating. "I think I talk too much."

"That's when you decided to go into nursing?" Steven asked.

"Yes."

"Omar's not bearded. He wears a baseball cap," Jerry said.

"In Senegal, most Muslims believe in the basic teachings of Mohammed, but their practices have been influenced by local religious beliefs. Still there are some who are very traditional."

"If you're not Rastafarian, why the dreadlocks?" Jerry asked.

"These are not dreadlocks. My hair is braided," Jacqueline said. "Dreadlocks are twisted like rope."

"What do men know about hair?" Gloria said. She nudged Jerry in the ribs.

"Don't feel bad, Jerry," Steven said. "I made the same mistake." He glanced over at his phone. Should he reconnect it? What if Chris was trying to call him? No, he'd wait until after they left. He'd call her.

After dinner, they remained at the kitchen table, sipping green tea from an assortment of dollar-store mugs.

Little Mary began to cry and would not stop, despite Gloria's efforts to console her. Jacqueline asked if she could take her. She took the crying child in her arms and went to the living room couch. She sang quietly to her. Within minutes, Mary, her thumb in her mouth, dropped off to sleep.

"We'd better be going. It's been a wonderful evening, Steven," Gloria said. She walked to where Jacqueline was sitting. "Would you be interested in baby-sitting?"

"I would be most pleased," she said as she handed Mary to her mother. "I love children."

As the Russos prepared to leave, Jacqueline said she too must be going. Steven retrieved her picnic basket. "You want to take what's left?" he asked.

"No, no. You keep it." She reached out and took Steven's hand.

Her grip was firm yet gentle. "Thanks," he said. "I do appreciate your thoughtfulness."

"I too had a very good evening. I hope to see you at the hospital soon. All the children ask after you."

Steven went to the door and watched silently as the Russos walked toward their apartment. Steven was still holding Jacqueline's hand. He had the urge to press it to his lips. Instead he withdrew it, awkwardly. As they stood side-by-side, he realized for the first time that in high heels she was an inch or two taller than he. He wished there were something about her that he didn't like, but nothing came to mind.

As they stepped onto the front steps she looked up at the full moon. Her dark eyes sparkled in its reflected light. She turned, her face inches from his. "The big bad wolf was not so bad. He did not eat me."

Steven smiled. "Not a wolf, but maybe a little bad." He had to fight the urge to take her in his arms. They stood facing each other for a moment. She smiled, turned and walked to her car.

As he watched her drive off, he thought of Chris, earlier that evening, driving along the same curving path, hurt, angry. Should he wait until morning to call her? No, it wasn't going to be any easier in the morning. He went back into his apartment and into his bedroom, where he reconnected his phone. He dialed Chris's number. It rang a dozen times. He was about to hang up when she finally answered. "Hello, Chris?" She didn't respond. She hung up.

He slipped off his shoes and jeans and settled onto the floor in the lotus position. He closed his eyes. The thought of Chris going to bed, angry and distrustful of him, filled him with a sense of loss and isolation. He recalled words from the Puja, the Buddhist Book of Worship. Words he had memorized, words to live by, goals seldom attained.

> *With deeds of loving kindness, with open-handed generosity, with stillness, simplicity and contentment, I purify my body. With truthful communication, I purify my speech. With mindfulness pure and radiant, I purify my mind.*

After much tossing and turning, Steven finally dropped off to sleep. He was suddenly awakened by the sound of breaking glass. He jumped from bed and went to the living room and flipped on the light switch. Something had been thrown through the window. A brick with an attached note lay on the floor. He read the note.

"If you return Mr. Amin's wife and child within forty-eight hours, no harm will come to someone you love. Someone in Zion."

Is this some kind of sick joke? Newspaper stories can activate all sorts of cranks. But the article had said nothing about Zion. Steven went to the phone, reconnected it and called his mother. My God! This is insane. It was midnight in Kansas, but he had to call her. He didn't want to startle her, but he had to make sure she was all right. Maybe he should ask her to go stay with his sister for a while.

Her line was busy. Why? He hung-up and redialed her number. She picked up on the second ring.

"Mother, are you okay?"

"Steven! I've been trying to call you for the past two hours. Someone called---a stranger---he had some kind of accent---he said I must call you immediately. He said you would know what it was about. What is it, Steven? What has happened?"

Chapter Thirteen

Steven opened his eyes. He was drenched in perspiration, his heart a pile driver in the center of his chest. The clock on his bedside table read 4 A.M. He jumped from bed and ran into the living room. There was no broken glass, no brick; the window was intact. He went to the refrigerator and peered in, not knowing what he was looking for. The mere sight of Jacqueline's spicy chicken gave him heartburn. He drank milk from a glass they had used as a cream pitcher at dinner. He returned to bed. It was just a bad dream, that's all. He drew the covers over his head.

The following morning, Steven sat at his kitchen table and began drawing up a list of things he must do:

Send Chris flowers with a note saying their relationship is too important to let a confluence of unintended circumstance come between them. Of course, he couldn't use those exact words. But that would be the general gist of what he had to say.

Do not think of Jacqueline.

Call the phone company and change to an unlisted number.

Call his mother to tell her he might be coming home for a while (In case they did decide to fire him. But not tell her that, not yet.

Call Ewing and tell him it was Dr. Murphy's idea to document the abuse. Admit he had not been exactly accurate when he had said it was all his idea. That he was trying to protect Dr. Murphy, but that she had insisted he tell it like it was.

Send Jacqueline a brief note thanking her for her thoughtfulness and great food. And that if he is reinstated, he will be happy to continue their morning rounds on pediatrics.

Call Gloria and thank her for the wonderful baked ziti, and thank her and Jerry for their willingness to spend an evening with one of the banished.

Call Clyde Gordon to get an update on the Reverend Jones' malpractice suit. And to set a time to talk with Clyde before his deposition, which was scheduled for the end of the coming week.

Search the Internet for information about laws as they relate to deportation of the spouses of foreign citizens here on student visas.

Shop for groceries, razor blades, toothpaste and incense.

Pay bills.

Do not think about Jacqueline.

As he completed his list, the phone rang several times. He let the calls go onto his answering machine.

Two calls were from Clyde Gordon. Steven called him back.

"We received a call from the secretary of the Algerian Ambassador. He said that under international law we are prohibited from taking Mr. Amin's child and wife from him with unsubstantiated accusations and without due process."

"Is what he says true?" Steven asked.

"I'm not exactly an authority on international law. I called our congressional representative and asked him to check it out. But that's not all. Mr. Amin has hired a lawyer who also called early this morning. He said a malpractice suit was being filed by Mr. Amin, naming you, Dr. Murphy and the hospital, alleging failure to insure the wellbeing and safety of Mr. Amin's wife and child."

How had the attorney learned of Chris' involvement? But then Steven recalled the hospital statement said Mrs. Amin was evaluated in the Emergency Department. It wouldn't have been difficult for the attorney to learn who had seen her there.

"But Mrs. Amin called the shelter herself and asked to be admitted. You can't just take someone there," Steven said.

"Amin's lawyer maintains that they have only our word that she wasn't coerced into going into the shelter."

"But why drag Dr. Murphy into this?"

"She saw Mrs. Amin in the ER. She enrolled her under a fictitious name in order to put off those seeking to find her."

"Will the hospital take disciplinary action against Dr. Murphy?" Steven asked.

"No. Dr. Ewing feels she acted responsibly, under the circumstances."

Steven was relieved. Still, she had been named in another suit because of him.

"You hear anything about the depositions in the Jones case?" Steven asked.

"Yes. That's one of the reasons I called you. I want you to come by my office at nine A.M. Monday morning. Bring a draft of your statement. I'll go over it with you. Your deposition is scheduled for three P.M. on Wednesday. Tell your story sequentially, exactly as you remember it. I'll review it, then ask you the kinds of questions I believe their attorney might pepper you with."

"Will Nathan Jones be there?"

"Probably not. You know, Dr. Johnson, if you and Dr. Murphy ever decide to go into practice together, you had better have a fulltime attorney as part of your group. We're cheaper on retainer than by the hour."

Steven could picture Clyde raking his mustache and laughing as he retold his little inside joke to his secretary.

"Actually," Steven said, "I've been considering joining the staff at Smithfield after my residency training."

After Steven hung up he added to his to-do list: Write detailed narrative of Reverend Jones encounter.

By noon Steven completed all of his phone calls and started on his detailed recounting of his two encounters with Reverend Jones. After completing the ten-page, double-spaced narrative, he printed two copies. He then began his statement about the Amin incident. As he wrote of the moment Anna lifted the veil from her forehead, his heart pounded as it had then. Her dark, penetrating eyes conveyed her shame and terror.

No, he was not dispassionate at that moment. Could he learn to balance empathy with the need to maintain professional distance? Most of his medical school professors had espoused and modeled a kind of intellectual empathy that did not cross into the emotional sphere. His fellow students had more easily accepted that approach than he.

Ewing was right. He hadn't exercised all the options available to him. But was his failure to consider alternative action the result of his emotional state? He would, as he gained experience, hopefully employ a broader range of options in his decision-making, especially in emotionally charged situations.

But even with training and experience, could he ever fit into the institutional mold? Where decisions are governed exclusively by policy, bylaws, and the fear of establishing precedents that do not fit into rigid parameters.

Steven could not recall his dad ever having talked of the importance of professional detachment. It was not the approach his father took with his patients.

It was seven P.M. by the time Steven completed his write-up of the Amin incident. He had told Chris that he would e-mail it to her. Ewing was expecting to have the report by noon the following day, but what if Chris didn't check her e-mail? Since she wouldn't speak to him on the phone, he decided he'd drop it off at her apartment. He had better call first. Maybe she wouldn't hang up on him this time.

He dialed her home number. The phone rang several times before she picked up.

On the drive to Chris's apartment, Steven stopped at a Chinese restaurant and picked up two takeout dinners. He balanced the bag of food between his legs as he rode his bike along the now familiar route to her townhouse. He had a copy of his report under his windbreaker.

He rang her front doorbell and waited. Was it hunger or anxiety that made his stomach rumble? What if she slammed the door in his face?

"Who is it?" she asked through the closed door.

"I have the report I've prepared for Dr. Ewing. I was hoping you might look it over. He wants it by noon tomorrow."

"Just a minute," she said.

As he waited he set the bag of food on the stoop. He removed the report from his windbreaker. When she opened the door, she was wearing a satin kimono. Her hair was wrapped in a towel, her feet bare.

"I just stepped out of the shower."

“I’d like to know what you think of this,” he said as he handed the report to her. She took it from him.

“Well, for one thing the food smells good.”

“Can I come in?” he asked. She shook her head.

“Okay. Give me a call after you’ve had a chance to review that stuff.”

“Oh hell, Steven, come on in. I should never have told you I love Chinese food.”

Chris and he sat at the kitchen counter as she read the seven-page report. She handled the chopsticks with the dexterity of a surgeon, allowing only an occasional grain of fried rice to drop onto the document. He fumbled with his chopsticks for a while, trying to imitate her technique, but finally gave up and grabbed a fork.

She finished the report. Set her pen aside. “You write well, Steven. Most of my comments relate to typos. I’m glad you included your visit to my office after you dropped Anna off in the ER. But you didn’t mention that I suggested she check in under a different name and that I had her change into different clothes, in case security was searching for her.”

“Okay. I’ll redo that section. Anything else?”

She dipped her egg roll into some hot mustard and took a bite. She blushed. “About last night...my reaction was a bit extreme.”

“It was honest.”

“I didn’t want to just storm out of there. I wanted to say something clever, I wanted to hurt you, to embarrass her. I’ve thought about it all day. It was childish. She took my toy. My plaything. I wanted to wrestle her for it.”

“It wasn’t what you think.”

“She’s lovely. Come on, Of course you’re attracted to her. She’s obviously got you in *her* crosshairs.”

"Her what?" He laughed.

"Well, so have I," she said. She stood, came to him and gently pulled him toward her. They hugged.

He whispered, "Your friendship means a lot to me."

She kissed him. Her lips were aflame. Was it passion or Chinese mustard?

Chapter Fourteen

The day following his father's funeral services, Nathan Jones, his wife, Gwen, his eight-year-old daughter, Yovonda, and his five-year-old son, Antonio, went to Smithfield's Pancake Heaven for breakfast. Nathan marveled at how little Smithfield had changed since his boyhood. Strict town ordinances had managed to keep the fast food chains from the center of town. Except for a shopping mall just beyond the town limits, franchised retailers were nowhere to be seen. The town's only supermarket had wooden floors, a brass cash register, and a checkout counter instead of stalls. He was greeted by the delicious aroma of fresh-ground coffee and the tangy smell of pickles in open barrels.

Stores along Main Street included: Miller's Paint and Hardware, Mother's Five-and Dime, Taylor's Department Store, Gus's Luncheonette, Bishop's Pharmacy and the town's only tourist attraction, the Silver Bullet Diner. Smithfield Hospital was located three miles south of town, surrounded by the rolling pastures of dairy and nurseries.

The last time the entire family had been to Smithfield was when Nathan's mother died. They had left the day after the funeral. Why hadn't he recognized the depth of his father's grieving? Gwen had suggested they stay. Work was his excuse. An important business deal was pending. His father would be okay.

He ordered the children's breakfast. Nathan looked about the crowded restaurant. Surrounded by a chorus of discordant voices, a mix of cloying odors and a blur of images seen through tear-filled eyes, Nathan said half aloud, "I'm sorry, Dad. I'm so sorry."

The waitress, his wife and the children turned to face him. Yovonda was first to speak. "Don't be sad, daddy. Grandpa's in heaven with Grandma."

Nathan returned to Smithfield several weeks after the funeral. His father's things had been placed into a spare room at the parsonage. Clothes, photos, a bag full of old prescription medicines and over-the-counter drugs, several boxes of books, an ancient Smith-Corona typewriter, a shoebox full of letters, another box with birthday and holiday cards. In a large, brown accordion folder were crayoned sketches of wide-eyed, stick figures with smiling faces. Some yellowed and brittle with age, others more recent, signed in block letters by Nathan's children.

Among the books, Nathan found a loose-leaf collection of his father's sermons. He sat cross-legged on the floor reading familiar stories and phrases. Some were handwritten in elegantly fluent script. Most were typed. The Corona's misaligned *S* reminded Nathan of the time as a child, he had stuck a screwdriver in the guts of his father's typewriter. The shaft of the *S* had been bent. His father had tried unsuccessfully to realign it.

As Nathan read his father's sermons, he could hear his sonorous voice, and repeated phrases filled the room. Nathan recalled the pride he felt seeing his father hold the assembled faithful in his spell; to move them to tears or laughter; and at the climax of many of his sermons, he'd admonish his congregation to be filled with the Holy

Spirit; to burst forth from the church to find a soul to do for, to love, to bring to God.

Among his father's books was a handsome, leather-bound journal that had been a gift from a parishioner. As a boy, Nathan had on one occasion been unable to resist reading the journal. His parents had gone somewhere. He stole into his father's study. He found that it was a kind of diary. With dates and talk of happenings. Comments about things he had read or heard on the radio. Postcards and snap shots pasted in here and there. He was a little disappointed how ordinary it seemed. But then he read an entry where his father was asking God to forgive him for something. Nathan hadn't gotten very far when he heard his parents at the front door. He heart pounded against his ribs as he replaced the journal in the desk drawer. He never again tried to read it.

Now, as he opened the journal, his hands shook. He was about to look into his father's mind, his soul. Did he have the right? He closed the journal and set it aside.

Nathan packed everything into drawer-sized boxes and loaded them into his car. He dropped the clothes off at a local thrift shop. He took the books and other personal items with him. On the long drive from Smithfield to New Haven, the journal sat on the seat beside him. Did it contain secrets he didn't want to know? If this were his own journal, would he want his children to read it?

Two weeks after Nathan Jones buried his father, he turned his attention to initiating a medical malpractice suit against Smithfield Community Hospital and the doctors who treated him. He contacted a consumer advocacy group based in Trenton, NJ. They referred him to the office of the medical ombudsman, who listened to his story and encouraged him to pursue legal action. He was given a list of the top five malpractice law firms in the state. He called the office of each of the attorneys and asked several questions about the firm's record of suits over the past three years. He decided to go with Delessandro, Lubson and Jones, whose offices were located in a twenty-story building a block from the state capital.

He spoke with Joseph Delessandro on the phone. The attorney was immediately interested.

"By all means," Delessandro said, "let's talk."

The glitzy building facade and lobby didn't prepare Nathan for the other-worldliness of the firm's offices. The high-ceilinged, walnut-paneled sitting area, as well as Delessandro's office, was lavishly furnished with oriental rugs, wall hangings, Japanese paintings, objects d'art and massive Victorian-style furniture. Nathan had the feeling he had entered a cluttered storeroom at Sotheby's.

Joseph Delessandro's intense blue eyes, dark skin, bulky build, and tiny voice were as discordant as his surroundings. It soon became apparent, however, that he would be a strong advocate.

"First of all," Delessandro said, clasping Nathan's hand with both of his. "Let me once again offer you my condolences for your father's premature death."

He led Nathan to a couch, where they sat.

"I've studied the relevant hospital records," Delessandro said. "There's no question that we have enough evidence to establish malpractice."

He rested his hand on a stack of folders. "It's all here." He hesitated. "But we may have more than just malpractice."

"I don't understand," Nathan said.

"Cover-up, obstruction of justice. Have you received a copy of the autopsy report?

"Only what the doctor told me. That he had severe coronary artery disease," Nathan said.

"Yes. The final report confirmed that," Delessandro said. "The report also stated that the neck injury and surgery that followed were not related to your father's death."

"How can they say that?"

"Exactly my reaction. I spoke with a cardiologist. Someone I often use as an expert witness. It's his opinion that although the heart disease was obviously present prior to the incident, that the trauma, subsequent blood loss and the stress of major surgery all combined to bring on the heart attack."

"But the trauma wasn't intentional. At least that's what they claimed," Nathan said.

"It's irrelevant whether the stabbing was unintentional. It still contributed to your father's death. My expert witness is prepared to testify that the events preceding the heart attack were causative factors."

"But a difference of opinion between the hospital pathologist and your cardiologist doesn't mean there was a deliberate cover-up," Nathan said.

Delessandro stood, returned to his desk, and picked up a slip of paper. He walked to Nathan and handed it to him. It was a copy of his father's death certificate. The cause of death was listed as myocardial infarction secondary to coronary artery disease.

"Notice, Mr. Jones, that although the certificate asks for the presence of contributory factors, the trauma was not listed."

Nathan looked again at the form. Yes, there were blank spaces where it asked for contributory causes.

Delessandro sat close to Nathan. He spoke quietly. “When someone dies from a criminal act or under suspicious circumstances, the county coroner must do an autopsy. The coroner has the legal right to do the autopsy even without consent of the next of kin.”

“So why didn’t the coroner do the autopsy?” Nathan asked.

“In cases where it’s obvious that a person has died from natural causes the coroner can opt to let the hospital pathologist do the autopsy.”

Nathan was confused. “What does it matter who does the autopsy?”

“For one, the coroner is more experienced in seeking out non-natural causes of death. Also, the pathologist is a hospital employee. In cases where the hospital may be responsible for the death, the pathologist has an obvious conflict of interest.”

“Are you saying the pathologist falsified his report?”

The attorney stood, walked to his desk and retrieved a folder. He opened it and sat on the edge of his desk.

Delessandro slipped on a pair of reading glasses. “The coroner received this faxed report from the hospital pathologist. Listen to this!”

The report described the basic facts that led to Nathan’s father’s neck injury, surgery and fatal heart attack.

“That is exactly what happened, as far as I know,” Nathan said.

“It’s what he left out that’s significant,” Delessandro said. “He failed to say that your father suffered severe blood loss and a punctured lung. That until the blood was replaced, your father’s heart was deprived of oxygen, that at one point his blood pressure dropped to shock levels.”

“My God,” Nathan said.

"That information in my opinion would have made it a coroner's case."

Nathan looked about the ornately cluttered room. He wasn't normally claustrophobic, but he suddenly felt the urge to rush to the window and throw it open.

"But why would the pathologist not want the coroner to do the autopsy?" Nathan asked.

"It would be admitting that the doctor and other hospital personnel, in the act of attempting to subdue a psychotic patient, inflicted injuries that led to his death. If the papers and patient advocacy groups were to get hold of that story, the hospital would have a public relations migraine."

A woman's voice on an interoffice intercom announced, "Mr. Delessandro, you're due in court in thirty minutes."

He leaned over and depressed the talk lever. "Yes. Yes, I know." He turned to Nathan. "When I explained to the coroner the actual extent of your father's injuries, he agreed the autopsy should have been done by him."

"Well, it's too late now," Nathan said.

"He said it's up to you, Mr. Jones. If you would consent to exhumation, he would agree to repeat the autopsy."

Nathan was appalled at the thought of digging up his father's body. "I don't see why repeating the autopsy is necessary to prove malpractice," Nathan exclaimed. "I'd rather drop the suit than disturb his remains."

Delessandro nodded. "I can understand how you feel. But if there is significant discrepancy between the pathologist's and coroner's reports . . ."

"I understand...damnit!" Nathan said. He stood, went to the desk, and leaned as close to Delessandro as the massive desk would allow. A vein on his forehead bulged. "No! I do not want to go in that direction. Do you understand?"

"Yes, Mr. Jones, I do. And there's even the possibility a repeat autopsy would reach the same conclusion as the one done by the hospital pathologist."

Nathan sat. He hadn't expected the lawyer to give up so easily. Was he afraid Nathan would seek another attorney if he pushed too hard for exhumation? "What happens next?" Nathan asked.

"I've scheduled depositions from Dr. Johnson, Dr. Murphy, Dr. Costello, the pathologist, the security guards and the patient who was in the room at the time of the assault. Probably take four-to-six weeks. I'll call you afterwards."

"I'd like to be there when the intern testifies."

"Really?" Delessandro asked. He seemed puzzled by Nathan's request. "In my experience, it's better to leave the depositions to the attorneys."

"It's just that the night I met with the intern and Dr. Murphy, I was shocked, angry."

"I want them to remember you as angry. If your words or body language reveal anything less, they'll doubt our resolve."

Nathan looked about Delessandro's lavishly furnished office. He was surrounded by relics that proclaimed the attorney's successes. They also bespoke what drove the man. "I know how and when to be stoic."

"Good," Delessandro said, as he checked his watch. "As you wish. I'll contact you as soon as we set the date and time of Dr. Johnson's deposition."

In the weeks following his meeting with the malpractice attorney, Nathan read through the entire loose-leaf collection of his father's sermons. A recurring theme was the importance of forgiveness and the necessity of making peace with one's brother. How would his father have wanted Nathan to react? Nathan recalled what a Jewish political leader had once said about their relentless pursuit of those who had committed crimes against the Jews in World War II. "I can forgive crimes committed against me personally, but I cannot forgive crimes against others. The pursuit of those who commit crimes against others is in the cause of justice."

How does one reconcile the virtue of forgiveness with the pursuit of justice? Is forgiveness a pure gift or must it be earned through the acceptance of the consequences of one's acts? Nathan struggled with this dilemma as he tried to decide if Delessandro was perhaps right in wanting to explore the possibility of obstruction of justice in the way the hospital responded to his father's death. The difference between a medical mistake and deliberate cover-up would move the charges from a civil case to the criminal court. He would wait to learn what the young doctor said in his deposition before he made that decision.

Nathan wondered if he should read the most recent entries in his father's journal, prior to attending the deposition. It would help him gain insight into his father's state of mind on the day he saw Dr. Johnson. And to learn what, if anything, happened over the next two weeks to throw him into a full-blown manic psychosis? Had he even kept up his journal writing those last months and weeks of his life?

On the day Delessandro's office called and told Nathan when the deposition was scheduled, he struggled with the decision to read or not to read the journal. That evening, after the children had been bathed and read to sleep, he took Gwen's hand and led her into a bedroom where his mother-in law stayed when she visited. He closed the door behind them.

"What?" she asked.

He led her to the bed. They sat. She raised her eyebrows, her eyes wide in mock astonishment. "Not here! It's where my mamma sleeps."

He laughed and gave her a hug. She had spent the day trying to instill the basics of the English language into the heads of third-year high school students, who were mostly interested in each other's bodies and probably even hers. She had resumed teaching after Antonio started kindergarten. She usually managed to be home when the school bus delivered the children to their front door. She helped them with their schoolwork, prepared dinner and after that invariably had papers to correct or lessons to prepare.

"The deposition's scheduled for Wednesday of next week." He went to his desk and removed his father's journal. "I'm driving to Smithfield on Tuesday." He sat beside her, the journal on his lap. "I'm trying to decide..."

"To read his journal?"

"I feel so damn guilty. It's like I'm twelve years old. It's like opening a door on things I don't want to see or have no right to see."

"You're afraid it'll reveal things that will change how you feel about him?"

"It's more about privacy."

"Yet you feel compelled ..."

"I want to do the right thing."

"I know that," Gwen said. "But I don't understand the connection."

"You saw that bag of medicines. He had leftover pills from years ago. What if he had taken some out-of-date medicine?"

"They didn't even realize he was a regular patient. If they had admitted him to the hospital, things might have turned out differently."

He took Gwen's hand. "What would you do?"

"I'd talk it over with you."

Chapter Fifteen

In reading the journal, Nathan was especially interested in the last year of his father's life. Each entry was dated and written with a fine pen in such small script that Nathan had to struggle to make it out.

> August 15, 1990
>
> Yesterday, as the sun in its flaming glory rose above the horizon, I held my beloved's cold, frail hand. "Don't you see them? Look, look how they fill the room!" she said. "The angels have come. How beautiful they are."
>
> I grasped her cold body to me. I commanded the angels not take her from me. I wept for my dear, dear Yovonda. A true saint who endured a ravenous cancer that spread through her body, her brain and even burst forth from the skin of her breast. And still she never cursed God; never lost faith. If my faith could be so strong.

Subsequent entries were sporadic and cryptic. More prayer-like than descriptive. He would not have anticipated the degree to which his mother's death had crushed his father's spirit, his love of his calling, his zest for the simple pleasures of everyday living. His entries told nothing of his daily life, of the people around him. Even calls from his children and occasional visits went unnoted. His world was constricting.

> November 15, 1990
>
> I cannot sleep and when I do terrifying dreams, dreams I cannot remember, will not let me rest. My body fills with waste; food has no taste and yet I consume large quantities with no joy. The children invite me for the holidays. I make excuses. They never talk of their mother. Have they forgotten her so soon? I cannot look at little Yovonda. I cannot say her name.

His entries more and more demonstrated his retreat into an inner darkness. He obsessed about cancer.

January 10, 1991

I feel that my body has been invaded by a malignancy. A cancer that at this moment is spreading, its ravenous appetite consuming my body as it did Yovonda's. I cannot wait for the cleansing fire of pain to prepare me for the angels of the Lord.

March 3, 1991

Today, Johnny Prescott, a longtime parishioner and friend, insisted I see a doctor; so, I went to the clinic at the hospital. They said my heart is failing. My body is filling with fluid. The doctor gave me three new medicines. He said there was no cancer. I do not believe him. I'm afraid to take the medicine. I'm shocked at the cost. I take only half of what he prescribed.

The next month there were several entries dealing with a group of parishioners who were trying to force him to retire. He is indignant. He's only sixty. Why do they plot against him? He will work harder. He visits the sick and makes social visits. His energy level goes up dramatically.

He again visits the doctor. He noted that his doctor seemed surprised at the reversal in his condition.

May 5, 1991

I have astonished everyone with my energy and the renewed vigor of my sermons. Still there are many who plot against me. A committee has been formed to *assist* in fulfilling the mission of the parish. But I can see through their fancy words. They will not succeed.

In June and July, he made daily entries. He talks of hearing voices. They tell him the anti-Christ is coming. He quoted passages from the Apocalypse that predict, in extravagant language, the end of the world and the second coming of Christ: *"Then I saw the beast come out of the sea, with ten horns and seven heads; on its horns were ten diadems; on its heads, blasphemous names---the beast was given words, uttering blasphemies against God."*

August 15, 1991

It is the first anniversary of Yovonda's death. Nate called. I admonished him to prepare for the Second Coming. My thoughts poured from me in such profusion that it startled poor Nathan. He insisted I see my head doctor. He pleaded with me to come and stay with them. He is a good boy, but he does not understand. There is nothing I cannot do.

August 16, 1992

Today Johnny Prescott came. He said Nathan had called and insisted he take me to the hospital.

I agreed to go, mainly to get something to help me sleep. I will not tell the doctor about my previous problems. If I do, he will send me to my head doctor. They will lock me in the hospital, give me strong medicines, and if that does not work they will give me electric shock treatments that will trash my brain into mush. They'll turn me into a zombie. I have energy. I have power. They shall not take that from me. The voices admonish me to be wary. *The good wheat shall be gathered and placed in the barn of the Lord. The weeds shall be gathered and burned*.

August 16, 1992

Yesterday I saw a young doctor in the emergency room. He was kind and I felt guilty about lying to him. I did not tell him about the voices or the boundless energy that I felt. I told him I couldn't sleep, had no energy or desire to live; that I desperately needed a medicine to help me sleep

The young doctor said he checked with a psychiatrist. He said he was giving me medicine to give me more energy and that would help me. He prescribed enough for a week and made an appointment for me in the psychiatry clinic. He said to call him if the medicine didn't help.

Still I had a fitful night. I'll double the dose tonight.

August 18, 1992

> I took four pills last night and still couldn't sleep. It's been three nights now. My hands shake so badly I can hardly write. Could the pharmacy have given me the wrong medicine? My thoughts race. The voices are becoming louder. They talk of devils and say to prepare for the Second Coming. The end is near, they chant. Prepare, prepare, the end is at hand.

"Prescott came to take me to my appointment. I refused to go. He pleaded with me. I ordered him out of the parsonage. The voices commanded I throw my medicines down the toilet. They are poison. *The weeds must not choke off the wheat. You must pull them up by the roots and cast them into the fire. The days of reckoning are at hand. The wheat will be gathered into the barns of the Lord. The weeds will be burned."*

That was his father's last entry. Nathan closed the journal. He felt a pervasive, penetrating sadness. God, how he wished he hadn't read it. Frightened, tormented, hateful words, not those of his real father. It was a demon disease that took possession of his mind, his soul.

It was apparent to Nathan that his father was already manic when he went to the hospital. He had covered up his true mental state to keep from being locked up. To get something to help him sleep he had presented himself as depressed. His father had deliberately deceived Dr. Johnson. But they should have known of his past history. As Gwen had said, if they had admitted him to the hospital, he would have received the proper treatment.

Should he drop the emergency room doctors from the law suit? Had they done the best they could under the circumstances?

The Jones' two-story brick colonial house was located on the outskirts of New Haven in a neighborhood that had sprung up almost overnight on what had been farmland. Its rolling forested hills and verdant pastures had been converted into half-acre estates, homes of young professionals and rising business executives.

Nathan was out of bed by six a.m. He slipped on a sweatshirt, shorts and sneakers and quietly left the house. His wife and children would be up by six-thirty. He'd be back in time to have breakfast with them.

He jogged his usual four-mile route that included a park, where he ran along a path that circled a small lake. He was not alone. Skimpily clad joggers, bikers in full racing regalia and waddling power walkers navigated the path in varying speeds and styles. The air was crisp. The lowering sun cast an elongated shadow that, like the hand of a clock, rotated about Nathan as he circumnavigated the lake, slowing as he slowed, speeding up as he picked up his pace. His body became a mobile sundial accelerating and decelerating the passage of time. And what would happen if he ran at the speed of light? According to Einstein, time would slow. Would his shadow separate from his body and take on a life of its own?

Nathan's thoughts switched from the theory of relativity to Jones verses Johnson, Murphy and Smithfield. What if the suit is successful and the doctors are convicted of malpractice, while Nathan concealed evidence that established the doctors had been deliberately deceived by his father? But if Nathan decided to drop Dr. Johnson and Dr. Murphy from the suit, he would have to tell Delessandro his decision was based on what he'd read in his father's journal. He didn't want to tell the lawyer about the journal. He would never permit him to read it.

If the hospital pathologist had omitted listing the stabbing as a contributory cause of his father's death, in order to deceive the coroner, that would constitute obstruction of justice. In Delessandro's opinion that would be a criminal offense. What if lawyers for the defense of the pathologist were to find out about his father's journal? God. He couldn't let that happen.

These thoughts played and replayed in his head as he lapped the lake over and over, losing count of time and the number of revolutions, finally dropping onto a bench panting, exhausted, undecided.

Chapter Sixteen

Steven rolled out of bed, took a shower, dressed and re-read the report he'd prepared for Ewing. He had made the changes Chris had suggested. He would drop off the report in Ewing's office when he went for his appointment with Clyde Gordon. He checked his watch. It was already eight-thirty. Not enough time to go out for breakfast. His stomach groaned. He ruled out the hospital cafeteria, where he might run into other housestaff. He opted for the hospital snack bar and a quick coffee and cinnamon bun.

Steven sat in a corner booth, his back to the entrance. He dreaded having to go over the Jones incident with Clyde Gordon, but the meeting with Jones' attorney was just a couple of days off. He had no choice. He wondered what Clyde was like after work. He was probably younger than Steven, yet he acted so damn middle-aged. Does he take off his clothes and lounge around the house in his briefs listening to jazz; sipping martinis? A "loose cannon," that's what Ewing had said Clyde called him. He could use a little "loose" himself.

"Hi, Steven."

Steven turned. "Jacqueline! Hi."

She was wearing her student nurse's uniform. Her finely braided hair hung to her shoulders. She was out of breath.

"I knew you would be here," she said, as she sat in the booth next to him.

"Rastafarian magic? You'll have to teach me how you do that."

"You avoid the cafeteria. You do not cook. It is too much trouble to go to town for breakfast."

"I like the magic theory better."

"I have no magic on Mondays."

"And the rest of the week?"

She smiled shyly. "I want to know many things. Learning is magic, is it not? You make something where there was nothing."

Steven sipped his coffee. "Learning is magic. I like that." He checked his watch. He had another ten minutes before his appointment with Clyde Gordon. "How did you get so wise?"

"My mother spoke in riddles. She told stories. If I asked her why my friend was being mean to me, she would ask, 'What color is the sky?' I would say it is blue. 'Always?' she would ask. 'Is it not black at times?' I would say only when there is no light. She would agree and tell me to think how I can bring light to the sky of our friendship."

"If she ever comes to visit you, I'd love to meet her."

"She will not come. She is afraid to fly. She says that if God wanted us to fly He would have given us wings. Maybe sometime you can come to Jamaica?"

"I'd love to," Steven said as he finished his sweet bun. "And if they fire me, I'll have the time, but if I get to keep my job, I won't have any time off for at least the next six months."

"Will you know soon?" she asked.

"In a day or two. Would you mind if I called you?"

She took a pen from his breast pocket and wrote her number on a napkin. "Do fishes like the water?" She smiled and slipped the napkin into his hand.

Clyde Gordon's small office was dominated by an antique roll-top desk. On an adjacent wall was a couch and small upholstered side chair. In one corner of the room was a bookshelf-sized fish tank. Colorful tropical fish appeared to float in air as they drifted lazily in their invisible sea. Morning light from a single large unadorned window flooded the room.

Gordon was standing by the fish tank as Steven entered. He motioned for him to sit, then went to his desk and picked up a yellow legal pad. He came and sat alongside Steven.

"You have your statement?" he asked.

"Yes, sir, right here." Steven handed him a manila folder. Gordon read Steven's description of his encounters with Reverend Jones. He occasionally made notes.

As Steven waited for Gordon to get through the long statement, he tried to imagine Dr. Ewing, Mr. Amin and Gordon in that same room, the day Anna went into the shelter. He was glad he wasn't there, and yet he would like to have met Mr. Amin. In his mind, he had conjured a small, stocky man with arched, bushy eyebrows, dark flinty eyes, and pouty, pampered, full lips accustomed to satiation. In reality, he was a young intelligent graduate student, from a family wealthy enough to send him to a prestigious, highly competitive, expensive American University. Why had he treated his child-bride so cruelly?

Gordon sat back, smiled. "I'm Mr. Delessandro, I represent the plaintiff, Nathan Jones, and I'd like to ask you a few questions. Tell me, Dr. Johnson, what has been the extent of your formal psychiatric training?"

"Several lectures, a one-month rotation on a psychiatric inpatient service as a fourth-year medical student, and many encounters with patients with psychiatric illnesses on the general medical ward and other services."

"No outpatient experiences dealing with depressed patients?"

"I did see a few clinic patients whose primary problem was depression."

"And did you personally treat those patients?"

"It was difficult to establish continuity. We usually referred them to psychiatry."

"Was there a single patient you saw exclusively on your own, that you diagnosed depression and initiated treatment?"

"No, but..."

"And what of a patient with the diagnosis of bipolar disorder? How many of those have you cared for in your extensive medical career?" Clyde asked.

As Steven contemplated that question he looked at the fish tank. He watched the exotic tropical fish dart about in their glass-bound cosmos, unconcerned about predators or lawyers.

"There are many diseases," Steven said, "that doctors go a lifetime and never see a single case. But the possibility of even the most obscure disease is part of the diagnostic process."

"I take it your answer is no."

"Right. I have never treated a patient with bipolar disorder."

"I see. It's clear you were totally unprepared by virtue of training or experience to treat either a depressed patient or one with bipolar disorder."

"I didn't say that."

"You're a new doctor, aren't you, Dr. Johnson?"

"Yes. I graduated from medical school in May of this year."

"That is why they place you under the supervision of more experienced physicians. Who was your supervisor in the ER?"

"Dr. Murphy was my attending."

"Wouldn't it be customary for her to also see the patient?"

"For new interns, yes. But she was tied up with a major trauma. I presented the case to her. She concurred with my diagnosis and recommended I call the consulting psychiatric resident."

"But the psych resident didn't see the patient either."

"No. He didn't think it was necessary."

"Dr. Johnson, I have here a copy of a directive issued by the hospital medical director that states the following: 'During the months of July and August, all emergency room patients seen by an intern must also be evaluated by the teaching attending and/or a senior resident or consultant.'"

"In practice, the degree of involvement of the supervising physician varies."

"Was it not deemed important that the attending see this severely depressed patient?"

"She believed it wasn't necessary," Steven said.

"And as things turned out she was obviously mistaken." Clyde looked through his notes.

Steven wished that Chris *had* seen Reverend Jones. She trusted his judgment. He should have told her that the psychiatry consultant decided not to see the patient. He had let her down, and now she was part of the suit.

"Let's move on," Clyde said. "The part of Reverend Jones's medical record that you had available to you was marked volume two. Is that correct?"

"Yes."

"Wouldn't that suggest that his primary record had grown so large it could not be contained in a single volume?"

"Yes." Steven concentrated on his breathing to help him remain calm.

"Yet you were willing to write a prescription for a potent medication for a presumed disorder you had never treated on your own, without being privy to the massive amount of information contained in volume one of his record."

"I did speak with Dr. Costello. He's a psychiatric resident. He concurred with my diagnosis and treatment."

"I see nothing in the record that indicates you spoke to him!"

"I recall the conversation in detail."

"Isn't it standard medical practice to document phone conversations with consultants?"

"Yes, but..."

"Of course, I understand. You forgot that. Yet you recall the conversation in great detail. Your memory is somewhat spotty, Dr. Johnson."

This is what the deposition will be like, Steven thought. He's asking hard but good questions. Yes, Steven thought, it's better for me to deal with my anger now than when I'm facing Jones's lawyer.

"How should I address that issue?" Steven asked.

"In your statement, you said it wasn't unusual to complete your charting between patients. That you intended to record the conversation but frankly got so busy you forgot. Just say 'I got busy, I forgot.' Direct, honest, non-speculative answers. What Delessandro is going to try to get you to do is to say something impulsive, stupid or contradictory."

Steven was developing a grudging respect for Clyde, his professionalism, and his purposeful insensitivity. But he still had to stifle the urge to give his droopy mustache a good, hard twist.

"Dr. Johnson, did it occur to you that Reverend Jones might not have kept his appointment with the psychiatrist?"

"I stressed to him how important it was."

"I didn't see that in your note. I see...that's something else you forgot to do."

"I spent almost an hour with the patient. I can't write down everything."

"Just the important things, I presume," Clyde said. "You perhaps didn't believe that his follow-up OPD appointment was important."

"I arranged for a follow up visit. I handed him an appointment card."

"Did you have his phone number?"

"It was on his chart," Steven said.

"Who was listed as his primary physician?"

"A doctor he'd been seeing in the medicine clinic."

"You could have called psychiatry or the patient to see if he had kept the appointment. Did you do that?"

"No."

"But you said it was important. Just think, if you had taken the time to call him, we might not be sitting here now," Clyde said.

"He was as likely to ignore my phone call as he did my effort to get him an appointment in psychiatry."

"Does someone in the Psychiatry OPD call no-shows?"

"I don't know," Steven said.

"Check that out before Wednesday," Clyde said. "Let's move on to your second encounter with Reverend Jones."

Clyde was right. A phone call may have made a difference. He recalled that his father had carried a small address book in his breast pocket. He called it his tickler file. Reminders to check out labs and pathology reports and follow-up calls to patients. Similar to Steven's index card tickler he used with his inpatients. With ER patients, a copy of the encounter is sent to a physician identified by the patient. The ER physician expected and depended on the person's regular doctor to do whatever follow-up was necessary. If Reverend Jones had told Steven the name of the doctor he had been seeing in psychiatry clinic, that person would have received a copy of the ER encounter.

"At the deposition, will I be able to refer to my notes?" Steven asked.

"Yes. I'll be there. We can confer before you respond to any question." Clyde went to his desk and picked up a letter opener. "This," he said, holding it up, "is a scalpel. Now I want you to stand and walk toward me."

Steven stood, and as he approached Clyde, the attorney suddenly raised the letter opener, thrusting it toward Steven. He instinctively jumped back.

"Isn't it possible that you raised the scalpel as Reverend Jones moved toward you?"

"I don't recall doing that," Steven said.

"You were frightened, things were happening rapidly. Are you absolutely sure?"

Clyde had hit on the one area that was most troubling to Steven. If he had put down the scalpel, would he have been better able to calm the Reverend? Steven turned from Clyde and went back to where he'd been sitting. He closed his eyes and tried to recreate the scene. "The honest answer is that I don't remember. I just see his face---the scissors raised over my head.

And then him crashing down on top of me." Steven opened his eyes. Clyde was perched on the edge of his desk.

"Is that what you'll tell Delessandro?" Clyde asked.

"Yes."

"Good. He can do less with that. He'll try to get you to speculate. Don't." He checked his watch. He stood. "I believe you're ready for Wednesday. Get a good night's sleep, a haircut, and dress so you look professional. Wear a fresh white jacket and tie."

Steven stood and extended his hand. "Thanks. You gave me a lot to think about." They shook hands. Clyde's grip was strong.

Steven decided to stop by the ER to see Chris. He wondered when her deposition would take place and if Clyde would rake her with hard questions. She didn't seem very concerned. He guessed that was the difference between being a valued, hard-to-replace attending rather than a barely housebroken, easy-to-replace intern.

When he found her tiny office empty, he went to the nurses' station in the ER. Martha was seated with a stack of charts. She looked up.

"Dr. Steve!"

"Hi, Martha. How are things going?"

"I've got a new intern to train. Otherwise okay."

Steven nodded. "Ride her hard, Martha, but go easy with the whip."

"You're looking for Dr. Murphy?"

"You do know everything."

"Her patient in room five just left. She's probably still in there doing her charting. She doesn't let it go like some people I know."

Steven closed the door behind him as he entered the exam room. Chris looked up.

“Sorry, I’m not ready for my next patient, sir.”

“I just spent an hour with Clyde Gordon. I desperately need a little loving.”

“Well, in that case...” She laid down her pen. “You had better make an appointment.”

Steven placed his arms around her. He pressed her against the exam table. Their faces were inches apart. They kissed. She arched her back.

“Your problem is obviously urgent," Chris said, "but I never initiate therapy without taking a thorough history. Tell me about the meeting.”

“We covered matters of extreme importance and significance to my future. But all I can remember is that he said I should get a haircut and try to look professional.”

“Yes, you could use a little dressing-up.” She used her fingers as scissors. “A snip here and a snip there. A white coat, your breast pocket filled with pens and tongue depressors, and of course, a top-of-the-line stethoscope draped around your neck.”

“Sounds like someone I’d trust with my life.”

She glanced toward the door, as she gently separated from him. She picked up the patient’s chart from the exam table. “I’d hate to have someone barge in and get the wrong idea about their boss.”

“How about tonight? Candle-lit dinner at your place.”

“I’m on call with a new intern. You know how that is.”

“How about tomorrow night? Rent a movie. Get some takeout.”

“Okay, seven-thirty, my place. You can pick out the movie as long as it’s not *X-rated* or has *gun* in the title.”

Steven went to the ER staff lounge. He had a whole day ahead of him and nothing in particular to do. A cup of high potency ER brew might help. He dropped a quarter in an empty can next to the coffeepot. He filled a Styrofoam cup, added a couple of cubes of sugar and cleared off a place to sit next to the phone. He was eager to hear what Ewing thought of his blow-by-blow account of the Anwar Amin incident. As he prepared to dial his number, Omar Diack entered the lounge.

"Hey, man, how are you doing?" Omar asked.

"Hi, Omar. I'm a man of leisure. Not a bad life."

Steven wondered how much Jacqueline might have told him about the chicken-jerky fiasco. Omar pulled up a chair and sat beside Steven.

"You know, Jacqueline is my cousin."

"Yes, she told me."

"I am like a brother to her. She tells me everything," Omar said.

A nurse came into the lounge and went to the supply cabinet. "Hi, Dr. Steve, what brings you here?" she asked, as she removed a package of disposable diapers from the shelf.

"Old friends and cheap coffee."

"More like cheap friends and old coffee. The average donation is ten cents," she said, as she backed through the door.

Steven's beeper went off. It was Ewing's number.

"You need to go?" Omar asked.

"No. It's just a call from God's secretary."

"Jacqueline says you invited her to have dinner with her in your apartment. She says you might be going to Jamaica to visit her mother," Omar said.

"Jacqueline called me and offered to bring some food. I invited her to stay for dinner. Jerry Russo and his wife were there."

"Jacqueline is pure as a young willow and as sweet as the toes of a honeybee. She is homesick and lonely. In Jamaica, it is serious business when a young man goes to speak with a girl's mother."

"She told me about her mother. She sounds like a fascinating person. It was just a casual remark."

"Jacqueline is very clever. She looks among the lines."

"I don't know what to say. We're just friends."

"She will be crazy if you say I have spoken with you."

"I won't mention it."

Omar stood and extended his hand. He pumped Steven's hand with vigor. "I like you, Dr. Steve. "But you must go slowly. She has little experience. I do not want to see her hurt."

After Omar left the lounge, Steven called Ewing's office. His secretary said Dr. Ewing would like him to stop by around noon to have lunch in his office and to discuss his statement.

Steven had an hour-and-a-half to burn. He headed for the hospital library. Since Mrs. Amin was not a US citizen, he needed to find out about immigration laws as they pertained to a non-citizen spouse whose husband, here on a student visa, had returned to Algeria, leaving her in the US. He didn't expect to find any hard-copy information on the subject. He went to the computer terminal.

There were ninety-eight hits for *immigration*. He browsed several of the sites. Most could not be accessed. Others were too broad and didn't discuss spousal abuse. He entered "battered women" at the search prompt. There were forty-four hits. He browsed a few sites. None covered non-citizens. He was getting nowhere fast. Perhaps another search engine would be more productive. He switched to “Dogpile.” Looked up “government directory” then went to “legislative branch.” He got nowhere. He entered “Library of Congress” as an Internet address. The “Library of Congress Home Page” popped up. Under legislative information, fifty bills were listed that pertained to immigration. Finally, one hit referred to immigration law as it applied to battered women. A number of congressional acts were listed. He printed out the “Battered Immigrant Women Protection 1999(H.R. 3083).” It was eight pages long. He read it carefully, highlighting a couple of relevant areas. It spoke of aliens who were the spouses or children of United States citizens or lawful permanent residents, criteria Mrs. Amin did not meet. Also, she had to establish extreme cruelty on the part of her spouse in order to qualify for exemption from deportation. He wondered if the shelter would make an attorney available to her. She’d also need expert witnesses to attest to evidence of extreme cruelty. Chris could do that. The statute did provide for a battered woman to apply for permanent resident status while she was still in the shelter. He checked his watch, gathered the papers he’d printed out and left for Ewing’s office.

Steven stood before Dr. Ewing's cluttered desk as he waited for him to look up from whatever he was reading. He motioned for Steven to sit. Clyde had liked Steven's report of the Amin incident. But that wouldn't guarantee that Ewing, looking at it from a medical perspective, wouldn't tear it to pieces. Ewing, dressed in a starched white lab coat, stood and walked around his desk. He sat alongside Steven. His expression was enigmatic, without a trace of the frustration and anger he displayed in their last encounter.

"I've been able to gather a quorum of the housestaff committee," Ewing said. "We're meeting tonight at six. I want this mess resolved as soon as possible."

Steven knew that the three housestaff representatives on the committee were the chief residents on the major services---medicine, surgery and pediatrics. That meant that Beck and Scully would be there. He might as well start packing.

"How much input do the housestaff representatives get?" Steven asked.

"Plenty. But don't look so glum. I received a telegram this morning from the president of WASA."

"WASA?"

"It stands for: *Women Against Spousal Abuse*. She said her group would picket the hospital if you were dismissed. That she would mobilize other women's groups. How they got wind of this so fast I'm not sure, but our switchboard's been flooded with calls--WASA members from all over the country."

"Will that intimidate the committee?" Steven asked.

"Let me say that it will certainly get their attention. As you probably noticed, more than half of this year's residency recruits are women."

Steven recalled that Chris had said that women's groups would be supportive of him. Had she contacted WASA?

"I've gone over your statement, Steven. You did a nice job recreating the sense of urgency you must have felt. In reading it, I felt I was there, caught in the same dilemma. As I told at our previous meeting, you didn't consider all your options, but it's obvious that your concern for the patient is what motivated you. You were willing to risk the censure of colleagues and the possibility of dismissal. I respect that. I would not have had the courage as an intern to do what you did. You placed the welfare of the patient before your own. You're an exceptional young man, Dr. Johnson. I'll do everything in my power to prevent your dismissal." Ewing placed his hand on Steven's shoulder.

How Steven missed his father at that moment. It was as though his dad were speaking to him through Ewing. Kind, self-effacing, generous, supportive words. Steven had to fight back tears. He recalled a Vietnamese poem by Le-Xuan-Thuy, in which the heroine shed “tears of pearls.”

Precious, transitory, passionate jewels to celebrate a moment when one soul touches another.

Chapter Seventeen

Steven was concerned that nowhere in the Battered Immigrant Protection Act did they describe a situation comparable to Anna Amin's. It spoke of aliens who were the spouses of United States citizens or lawful permanent residents. By implication it seemed to exclude spouses of temporary residents, such as people here on student visas. There must be thousands of spouses of non-citizens under those circumstances. Why wouldn't the law protect them? Could the Algerian government demand her extradition? Anna was going to need a hell of a good lawyer.

Steven stopped by Gordon's office to talk with him about his concerns and to give him a copy of the bill he'd downloaded from the Internet. While Gordon read the eight-page report, Steven walked to the aquarium to get a closer look at Clyde's collection of exotic fish. The bottom of the tank was an elaborate Japanese landscape with pagodas, bridges and tiny bonsai trees.

"You're right," Gordon said, tapping the document, "this doesn't specifically cover a woman in Mrs. Amin's situation. I believe the INS would reject her application for adjustment of status. I'm afraid she's subject to deportation."

"They can't do that. Her life is in danger if she returns to Algeria." He walked over to Gordon's desk. He slumped into a side chair. "How can they deport her if she's here legally?"

"You haven't heard?"

"What?" Steven asked.

"Anwar Amin's attorney called this morning. He said that his client has taken a leave of absence from his studies at Princeton. He'll be arriving in Algiers this afternoon."

"And her visa is only valid as long as he remains in the United States?" Steven asked.

"Exactly his intent."

"But her problems developed while she was legally here."

"She can appeal on those grounds, but it's rare to reverse an INS decision," Gordon said.

How was she going to afford an attorney? Steven wondered about women's groups, like WASA or even the Civil Liberties Union. Maybe he *should* talk to the reporters. Mention that she needs legal representation.

"I can't just do nothing and let her be deported," Steven said.

"I understand how you must feel," Gordon said, "but that's exactly what you're going to do. Nothing!"

"You don't really care what happens to her, do you?"

"If she returns to Algiers, Amin is likely to drop his suit against you, Dr. Murphy and the hospital."

"Is that all you care about?" Steven asked.

"That's what I'm hired to care about."

Steven's face reddened. He had gotten himself into this bind and now the straps he felt about his chest began to tighten. It was hard to breathe. He wished that Gordon had looked into Anna's eyes as he had. He would then understand why Steven felt compelled to do whatever he could to help her. He had almost begun to like Gordon, but this was too much. He stood.

"It was my impression that I was hired to look out for my patient's, not the hospital's, welfare."

"The hospital's and the patient's welfare are parallel objectives," Gordon said.

"Not always. Sorry to have taken up your time." Steven headed for the door.

"Doctors come and go," Gordon shouted. "The hospital's part of this community."

Steven fought the urge to slam the door shut behind him. His path to the elevator took him past Dr. Ewing's secretary. She occupied an open area where several workspaces were separated by five-foot high glass partitions.

"Dr. Johnson, I was about to call you."

"Hi."

"Dr. Ewing said he'd call you tonight after the housestaff committee meeting. Where can he reach you?"

"I'll probably be in my apartment all evening, but I'll be wearing my beeper just in case."

"Good. I have both those numbers."

In the hospital library, Steven grabbed several pediatric journals and spread them on a large oak, glass-topped table. He pulled up a heavy oak chair with red leather armrests. He might be back on the pediatric ward in four days, and Scully, from what Jerry Russo had told him, was bound to ride Steven pretty hard. He'd better familiarize himself with the recent medical literature, especially the editorials. They usually got into the more controversial issues, the kinds of things Scully was likely to bring up on rounds. Review articles that compared and analyzed several studies were of most interest to Steven, rather than a single point of view. Doctors, deluged by drug company promotion and their natural desire to try new medication, were impressed by studies that supported the drug company claims. But studies dealing with therapeutic efficacy of medicines are often supported by grants from pharmaceutical companies.

"Read the fine print" his father would say. "Don't be the first to try the new or the last to give up the old.

Steven's stomach began to grumble. He glanced at the wall clock. It was two P.M. He had been reading for three hours. Too late for lunch in the cafeteria...three hours until the housestaff committee meeting. He wished he could be there. Maybe he should talk with Scully before the meeting. After all, he was a representative. He wondered if Scully would have read the report he had given to Ewing. But even if he had, it wasn't the same as a face-to-face meeting. There was a phone in the library, but it was at the librarian's desk. No privacy there. He could just stop by the pediatric ward and take his chances on seeing Scully. But again, there would be other ears. It could be awkward for both Scully and him.

Whatever Scully said was bound to have a significant impact on the committee members. It wouldn't look good if Scully said Steven hadn't made any attempt to contact him. Steven decided to call Scully as soon as he got back to his apartment, but first he'd better get some lunch and do a little grocery shopping. His apartment's cockroach union was threatening to picket.

On the way to the hospital snack bar, Steven used an intra-hospital phone to page Dr. Scully. Moments later, he was on the line.

"Steven Johnson! Well, what do you know? Thought maybe you'd have headed back to Kansas. I'm busy as hell so make this quick. I'm short of help. Some people aren't pulling their weight."

Scully was obviously speaking loud enough so those near him could hear what he was saying. Steven wanted to make the conversation as short as possible.

"Are you going to the committee meeting?"

"I can hardly wait. Beck will be there also. Last time I saw him he was busily stropping a scalpel."

"Can you meet me in the snack bar? I'd like to explain some things to you."

"I've read your report—do you have something to add to that?" Scully was still speaking in a stilted voice one uses when addressing a larger audience.

"You're on the committee to represent the housestaff interests."

"I represent the housestaff as a whole. You know what they say about a bad apple."

Steven concentrated on his breathing. He took several breaths.

"You still there?" Scully asked.

"Actually, Clyde Gordon thought it would be a good idea for us to meet." It wasn't exactly a lie. Gordon had asked if he and Scully had talked since Steven's suspension. Gordon just shook his head in disbelief when Steven said they hadn't.

"Hmm. Okay, Johnson. I don't see what's to be gained, but I'll meet you there in ten minutes. Will you be bringing your lawyer?" He laughed. He didn't wait for an answer to his question. He hung up.

Steven picked up a pimento-cheese sandwich, a carton of milk and a package of chocolate chip cookies. He sat at a booth. A half hour passed. He wondered if Scully really intended to come. Scully hadn't sounded exactly open-minded. Steven tried to convince himself that the meeting wasn't that important. It might even make matters worse. And had Scully made up that business about Beck being out to get him? He checked his watch. He'd give him another ten minutes. His thoughts drifted to Anna Amin. How would she learn that her husband had returned to Algiers and, in so doing, invalidated her visa? He had to get in touch with her somehow. Chris might be able to help, but did he really want to get her more involved?

Steven was startled when Scully slipped into the booth opposite him. He hadn't seen him approach.

"I need to get to closeout rounds before the meeting," Scully said. "You've got ten minutes."

"I'm sorry about missing calls. I intend to make those up if I'm reinstated."

Scully's starched white coat was as stiff as armor. As he drummed his fingers on the table-top, Steven noticed for the first time the extraordinary length and delicacy of Scully's fingers. Steven imagined him as a giant hard-shelled insect. A praying mantis came to mind.

"Making up the missed call is a given, Johnson." He removed his glasses. He chewed on the ear-piece. "You know what I don't understand is why you went out of your way to make me look bad."

"I'm sorry you felt that way. But what I did wasn't about you."

"You should have come back and told me about the abuse. We could have handled it together. Instead you left me to rant and rave, thinking it was all about the circumcision."

"I was convinced I didn't have time."

"It was knee jerk. Unprofessional." He stood and looked at his watch. "I have to go."

"Is that what you intend to say at the meeting?"

"I'm not sure what I'll recommend."

Steven watched as Scully loped toward the exit. His spidery fingers, long legs and narrow face brought to mind a textbook photograph of a young man with a rare hereditary condition called Marfan's syndrome. Why hadn't he thought of it before? Abe Lincoln was believed to have part of the syndrome. He tried to picture Scully with a beard.

The most serious and commonest complication of Marfan's was progressive weakening of the aorta. A time bomb just waiting to go off in the center of the chest. Certainly, Scully was aware of his condition. Or was he? He should be getting periodic chest films to track the size of his aorta. Surgical intervention could prevent sudden death from rupture.

What was Steven to do? Send Scully a note saying he might have Marfan's syndrome? That he should have a careful cardiac evaluation? If Scully were already aware of it, he might be offended by a note from Steven. For the present, Steven thought, I have enough to worry about. Besides, if he really has Marfan's, he would never have gotten through medical school without someone making the diagnosis. He must know.

Why had Steven diverted his thoughts to Scully's problems? At least it was better than dwelling on what was to come next for him. In little more than an hour the housestaff committee would meet to decide Steven's fate. Nothing as dire as an insidiously expanding aorta, but still, the thought of it made Steven's brow moist. His hands grew cold.

Chapter Eighteen

Steven had at least three hours before he would expect to hear from Dr. Ewing about the committee's decision. As he strolled along the path toward his apartment, he decided he'd call the battered women's hotline to leave a message for Anna, informing her that since her husband had left the country, her visa was no longer valid. It was a clear brisk evening. The sky to the west was lighted by a crescent flame; a residual image on the retina of the horizon. A great night for a ride on his bike, Steven thought, as he approached his apartment and glanced at his faithful but neglected Honda Shadow.

The phone was ringing as Steven entered. He rushed to his bedroom and picked up the receiver. He was surprised to hear Chris's voice.

"Hi, Chris. I thought you were working tonight."

"I am. Things are crazy here. I'll have to make this short. You'll never guess who I ran into today."

"I wish it were me."

"Nathan Jones. You know, the preacher's son."

"Did he recognize you?"

"Yes. We were in line at the supermarket. He said he wanted to talk. We went to the diner for coffee."

"That's amazing. You know, I've thought of calling him."

"He said that he came to town to be at your deposition on Wednesday."

"I don't know if I like that. It's going to be hard enough without him being there. God, he was angry the last time we met." Steven slipped to the floor. He leaned against his bed.

"He's past that. He talked about his father, growing up in this town...excuse me a minute, Steven."

He could hear her speaking with someone, probably the intern.

"I have to run. Russo has a patient who's crashing. Call me after you hear from Ewing. Bye."

Steven slipped off his shoes and began to undress. It had to be pretty unusual for a person in the process of suing someone to want to have a friendly little talk. What did it mean? Steven adjusted the water temperature, then entered the shower. He was fully sudsed when the phone rang. He decided to let the answering machine get it. It was too soon for Ewing to be calling. He could hear his recorded answering message, then nothing. Probably a wrong number.

He dressed and looked up the battered women's hotline number in the phone book. He dialed it. A woman answered.

"This is Dr. Johnson. A mother and her newborn went from Smithfield Hospital directly into a shelter."

"I recognize your voice, Dr. Johnson. I've spoken with you before. I'm sorry; I can't confirm or deny any such person is at the county shelter."

"I need to get a message through to her."

"I can't guarantee she'll get the message since she may or may not be there."

"She's in this country as the spouse of a man with a student visa. He has returned to Algeria, so her visa is no longer valid and she's subject to deportation. She needs to get an attorney, so she can apply for lawful permanent resident status."

"Slow down, Dr. Johnson. She needs to apply for what?"

"Lawful permanent resident status. She must move fast because her husband's attorney will no doubt notify the INS."

"We heard from the INS today. The agent demanded to know if this woman was at our shelter."

"How would they know?" Steven asked.

"Probably through the local police. The INS can be pretty damn intimidating when they want to."

"What did you tell him?"

"Nothing. He threatened to get a court order to force us to comply."

"Can they do that?"

"Yes. We contacted an attorney who does volunteer work for us. She said the INS has seized women from shelters and deported them."

"My God!" Steven said. "They know she can apply for permanent resident status under the new law. That's why they're moving so fast. I wonder how soon they'll get the court order."

"Our lawyer said that they have to prove to a judge that she's no longer a legal immigrant before he would order us to reveal her location. Then they'll have to go back to court for a search warrant. It could take a day or two."

"But it might take weeks for an application for permanent resident status to be approved. Can't a lawyer representing her get an injunction to block the INS's action?"

"There isn't time for that. Dr. Johnson. But if a client were not to feel safe in a particular shelter she's free to leave. If she then voluntarily chose to go to another facility, that's certainly her prerogative. Of course, I'm not admitting that she's here or ever was here."

"Could the court force you to reveal her new location?" Steven asked.

"We can't tell them what we don't know. She could be any place. Such a transfer would be done so that no one here would know where the client had gone."

"How is that possible?"

"She's dropped off in a public place. Someone picks her up a little later. Then takes her to who knows where."

"Might that happen today?" Steven asked.

"It might have already happened, doctor."

Steven didn't know what to say to express his admiration and gratitude. He had images of an INS swat team descending on the shelter. This was a very brave lady. "Anyone ever tell you you're wonderful?"

"Just doing my job."

"I wish you were here so I could give you a big hug."

"After things cool down, who knows? I might get sick. Need a doctor."

Steven laughed. "If I'm not fired, I expect I'll be here a long time. You'll know where to find me."

Steven was eager to talk with Chris, to learn more of what Nathan Jones had to say and to tell her about the likelihood that

Anna had probably escaped seizure by the INS. He lay on the bed, his hands cupped behind his head, staring absently at the ceiling. What would become of Anna? Even if she were to get permanent resident status, she was a mere child with a baby to raise. Cut off from her family; her home. Had he done the right thing for her? Would her husband ever really give up on wanting to get his son back? He wished he could have taken her home to his mother. He was certain that she would grow to love Anna and the baby. They would have a home. But for anyone looking for her, it would be too obvious a place.

The phone rang. Steven jumped to answer it.

"Hello, Steven."

He recognized Dr. Ewing's voice. "Yes, sir."

"Relax, Steven. You're not fired."

Steven had prepared himself for the worst. His voice shook with emotion

"Thank you, Dr. Ewing. I..."

"Don't thank me. The housestaff representatives came out strongly in opposition to dismissal. I couldn't have swung the program heads around without their support."

Steven was stunned. Beck and Scully supported him! Why the about-face?

"The committee did decide to give you an official reprimand," Ewing said. "It will be part of your permanent record. It virtually eliminates your chances of getting a residency slot here at Smithfield."

"What will they enter in my record?"

"That you are officially censured for flagrant insubordination and actions contrary to established hospital policy. The statement also stipulates that any future conduct deemed by the committee as contrary to established ethical or policy standards will constitute grounds for immediate dismissal."

"When can I start back?"

"They left that to my discretion. Then Scully said he'd like you back as soon as possible to relieve the other housestaff of extra call nights and to reduce patient loads for the interns."

"My deposition is on Wednesday."

"I know. You can return to the pediatric service the following day."

"I'll be there. By the way, Dr. Ewing, did you know that Nathan Jones is in town and will be coming to the deposition?"

"I'll be damned. That's a bit unusual. Probably a micro-manager who's unwilling to leave it entirely to his lawyer. I don't think you should be concerned about that. Just tell it like it was."

Steven didn't agree. It would be much harder for him to go into all the gory details with the preacher's son sitting there. He wondered if the committee had discussed Chris's involvement. "Sir, was Dr. Murphy's role brought up.?"

"That's executive committee business. But it's really a non-issue. Once you brought the patient to the ER, Dr. Murphy had no choice but to proceed as she did."

Steven was too excited to sleep. He was eager to talk with Chris, maybe ask her to stop by before heading to her apartment. He wanted to call Jerry Russo to see if he had any idea why Scully and Beck came out strongly in his favor. Had he promised Jacqueline he'd call her as soon as he heard from Ewing? Or had she said she'd call him? Omar Diack had asked him to go slow with Jacqueline. He didn't want to pursue her and yet he couldn't deny his fascination with her. He had no experience oscillating between two relationships, like a physics-lab pith ball, drawn one way and then another by invisible, mysterious forces.

He stripped to his shorts, lit some incense and sat on the floor in the lotus position. He slowly cleansed his mind of all thought. As his body relaxed he was transported to his private place of peace, a universe free of predators and self.

Steven extended his arm, placed his hand on the phone, hoping the jarring insistent noise would cease. Finally, he sat up. He picked up the hand set.

"Steven? It's Chris."

"Hi." He squinted at his bedside clock...six-thirty A.M.

"Sorry to call so early. Jerry's had four admissions. We just tucked away the last one."

"It's okay," he said, trying to sound convincing.

"I go on duty in the ER at eight and wondered if we could meet for breakfast. Celebrate the housestaff committee decision--and there's something we have to discuss--it can't wait," she whispered.

"What? What is it?"

"I can't. Not over the phone."

"Sure, seven at the Silver Bullet?"

"No, let's meet at the hospital cafeteria, in case the intern needs me. I'm not off call until eight."

Chapter Nineteen

Steven entered the cafeteria; spotted Chris seated in a far corner; grabbed a cup of coffee, toast and a scoop of scrambled eggs; and walked to her table. She was wearing fresh scrubs and a white lab coat. She looked remarkably perky for what must have been a horrendous call night. She raised her orange juice in a toast.

“To the housestaff committee’s wise decision.”

Steven sat. He clinked his coffee mug against her glass. “Ewing said the reps made the difference.”

“I’m not surprised," Chris said. "One of the interns told me that the entire housestaff met late yesterday afternoon. She said Jerry Russo came out strongly in your support. He said that he’d personally be looking for another job if you were released.”

“I can’t believe he said that. He’s got a wife, a baby--why would he risk so much for my sake?”

“People underestimate Jerry," Chris said. “There’s a tiger beneath that teddy-bear exterior of his. He caught Scully and Beck off balance.”

Steven recalled a favorite Taoist proverb:

Prey passes the tiger who

Sometimes merely looks,

Sometimes pounces without hesitation

But never fails to act.

They ate in silence for a few minutes. There's risk in acting, he thought. It takes courage to trust your instincts. And if you stop to measure the consequences of action, the opportunity often passes, at times never to return. So often the foolish and the heroic act are one and the same. The outcome determines which.

Chris broke the silence. "Apparently, Anwar Amin has friends in high places."

"What do you mean?" he asked.

"Two FBI agents stopped by the hospital at midnight for a friendly chat."

"FBI! About what?"

"He said you and I are running the risk of being charged with obstruction of justice in plotting to help an illegal alien evade the INS."

Steven smiled. "Come on, Chris, you're joking."

"I wish I were. He said he has a transcript of a telephone conversation that clearly incriminated us."

"My God, this is too much. How would they know that unless they had tapped my phone? And besides, your name never came up."

"It didn't have to. I called the shelter when I heard Mr. Amin had left the country."

Steven studied Chris's face. He wondered what else she hadn't told him. What exactly was her connection with the shelter? "What did you say?"

"That Mrs. Amin and the baby were now subject to deportation. I suggested she be sent off to another location,"

Chris said. "The second agent, who had been silent until that time, pulled a pad from his pocket and read me those exact words. He said they wouldn't charge me with obstruction if I cooperated with them."

"I can't believe they'd go to such lengths over a deportation case. Especially since they know the woman's been abused."

She looked about the cafeteria, then her gaze settled on a well-dressed man in a business suit, sitting at a table across the room. Her eyes narrowed.

"It must be the shelter number that's being tapped," Steven said.

"Maybe even yours and mine."

Steven followed Chris's eyes. He saw a man in the business suit, leaning over a folded newspaper, a pencil in hand. Probably doing a crossword puzzle.

Steven had never thought what it must feel like to know someone had listened to, or even recorded your private conversations. He felt violated, angry. They must know the dangers Mrs. Amin would be exposed to if she were to be deported. Why pursue her with such vigor?

"What did he expect to gain by confronting you?" Steven asked.

She glanced over her shoulder. She opened her mouth as though to say something then changed her mind. Steven felt the muscles in his neck and back tighten. This wasn't really happening. She shifted her chair so that her back was to the man.

"The agent who did all the talking said that if I could find out where she had been taken, that they wouldn't press for an obstruction of justice charge."

"Didn't you tell them we have no idea where she might have been taken?"

"They know it was I who took her to the shelter initially. They believe I'm part of the system." She stared at her half-empty coffee mug.

"Are you?" he asked.

She pulled her chair closer to his and spoke in almost a whisper. "I'm...I'm sorry, Steven. I haven't been up front with you about me and the shelter."

"I wouldn't expect you to."

"I've gone there many times to examine women and document abuse. I'm an adviser to the shelter. I know how things work. I arranged for Anna's transfer."

Steven was dumbfounded. Had she lied to the FBI agent? Maybe she did know where Anna had been taken. "You do know where she is!" He said it louder than he meant to.

"My God! Steven."

Steven's face reddened. "I'm sorry." He leaned forward and whispered, "Do you?"

"It's kind of like roulette. You start the wheel spinning. You don't know where the little ball will land."

"Do you believe they'll be able to track her down?"

"Yes, if she's in another shelter. Local police know the location of shelters. I'm sure the FBI could pressure them into cooperating. The agent said Mrs. Amin could be facing kidnapping charges. She's denying her husband access to his son without first gaining legal custody."

"That's insane. They're just trying to intimidate you."

"I said the same thing. He cited a case in South Carolina where a woman ran off to Canada with her nine-year-old son.

They eventually caught her. She was sentenced to five years in prison. Her abusive husband gained custody of the boy."

Steven shook his head in disbelief. He glanced across the room. "Is that guy sitting over there one of the men who talked with you last night?"

"No. But he came in when I did, and he's been staring at me."

Steven covered her hand with his. It was cold. She turned to face him.

"Be careful, Steven. Don't call the shelter. You've done all you can for Anna." She looked at her watch. She stood. "I have to go. Don't forget, we have a date tonight."

"You haven't told me about your meeting with Nathan Jones."

"I'll fill you in later."

Steven watched her exit the cafeteria. The man she had been concerned about also watched. Moments later the man rose and left. Was it just a coincidence or was he following her? Why? She had told the FBI agent she knew nothing of Mrs. Amin's whereabouts. Still, they *were* in a race against time. They needed to deport her before she would be able to obtain permanent resident status. With thousands of shelters scattered across the country, it could take them weeks to locate her. They were probably hoping Chris would somehow lead them directly to her.

Chris had said something that bothered Steven. "If she's in a shelter." If she's not, where would they have taken her? He tried to place himself in Chris's position. Where would she have taken Anna? Family members would certainly be checked out by the FBI. He thought of the Underground Railroad used to help escaped slaves to flee their masters. Was that what Chris meant when she used the analogy of roulette? Did an underground railroad exist for abused and battered women?

In two days, Steven would be starting back on pediatrics. He had a day and a half to sharpen his baby skills. He also had better begin studying for his State Board Examination. It wasn't until spring, but it was a comprehensive, two-day exam that covered both the basic sciences and the major clinical specialties. And soon after that he'd have to take the second part of his National Boards.

He wondered if the library kept an archive of previous Board questions or at least Board Examination study guides. It was daunting to contemplate reviewing four years of intense study.

Dinner with Chris wasn't until seven. He wouldn't have much down time during his internship, so he had better take advantage of this opportunity. On leaving the cafeteria, he navigated past a stream of visitors and hospital employees. He took a stairway to the ground level and passed through a door marked "employees only." He headed down a long, deserted corridor leading to an elevator that serviced the hospital's administrative wing. Steven walked a gauntlet of black-and-white photographs of stern-faced, hospital founding fathers, whose steady, unblinking eyes followed him as he hurried along.

As he waited for the elevator, he scanned a bulletin board that listed the noon conferences. The pediatric conference was "Failure to Thrive." He decided to attend. He was interested in the topic. Also, it would be a good chance to show that he was eager to get back to work. The fact that Jacqueline would most likely be there had no influence on his decision to attend. Or had it? The elevator doors opened. He was face to face with Dr. Ewing.

"Dr. Johnson! Were you coming to see me?" Ewing asked.

"No. I'm going to the hospital library."

"Nice haircut, Steven. Almost didn't recognize you. I'll see you in my office at nine A.M. sharp."

"Yes, Sir."

"Clyde tells me your meeting with him went well." Ewing placed a hand on Steven's shoulder. "I've dealt with Jones' attorney before. He can be a bit intimidating. You'd better get a good night's sleep."

Chapter Twenty

Steven was more disappointed than he would like to admit, when Jacqueline failed to show up at the noon lecture. The series was part of the student nurses' curriculum. They were excused from other duties in order to attend. Was she out sick? Maybe he'd better call her later. But just before the conference began, Jacqueline came into the room, escorting a tall slim woman carrying an infant. The woman held the baby to her breast, its head nestled on her shoulder. The mother looked to be in her late teens. Her blond hair hung to her shoulders. Jacqueline led her to a seat in the front row.

Russo presented the nine-month-old infant's history. The child was far below her expected weight. She was unable to sit unsupported. She was bottle fed and often regurgitated her feedings. Milk intolerance was suspected, and the infant had been switched to a non-milk formula. But she still failed to gain weight and continued to throw up after eating.

The mother of the child, a single parent, worked in a local nursing home as a nurses' aide. While the mother was at work, the child stayed with a neighbor. The woman had three small children of her own. Russo and Jacqueline had made a visit to the child's home, as well as that of the caretaker.

Steven was impressed by the thoroughness of Russo's presentation and delicacy with which Jacqueline interviewed the mother. The audience was also given a chance to question the mother before Jacqueline escorted her from the room. After the mother left, Russo ran through a list of possible causes for the infant's failure to thrive. He presented physical, as well as laboratory findings. Neglect verses metabolic or physical causes were debated. When Russo declared that abdominal examination was unremarkable, most of the clinicians present were inclined toward the neglect theory. But the diagnostic clincher was a barium swallow that confirmed the presence of pyloric stenosis, an anatomic obstruction to the outflow of food from the stomach to the small bowel...a potentially fatal condition if not diagnosed, but curable by timely surgical intervention.

"You should have been able to feel the mass on abdominal examination," a grey-haired clinician insisted.

The attending came to Russo's defense. "I also couldn't feel a mass prior to seeing it on the barium swallow. In my experience, the mass is not palpable in about twenty-five percent of cases."

As the conference broke up, Jacqueline waved and smiled at Steven, who was seated in the rear of the room. He caught up to her in the hall.

"Hi. Nice job interviewing the mother," Steven said.

"She was very nervous. She was certain the doctors blamed her for the baby's condition."

"Probing for abuse or neglect without making the parent defensive is tough," Steven said.

Jacqueline looked about. "It will be good to have you back."

"I'm a bit nervous. The count's no balls and two strikes."

She looked puzzled for a moment, and then smiled. "Be careful, Steven," she whispered. Not waiting for a response, she hurried off.

What was she talking about? The Jones deposition? She couldn't know anything about Mrs. Amin. God, had the FBI questioned her?

Someone tapped him on the shoulder. He jumped.

"Caught you staring. Can't say I blame you. She's a number."

Steven gave Russo a high five. "Decent thing you did for me at the meeting."

"No big deal. Besides, it was Jacqueline who asked me to speak up for you. Of course, I would have done it without her asking. The lady's got a big-time crush on you."

"She's a warm, sweet person. We're just friends."

"Watch your step, buddy. She'll work a little Rastafarian magic and before you know it, you'll be on your way to Jamaica to meet Mama."

"I'll have to watch out for home-baked cookies."

A cool breeze carried the scent of ripening apples that brought to mind the smell of new books and erasers and the excitement Steven had always felt at the beginning of a new school year. Steven searched the hillside that bordered the hospital property. He spotted an aged apple tree, its fruit glistening in the mid-day sun, its gnarled limbs arching as they strained to hold onto their precious yield. As he drew closer he could see that many of its apples were already on the ground. Reaching up, he plucked a ripe apple from a low branch. He rubbed it on his shirt sleeve before taking a bite. It was crisp and delicious.

He had to watch his step. The ground was alive with bees, feasting on rotting fruit. He reached up and picked four apples to take along to his apartment. Suddenly a swarm of furious yellow jackets, a cloud of miniature buzz saws, rose from the ground. Every exposed part of his body felt their anger. He dropped his apples and began to run, instinctively heading for the ER. He could feel his lips and one eye beginning to swell. Growing up, he had been stung many times, but never before had he had so many bites. His flailing arms failed to discourage his pursuers, several of whom had gotten under his shirt. He smacked at his chest with his fists. One eye was already swollen shut, the other a mere slit. His chest, caught in a vice-like grip, refused to admit air. Blinded by massive edema of his eyelids, he continued to run in the direction of the ER entrance, where he collapsed into someone's arms.

When Steven awakened, Chris was sitting on a stool beside his stretcher looking through a chart. He was hooked up to two IVs. "Hey," he said. His speech was slurred. He sounded drunk. He tried to smile, but his face couldn't quite pull it off. His throat was an open sore.

She smiled. "I was on the ER receiving platform waiting for an ambulance to arrive. I saw you walking up the hill. I saw you tearing down the hill...figured it might have been the bees."

"I anaphylaxed?"

"That you did. Thirty-seven stings. That’s a lot of bee juice."

"I ate one of their apples. The little bastards never learned to share." He tried again to smile. This time his face worked a little better. "How bad was I?"

"Your BP was zippo. Pulmonary edema. Stridor. Benson wanted to do a trach. But I was able to get a tube down. We loaded you with epinephrine, steroids and antihistamines."

"What's in the IVs?" Steven could barely keep his eyes open.

"Dopamine in one. Steroids in the other. Probably be able to stop the dopamine by morning."

"You saved my life." Steven looked about the curtained-off cubicle. "I'm still in the ER...how long have I been out?"

She checked her watch. "It's half past six. You came in around one thirty."

"I can't remember a thing."

"Good, because Jacqueline came by. She held your hand for an hour until I chased her off. Ewing and Russo came by. Actually, just about all of the interns. You have more fans than you realize." She took his hand into hers. She brought it to her lips.

"What are my chances of making it to the deposition tomorrow morning?"

"Zero. You're in the ER on a 24-hour admission. I didn't want to give you up to the floor."

"Will they reschedule the deposition?" Steven's eyelids refused to remain open.

"They already have your written statement. But Jones' lawyer may press for a delay. After the meeting, Clyde told me the hospital would consider settling the case out of court if the physicians were not part of the suit. He said that malpractice juries usually show more compassion for doctors than they do for hospitals. Hey, you still with me?"

He nodded. He spoke with his eyes closed. "But I'm supposed to start back on the ward . . ."

“Shut up and go to sleep. I'm going to get a bite to eat. I'll check back with you later."

Chris picked up a boxed meal the cafeteria staff had put aside for her. Fried chicken, mashed potatoes and green beans with bacon bits. She got some ice water and picked out a table off by itself, away from the noisy clusters of visiting family members.

She wished she could let Steven in on what was happening with Anna, but she couldn't involve him any more than he already was. Besides the legal risks, his job at Smithfield was so tenuous it couldn't withstand even a minor jolt. As she picked at unappetizing food, she recalled the spiraling events after she learned that Anna's husband had left the country, effectively invalidating her visa.

She had dialed the unlisted shelter number. Helen came on the line. "How's Rosebud doing?" She knew Helen would recognize her voice.

"Who is this?"

"I must have dialed the wrong number. Sorry to have bothered you," Chris said. She was glad she had set up the code words at the time she dropped off Anna and her baby at the shelter. She had just told Helen that now was the time to get Anna and her baby out of there. She had already spoken with Omar and asked if he would be willing to help. She went to the nurses' station. Omar was charting. He glanced at her. She nodded. He knew exactly what he had to do. When his shift ended, he headed for a local fast food restaurant. He picked up Anna and her baby and brought them to Jacqueline's apartment. Chris hadn't wanted to involve Jacqueline, but she had no other option. Her own place was too obvious, and Anna couldn't stay in Omar's apartment. It was Omar who had suggested Jacqueline. She was renting a garage apartment in a quiet neighborhood, within walking distance from the hospital. The stairs leading up to the second-floor apartment were on the side away from the front entrance. The adjacent property was set back, obscured by trees and shrubs. No one would see her enter.

Omar often gave Jacqueline a lift, especially when the weather was too bad for her to walk. The neighbors or Jacqueline's landlady wouldn't be concerned seeing his car pull onto the drive and park in front of the garage.

Omar gave Anna the apartment key. He remained in the car until Anna and her baby were safely inside.

After work, Jacqueline left the hospital, stopping to buy some groceries before heading home. It was seven. She wondered if Anna was already in her apartment. Was she a vegetarian? What would she feed her?

She knew Anna and the baby would only be with her a short while. Living on her own wasn't as great as Jacqueline had thought it would be. She missed her family, especially her mother and sisters. It was going to be fun to be with someone close to her age. She thought of Steven often. Especially at night when she lay in darkness. She imagined him in bed with her. His strong arms holding her close. His breath warm on her cheek as he told her of growing up in Kansas---Kansas. She liked the sound of it. All she knew of that part of America was from the movie, *The Wizard of OZ*. She imagined herself as Dorothy and Steven the son of a wealthy farmer. He would travel to the Land of Oz; rescue her from the clutches of the wicked witch. She would climb onto the back of his Honda shadow, holding him tightly as they roared through the sky, back to Kansas where they would live on a great farm. They would have vast fields of wheat and corn and horses. Many horses.

Was she falling in love with Steven? Or was she just lonely? Still, she never felt like this before. She looked constantly for him in the halls of the hospital. And when she saw him it took great effort not to rush to him, with no idea what she would do if she had. What did he think of her? Omar says that Steven thinks of her as a young sister. But how does he know? She recalled the night she took food to Steven's apartment. As she left he had taken her hand. The look in his eyes was of longing and a touch of sadness...not that of a brother.

Jacqueline climbed the stairs to her apartment. As she opened the door she heard Anna quietly singing to her baby. She was sitting on a side chair in the living room. A large cloth bag on the floor beside her, her baby was at her breast. She was wearing blue jeans, a flannel shirt and a baseball cap pulled down low over her forehead. She quickly covered the exposed part of her breast as Jacqueline entered.

"I'm Jacqueline."

"Omar told me of you. It is an honor to meet you."

She couldn't be any older than seventeen, Jacqueline thought. What would they talk about?

"Please, feed your baby. I have to put these groceries away. Are you hungry?"

"I am always hungry since I started feeding my son."

There was no separation between the tiny kitchen area and the living room. She placed a bag of groceries on the counter. She removed a carton of eggs, milk, butter, a package of chicken, a carton of tofu, a green pepper, a yellow onion, broccoli, and a package of carrots.

"Do you eat meat?" Jacqueline asked.

"I can only eat halal."

Jacqueline was puzzled. “Is that a kind of meat?”

"It can be any meat except pork. It is prepared at the market in a certain way. In Princeton, there is a Muslim community. Halal can be purchased in a market close to the mosque."

Jacqueline was certain Smithfield would not have such a market. She must speak with Omar. She wondered where the nearest Muslim market might be. “What of vegetables, fish, milk and cheese?”

"I am imposing on you. You are kind to be concerned about my diet. Cook your customary food. I will eat all but the meat of animals and shellfish.”

“Did your husband observe the Muslim diet?”

Anna shook her head. “He ate and drank what he pleased. He pretended to be a devout Muslim only to win my father's favor. While he courted me, he went to the Mosque. He prayed five times daily. He gave me fine jewelry. After we married he ridiculed my father. He sold my jewelry to pay off gambling debts.”

Jacqueline sliced the pepper into thin strips. She quartered and peeled the onion.

Anna's baby stopped sucking and dropped his lips from her breast. Anna rested the baby on her lap as she adjusted her bra and buttoned her shirt. She raised him to her shoulder, gently patting his back. He expelled a loud burp. She and Jacqueline laughed.

Jacqueline was surprised how open Anna was, talking of her family. "Did you love Anwar when you married?"

"I was not yet sixteen. It was all arranged. I hardly knew him. I pleaded with my father." She lowered her eyes. "My father is a good man. He believed he was doing what was best for me. Anwar was from a respected Muslim family."

Jacqueline diced the tofu and carrots. She placed a wok on a gas burner and poured in an ounce of peanut oil. "You were forced to marry?" she asked.

"No. In Islam, the woman must consent to marriage. I agreed to please my parents."

From what Steven had told her, Jacqueline knew that Anwar had renounced Anna and that was tantamount to divorce. "Are you still legally Anwar's wife?" Jacqueline asked.

"There is a three-month waiting period to be sure the woman is not pregnant. If the wife has a suckling child, the divorce does not take effect until after the child no longer nurses."

"That could be a long time. Some males never stop," Jacqueline said.

Anna smiled. Then she began to giggle and soon her laughter turned to tears. "It is good to laugh again."

"Yes," Jacqueline said, "and sometimes it is necessary to cry. Especially when preparing onions."

"I would like to help."

"My kitchen is too small for two. Anna, would it be possible for you to get back with your family in Algiers?" Jacqueline asked.

"When a man renounces his wife, it brings shame on the family. I cannot live at home. I have younger sisters. It is the oldest who must marry. He has told my family lies. That I walk the streets without a veil. My father cannot take me back. It is impossible. Anwar will take my baby from me. He would never give him up." Tears filled her eyes. "I will be forced to live like a beggar."

Jacqueline removed the wok from the burner. She walked to where Anna was sitting. She sat on the floor beside her, placing her hand on Anna's.

"You have done nothing to shame yourself."

"He said I wore Western clothes, painted my face, and walked the streets. That I neglected my daily prayers."

"How do you know he said those things? Have you spoken with your parents?"

"Yes. I called from a pay-phone. My father accused me of terrible things. I pleaded with him. He wouldn't listen."

"Why would he believe Anwar and not you?"

"I should have called him sooner. When Anwar left the United States, he went directly to my parents. He showed them something from an American newspaper that said I left the hospital with a young doctor."

Jacqueline still didn't understand. Her own parents would trust her before someone outside the family.

The baby awakened and began to cry as though in pain. Anna felt his diaper.

"Is there a place I might change him?"

Jacqueline pointed to the bathroom door. "The counter next to the sink is wide enough. While you change your baby, I'll prepare dinner. A full stomach quiets the soul."

Anna smiled through her tears. "So too does a dry diaper." She picked up a large cloth carrying bag and took it and her baby to the bathroom.

"Shower if you like," Jacqueline said. "There is a clean towel on the rack."

Jacqueline watched as Anna left the room. Despite her tiny stature and obvious gentle nature, she must possess great inner strength, Jacqueline thought...to leave her husband despite the consequences.

Jacqueline placed the tofu, chopped peppers, broccoli and onions in the hot oil. As she stir-fried the vegetables and tofu, her mind remained on the events of the morning Anna's baby was supposed to be circumcised. At the time, it had seemed Steven did the right thing to place Anna into a shelter. But now Jacqueline wondered if he had acted too soon. Wouldn't it have been better for Anna and her baby to go back to Algiers with Anwar when he finished his graduate work at Princeton? She could have gone to her family and showed them proof of his abuse. Exposed him for the hypocrite he was. Her family would likely take her back and even fight for her to have custody of the baby. Was it too late to go to the family and explain Anna's predicament? Could she go to Algiers, bring Anna's X-rays and the photographs taken in the ER? But there was risk in such a plan. Anna might still lose her baby. And what if Anna's family did not believe Jacqueline's story? Still, it might be worth the risk. She must talk with someone...certainly not Steven. He was already in danger of being fired. Who else was there other than Dr. Murphy and her cousin Omar? First, she would talk with Omar. He could be trusted not to tell Steven. Besides, Steven might be hospitalized for several days. He could do nothing to help. She wondered if he had as yet awakened. She would call the hospital after dinner.

Anna came into the kitchen, a towel wrapped about her head like a turban, the sleeping baby resting its head on her shoulder. "Please, there must be something I can do?" Anna asked.

"This time you watch. At the hospital, they say: 'see one, do one, teach one.' It is also a good rule for the kitchen."

"Omar said you are a nurse."

"A nursing student. I had the classroom work in Jamaica. Now I must work two years in hospital."

Jacqueline added minced garlic and spices to the wok as Anna watched. "My mother prepared these spices for me."

"I am sorry to make trouble for you."

"You are the same age as my younger sister. Her name is Camille. It is good not to be alone. How old are your sisters?"

"Aissa is fourteen. Leila is twelve."

"And your brother?"

"Tahar is the oldest. He will soon be eighteen."

"Anna, I do not know your family name."

"Yacine. I will be glad to have it back." She watched as Jacqueline scooped the sizzling stir-fried vegetables into a bowl.

"Omar said I will be here only a few days. He is going to find a Muslim family willing to have me and my baby live with them. He said there are many of the Muslim faith in New Jersey."

And what of her own family? Jacqueline thought. Would Anna never see them again? Would she live in constant fear of being discovered? Reuniting with her family seemed the best possible outcome. *I must think on that. There must me a way.*

Chapter Twenty-One

Steven was awakened by the familiar chorus of hurried steps, banging trays, creaking cart wheels and intrusive voices fueled by caffeine. He was still attached to an intravenous line, but the Foley catheter, thank God, had been removed.

An attendant dropped a breakfast tray onto his bedside stand. "Good morning, Dr. Johnson. Another beautiful fall day."

It was an effort for Steven to speak. "Good morning," he said hoarsely. "What day is it? Wednesday?"

"No, doctor, Wednesday's come and gone."

Steven couldn't believe he had slept through the entire day. Reluctantly he removed the lid from his breakfast tray. The smell of coffee, scrambled eggs and bacon reminded Steven that he hadn't eaten in over two days. But swallowing was so difficult and uncomfortable; he gave up trying after a couple of bites. He lay back on his pillow staring absently at the ceiling, feeling very sorry for himself. Moments later Chris entered his room. Her warm smile and cheerful attitude reassured him that he would most likely survive his encounter with the army of yellow jackets. He sat up, trying his best to smile back, but the muscles of his face felt as though they had been pumped full of Novocain. His lips were puffy and sore.

"How am I doing, doc?"

"We stopped the Dopamine yesterday. You're on a steroid taper. We'll switch to oral steroids tomorrow."

"I'm out of here in the A.M?"

"Maybe." She sat and squeezed his hand. "Nice having you under my control."

"I'm at your mercy."

"You ever react to bee stings before?"

"Never like this. Just localized reactions."

"You're going to have to carry a syringe of epi around with you from now on."

"Do you believe the desensitization shots are worth all the trouble?"

She nodded. "It's at least a five-year ordeal. But I've seen it work wonders. By the way, I called your mom."

"You did? Was I that bad?"

"I told her you'll be back to your old self in a couple of days."

"How'd the deposition go?"

"Delessandro insisted he had the right to question you in person. He wanted to reschedule the hearing. I'm glad Nathan Jones was there. He said it wasn't necessary. That he had already decided to drop you and the ER staff from the suit."

Steven was incredulous. "Damn. You were right. You said he might. How did Ewing react to that bombshell?"

"Controlled, but I could tell he was pleased. Of course, they're still going after the hospital, so he wasn't ready to do a celebratory jig."

“I’m glad...no, I'm thrilled that you and I aren't getting sued. Still, I feel I should have followed up to make sure the preacher kept his appointment."

"You obviously enjoy beating up on yourself, so here's some bad news..."

"Oh?"

"Delessandro will be calling you and me as his witnesses. He feels our testimony can be used to build his case against the hospital."

"He can do that?"

"He seems to think so."

Steven sank back on his pillow. "God, can’t we take the fifth? After all, we do work for the hospital."

"I don’t believe that would work. After Delessandro and Nathan Jones left, Clyde and Ewing and I discussed our potential testimony. Clyde said to refuse to render any opinions or engage in speculation."

"Can't a witness be in contempt of court for refusing to answer a question?"

"Aye, there's the rub. Changing the subject, I assume that you had a pretty good reason for not making it to dinner at my place two nights ago?"

"Nothing short of anaphylaxis could have kept me away."

She kissed him on the cheek. "I must run. There are lives to be saved." She headed for the door.

"A lame excuse for leaving a patient with so many questions and concerns. When can I start on my pediatric rotation?"

"Monday at the earliest. Massive doses of steroids have suppressed your immune system. You'll be at risk on the pedes ward."

"Hey wait. What about Anna?"

"I'll be back this evening. We'll talk about it then." She threw him a kiss and exited.

He pushed the nurse call button.

"Yes, Dr. Johnson?"

"Would you remind Dr. Murphy to leave an order for me to get out of bed?"

"She already has. PT will be here in about thirty minutes. Don't try to ambulate until the therapist arrives."

He picked up the phone and started to dial his mother's number, then remembered it wasn't yet seven in Kansas. He decided to call her later.

Why hadn't Chris said something reassuring about Anna? Had the INS caught up with her? He knew he should remove himself from that situation... but how could he? He'd gotten her into that mess. He dialed his own telephone number to check his messages. There were two. One from Gloria Russo inviting him to dinner the following Sunday evening. He listened to the second message.

"Hi, Steven. This is Jacqueline. The pediatric staff, and especially the student nurse assigned to the service, are all looking forward for you to join us on Friday. I hope the deposition goes well."

Chris had mentioned that Jacqueline had been to see him. He couldn't recall her being there. He wanted to call her, but she was probably making morning rounds with the pediatric team. He hoped she would stop by during lunch. There was no denying his attraction to Jacqueline. She was kind, gentle and wise beyond her years. He was flattered and frankly puzzled why she was so aggressively pursuing him. Omar was right. He must keep their relationship that of friendship, nothing more. But would Chris tolerate even that? He was living a perfect male fantasy.

The dilemma of having to choose between two charming, beautiful, intelligent women, both of whom for some strange reason saw him as a person worth the chase.

The chase reminded him of his desperate race down the hill, pursued by hundreds of miniature assassins. If Chris hadn't been there as he collapsed unseeing and unseen, he would surely have died. He lay back on his pillow, his hands suddenly cold; his palms moist. Of all the people in the hospital, it was Chris who had seen him stumble down the hillside. Had his life been spared by pure chance? Or did God have other plans for him? Was Chris part of that plan?

A male attendant pushed a wheelchair through the door of Steven's private room.

"Come to get you to PT," the man said.

To Steven's surprise he felt wobbly and light-headed as the attendant helped him from the bed. He attached Steven's intravenous bag to a pole mounted on the back of the chair.

"We'd better stop at the nurses' station," Steven said. "That bag's close to empty. I don't want it to run out while I'm at PT."

The attendant had Steven's medical record tucked under his arm.

"Mind if I look at my chart?" Steven asked.

The man shrugged and handed it to him. Steven flipped to the medication record. He was shocked to see the massive doses of steroids he had received. He read Chris's initial notes and those of an anesthesiologist and a consulting medicine attending. It was strange seeing himself subjected to cold clinical analysis. Even Chris's entries didn't convey the anxiety and terror she must have felt. He was starting in on the nurses' notes when he arrived at physical therapy. He handed the chart to the therapist, a middle-aged ruddy-faced cheerful man.

"You don't want to read that stuff. Makes it sound like you're dying."

"I apparently came pretty damn close."

The physical therapy session went well. Although a little shaky at first, Steven was soon walking without assistance. But his whole body was one massive sore from the dozens of bee stings.

"What you need is a hot whirlpool bath."

"Who doesn't?"

Steven eased his way into the bubbly water, slipping off his hospital gown as he did.

"This is great," he said. He closed his eyes, resting his head on the edge of the stainless-steel tub.

"Mind if I join you?"

He opened his eyes with a start. Chris was standing next to the tub. The somewhat opaque water afforded her only a blurred version of his naked body.

The attendant was working with another patient, separated from Steven by a curtain. "Hate to be a killjoy, but hospital policy states that only patients are allowed in the whirlpool."

"Damn bureaucracy," Chris said.

Steven wanted to ask her about Anna but couldn't, with the therapist just beyond the curtain. Besides he wasn't confident Chris would tell him the whole truth.

"You should have seen me on the parallel bars. I did great."

"He did okay," the therapist said. "But I'd hold the prisoner another day."

"God says you have to stay another day, Steven," Chris said. "Should I bring in your little Buddha?"

"Not funny. I hate being a patient."

"Remember that when you're the one writing the orders."

"Can you stop by my room this afternoon?" Steven asked.

"Sure. And if you can do ten one-arm pushups I'll discharge you."

The unseen therapist said, "The lady's my kind of doctor."

Late that evening Jacqueline heard a car pull onto the drive. She could tell from the tap tap sound that it was Omar's. She opened her apartment door as he was about to knock. His expression did not convey a successful mission.

"Where is Anna?" he asked.

"She was breast-feeding the baby. They both went off to sleep. She is very tired, so speak softly. Are you hungry?"

"No. I ate on the way. I met with the Mullah of a Mosque in Hoboken. He knew immediately who I was talking about. He said he read about the incident in the *Newark Star Ledger*."

As he spoke, Omar walked to the refrigerator and peered inside. "I guess I am a little hungry."

"There's leftover stir-fried vegetables."

Omar was already removing the bowl from the fridge.

"Let me heat that."

"No, no. I like it cold."

Jacqueline got him a fork and poured him a glass of milk. "I have some tea already made. I will heat it." She went to the stove. "Did you find a home for Anna?

"The Mullah was very kind. He understood the predicament we faced. He explained that his community consisted mostly of moderate Muslims and that among them he could no doubt find a family willing to take in Anna and her child. But, as in any community, there are those who hold extreme views. Those few voices have spoken out in support of the father. They believe it an abomination that the hospital took his son from him. That his wife has brought disgrace on herself and other Muslims. If she is discovered by them, they would not hesitate to expose her."

"Couldn't a Muslim family say she is a cousin recently widowed, in need of a place to live?"

"I posed the same question to the Mullah. He said his people are fearful of the INS. Some are undocumented. Others are trying to get family members into the country. The Mullah feared there would be reprisals if it is discovered his community is harboring someone the INS seeks to deport."

"He refused to help?"

"Yes, and now I do not know what to do."

"I believe I know a way," Jacqueline said. She poured him a steaming cup of tea. It was her mother's secret blend. He needed something warm in his belly to incline him favorably toward her idea. "If Anna's own family can be convinced that Anwar is a lying hypocrite... that he beat her."

"And how are we to do that?"

"I will go to Algiers. Visit her family..."

"No! I will not allow it," Omar said. "Besides why should they believe you, a stranger?"

"I will bring X-rays, photographs and a copy of Dr. Johnson's description of what happened."

"Even if they take her in, Anwar will take the child from her."

"Yes, that is a risk. But her family is respected and has the means to hire a lawyer. It is possible she will be able to keep her baby or at least get joint custody."

"What do you know of such things?"

Omar was right. She knew little of Anna's culture and Islamic laws. "Isn't it better for her to be with her family, even if she does lose her child, than to live in constant fear of being discovered? Or having him torn from her when he is older?"

Omar sipped his tea without responding. What was in his mind? Jacqueline's mother had asked him to look after her. Would he insist on talking with her mother before even considering letting her make the trip to Algiers?

"I must think on this," Omar said. "You must not talk with anyone."

"We mustn't wait too long."

"And how are you to get her X-rays and hospital reports?"

"I can ask Dr. Johnson."

"No! He is already in too much trouble."

"You're right. I can go to the X-ray department and say we need her films for a conference. I can get her chart from medical records."

He glanced toward the bedroom where Anna was sleeping. He lowered his voice. "I was foolish to bring her here. I will talk with Dr. Murphy. It is not too late to get her to another shelter."

"No. They will find her. Then everything Steven has done will be wasted."

"This is about Dr. Johnson, not Anna?"

Jacqueline didn't know how to respond. "I must confess that at first I merely wanted to help him. Impress him. But now I have met Anna and her baby. It is different."

"And you and Steven are very different. Have you thought ahead? How would your family look on him? How will his look on you?"

"For now, it is enough that we are friends. Please, Omar, I want to do this for Anna."

Omar poured himself more tea. He shook his head as he thought about what Jacqueline said. "You say you will bring her medical record with you. That is privileged information. You will be dismissed if you are discovered."

"I can copy the contents of her chart and immediately return it."

"Yes...that would work. But you cannot take the X-rays from the hospital. Besides it is not necessary. The reports will be on her chart."

"How soon will you decide?" She studied his profile as he drank his tea. He looked so much like pictures she had seen of her father when he was a young man.

"I'll stop by tomorrow evening after work."

"Will you call my mother?"

"When you came to Smithfield, your mother said she was trusting you to my care. If I'm crazy enough to allow you to go ahead with such a risky plan, it will be my decision to make." He stood and put his arm around her shoulder.

"I could be there and back in three or four days. You must let me do this."

Chapter Twenty-Two

Steven was in bed eating breakfast when Jacqueline knocked and entered his room.

"You are looking much better," she said.

His facial swelling had mostly resolved. He was grateful for the three-day beard that partially obscured the ugly clusters of insect bites that covered his face and neck.

"And you could not possibly look any better," he said.

"I'm not sure how one is to take that?"

He laughed. "You're such a careful listener to words. Omar says you read within the lines."

"Your bed is a mess." She straightened the bedspread tucking in the corners. She puffed up his pillow. "There now, it looks better. When will you return to the pediatric service?"

"Dr. Murphy says not until Monday."

"Why so long?" she asked.

"She said something about my immune system. She's afraid I'll catch the measles or worse yet, the mumps."

Jacqueline smiled. "You're in good spirits, for one who has been through so much."

"I cry when I'm alone."

"I would like to stay," Jacqueline said, "but rounds will begin in five minutes. Dr. Scully will not be happy if I am late."

"His bark's louder than his bite. He actually supported me at the housestaff committee meeting."

"Barking is more often a sign of fear than courage."

"Sounds like more maternal wisdom," he said.

"There is very little I make up."

"Thanks for talking with Jerry Russo before the meeting."

"I didn't mean for you to know."

"Why?" he asked.

"If you do something for someone, and they know it, they will feel an obligation to you. It is better they do not know."

"You are too much."

"Is it good to be too much?"

"Yes."

She looked at her oversized quartz wristwatch. "But it is not good to be too late. I will stop afterwards. There are things I must ask you." She turned to leave.

"What?"

She glanced over her shoulder. "It can wait."

After she left, Steven gazed out the hospital window as he sipped his tepid coffee. The phone rang. It was his mother.

"Steven? It doesn't sound like you."

"I'm a little hoarse, Mom. But I'm feeling great. Getting ready to be discharged."

"I was so worried. I kept thinking of the time your dad went out to see a farmer, who collapsed after having a bunch of stings. Daddy gave him some kind of injection that saved his life."

Steven knew the story. It wasn't his dad's regular patient. He had told the man he had better see his regular doctor and get shots and carry medicine with him at all times.

"But a couple of weeks later," his mother said, "the man had but a single sting, and was dead before daddy got there."

"I'm doing fine."

"You be sure to take the shots."

She sounded somehow different, tremulous. "Yes, Mama. How are you doing?"

"People keep asking if you're coming back to Zion. You'd have a ready-made practice, Steven."

"Mother, I still have three or four years of training."

"All your daddy had was an internship."

"It's different today," Steven said. "You can't get hospital privileges without specialty training."

"The nearest hospital's in Great Bend. That's where daddy sent his patients."

"There's so much I still have to learn," he said.

There was a long silence.

"Don't listen to this old lady. You've got your own life to live."

From the slight tremor in her voice he knew she was on the verge of tears. "Have you heard from Claire lately?"

"Oh, yes. She calls once a week. Not like some people."

"I love you, Mom. I promise I'll call more often."

Steven wished he had chosen a hospital closer to home. He studied the view from his window. The sky was cloudless. Morning sun flooded his room. Leaves on a grassy hillside adjacent to the hospital tossed in a gusty fall breeze. He had three days before reporting for duty. There was no chance for him to see his mother before Christmas, and even that wasn't a certainty, with all the time he had missed. Why not fly to Zion? Leave early Friday morning. Return Sunday night. He'd probably have to pay dearly for a last-minute ticket. Maybe Chris, on her fat attending salary, might be talked into lending him a few bucks. He picked up his phone and asked the hospital operator to connect him to a local travel agent.

Throughout the day, Steven made a pest of himself walking up and down the hall, buttonholing whichever nurse he could find to ask why Dr. Murphy hadn't come by to discharge him. They didn't know and weren't about to call her. He also needed to hit her up for five hundred dollars. Enough for the round-trip fare and a car rental.

At five-thirty she barged into his room and flopped onto the bedside chair. Steven, fully dressed except for his shoes, was propped up in bed, the television remote in his hand. He clicked off the television. "Hey, about time."

"What a day. It was like a Saturday night at Cook County General."

"Good. You made a lot of money. I need five hundred dollars."

"I'm on a salary, remember? And what do you need five hundred dollars for?" She slipped off her shoes and propped her feet on the edge of the bed.

"Doctor, your bedside manner is a bit unusual." He began to massage her feet.

"That feels great. You didn't answer my question."

"I've decided to fly to Zion for a quick visit. It may be a while before I get a chance."

"You want a check or cash?"

"Neither. Would you call my travel agent and put it on your credit card? She's tentatively got me booked on an early morning flight."

"It sounds very rushed. Is something wrong?"

"I spoke with my mother earlier today. She sounds very down. Maybe depressed. I may want to get her to a real doctor."

"My purse is in the ER. I'll call before I leave the hospital." Chris slipped on her shoes.

Steven gave her the travel agent's number. "And fill me in on Anna Amin."

"She's playing musical shelters. What can I say?"

"Why should I believe you?"

"Have I ever lied to you?"

"Yes."

"Technically speaking, I didn't. I merely didn't tell you the whole truth. And you'd better shave before getting on that plane. You look like a terrorist."

"You haven't answered my question."

"Oh, I almost forgot." Chris reached into her lab coat pocket and handed Steven a small plastic container. "Here's your sting kit."

Steven popped open the small plastic box. It contained a pre-loaded syringe and a couple of tablets.

"There's enough there for two shots of epi. The pills are antihistamines."

"Hope I never need to use it. About the loan, I'll pay you back as soon as I get my next paycheck."

They both stood. He put his arms around her and drew her to him. Their lips met for a long steamy encounter. She pulled away. "Wow. Must be the steroids!" Chris said. "Maybe I should keep you on a maintenance dose."

He walked her to the door. Hadn't she said there was something they had to talk about? "Wait. What is it you wanted to tell me?"

"I can't, I haven't made up my mind."

"About what? Anna? The malpractice suit?"

"No. It's personal."

"You can't leave me hanging."

She turned and walked to the bedside chair and sank into it dejectedly. "I've had a job offer. Johns Hopkins is looking for an assistant director of an Emergency Medicine Program in one of their affiliated hospitals: St. Joseph's in Baltimore."

Steven sat on the arm of the lounger. "I didn't know you were looking."

"I wasn't. I met the program director a few months ago at a medical meeting. I had presented a paper. He invited me to dinner."

"Young, handsome devil?"

"Actually, a handsome grandfatherly type. Afterwards he wrote and said the assistant director position was open and invited me to come for an interview."

Why hadn't she told him this before? He stood and walked to the door of his room. He glanced down the corridor. It was busy with the usual clutter of carts, doctors, students and nurses.

"Well, what do you think?" she asked.

"Sounds like a marvelous opportunity. You're a great teacher. I assume it's an academic position?" He walked back and sat on the arm of the lounger.

"Tenure track. The medical school dean has agreed to offer me the rank of Assistant Professor."

Steven was happy for her, but he couldn't imagine life at Smithfield without her. "When's the interview?"

"I went down in July. He called me a couple of days ago and offered me the job. I'd actually be taking a cut in salary, but they have a great benefit package."

July! Why hadn't she mentioned it? He was afraid to ask. "You accepted?"

Her eyes filled with tears. She shook her head. "I told him I had to think about it for a few days. It's an incredible opportunity."

He squeezed her hand. "Hey, Baltimore's not that far away. When would you start if you accept?"

"Depends on how much notice I give Smithfield. Probably the first of the year." She grasped his hand. "Steven, Hopkins has a great pedes residency."

"It's a very competitive. The way things have been going at Smithfield..."

"But your medical school record was outstanding," Chris reminded him. "If you ace the State and National Boards . . ."

"A pretty big if."

"Would you consider finishing out your internship at St. Joe's in Baltimore?"

"How would that be possible? I have a contract here."

"They wouldn't hold you to it. I could make offering you a position a condition for accepting their offer."

"Why jeopardize your chances for something so iffy?"

"As another Irish lady once said, 'a good man these days is hard to find.'"

"Baltimore's a straight shot on 95."

"But completing your internship at St. Joe's would increase your chances of landing a pedes residency there."

Sounds like she has things all planned out for me, Steven thought. "I've been thinking maybe I'd practice for a year or two after my internship. Do my specialty training later. There's a ready-made practice waiting for me in Zion. No investment or hassle. Just move in and start seeing patients. A chance to pay off debts."

They sat for a long time holding hands. Neither speaking. Steven had no desire to practice in a large city like Baltimore. It hurt that she hadn't mentioned the job interview sooner. How could she keep such a big decision to herself?

Someone banged on the door, then pushed into the room without waiting for a response. An attendant carrying a meal tray plopped it on the bedside stand. He removed the insulated lid. Steam rose from a slab of meatloaf, a pile of pale green peas and breaded okra.

Chris grimaced. "How about I take you out for a real meal?" she asked.

He nodded. "I'll be ready before the ink dries on my discharge orders."

"You're already discharged, Steven." She stood. "I have a couple of patients to sign out. Meet you in the lobby in fifteen minutes."

Chapter Twenty-Three

After making a connecting flight from Kansas City to Great Bend, Steven rented a red convertible for the thirty-five-mile drive to Zion. He had called his mother from the Great Bend airport to tell her he was on his way. She scolded him for not letting her know sooner. But she sounded really happy.

Their home was only a few blocks from downtown Zion. The vintage 1930s two-story white-clapboard duplex with black shutters had a large covered porch that ran across the entire front of the house. They lived in one half of the duplex; his father's practice was housed on the other side. There was a patient parking area on the side adjacent to the office. A separate entrance had been built just off the parking lot.

Except for a sloping lawn in the front, the two-acre lot was mostly wooded. His mother was standing on the front porch as he pulled in front of their detached garage.

He ran up the wooden steps and embraced her, lifting her off her feet. He was shocked how light she felt. Her cheek was moist with tears. Although it was almost noon she was still wearing bathrobe and slippers.

"You okay, Mom?" he asked as they entered the house. He half-expected to smell coffee and a baking apple pie. But instead the house smelled of mold and dust. The foyer table was overflowing with unopened mail.

"I haven't been sleeping all that well. Sorry the place is such a mess."

Her gray-streaked, dark brown hair looked as though it hadn't been combed.

"You must be hungry. Take your bag to your old room."

His bedroom looked out on the office parking area. He set his bag on the bed and removed a box of chocolates that he had bought at the airport. The room was musty, but didn't look much different than it had when he last lived at home. The quilted bedspread made by his grandmother looked more worn than he remembered. The colonial maple furniture had darkened with age. He ran his hand over the pineapple finial on the bed post. The oak floor was bare except for a small braided rug.

After a quick shower and a change of clothes, he grabbed the box of candy and went into the kitchen. His mother was standing over the stove stirring what smelled like chicken soup. He set the candy on the table.

"Can I help?"

"Sure. Get out a couple of bowls, spoons and napkins."

As Steven set the table, he noticed smoke coming from the toaster. He popped out two charred pieces of bread. He adjusted the toast dial and stuck in two more slices. On the counter was a large cardboard box filled with canned food.

"You want some tea?" his mother asked.

"No, thanks, I'll just have a glass of milk." He was surprised to see that the refrigerator was bare except for two loaves of bread and a half-gallon of milk. He opened the freezer door. It was crammed with cartons of Breyer's vanilla ice cream.

"You eat out a lot, Mom?"

"Mostly never, unless Glady comes by and drags me someplace. She and Ned are doing just fine. Just got back from a California trip to see their daughter. Judy had another baby."

Judy was a year older than Steven. He had a big-time crush on her when he was a junior in high school. She had a weak right eye that sometimes drifted off on its own. He thought it made her look sexy.

"Glady's always scolding me to get out and do like we used to when your father was alive. Your father got to like square dancing in his later years. Glady and Ned have taken up ballroom dancing at the YMCA. I don't see any sense to it."

She ladled some chicken soup into their bowls. They sat at the table.

"It's delicious. You always made the best chicken soup."

"It's store-bought. Most everything I eat comes from one can or another. I don't enjoy cooking anymore. I can't seem to set my mind to it. Everything burns. Besides it just isn't worth it. Not for just one person."

"I noticed there's plenty of ice cream in your freezer."

"Breyer's Vanilla was always your father's favorite. I like to keep some on hand, just in case."

"In case what?" he asked.

"I know you're going to think I'm crazy. But when I'm at the kitchen sink and look out back, sometimes I can see your daddy chopping and stacking wood, or fussing in his vegetable garden like he always did."

"You've probably seen him do that hundreds of times."

"I see him clear as day. It's not my imagination. When I told Glady, she right off wanted to take me to the doctor's."

Steven had just swallowed a mouthful of soup. It gathered into a painful bolus in the center of his chest. On a psychiatry rotation in medical school, his instructor had once told Steven that it wasn't uncommon for widows to see their husbands in the months and even years after their death. It's a kind of dream-like state halfway between sleep and wakefulness. He stressed that you must distinguish it from hallucinations associated with clinical depression or psychoses.

"You have that same look Glady got when I told her."

He reached out and held her hand. "I believe you, Mom. I believe you really see Dad."

Tears filled her eyes. "I'm glad I told you, Steven."

"What worries me is how you let yourself go. You've lost weight. You're not eating right. When was the last time you had your blood pressure checked?"

"I don't like the way the pills make me feel. Besides, my mother had high blood pressure, and she lived to be ninety."

"I'm taking you to the doctor today."

"Can't get to see Doctor Heinrich the same day unless you're dying."

"Please, Mom. He doesn't even charge you. You've got nothing to lose."

"I don’t want to go.”

"You leave me no choice; I'll call Claire and tell her everything. She'll probably come with the kids and stay with you."

"My God, Steven, she'll give me no peace."

He stood and went to a wall phone just beyond the kitchen door.

"Okay. Okay, call him."

When Steven explained the situation to Dr. Heinrich, the elderly doctor agreed to work her into his busy schedule.

After the visit, Dr. Heinrich called Steven into his consultation room. Steven's mother sat passively as they discussed her condition.

"I drew some blood to check out her thyroid function."

"What about lipids, folate and B12 levels?" Steven asked.

"Yes, that's part of my screening panel."

Steven was impressed. "Could you send me a copy of the report?"

"Of course. But I fully expect those tests to be normal." He turned to Steven's mother. "Miss Lilly, I believe your primary problem is depression. And you were right to stop the blood pressure medicine. It probably made matters worse. Your pressure surprisingly is only slightly elevated. I'm starting you on a medication that will immediately help you sleep. In a week or two you should be seeing an improvement."

It had been years since Steven had heard anyone call his mother Miss Lilly. It struck a resonant chord deep inside him. He could hear his father's voice saying, "Miss Lilly was the prettiest girl in Zion!"

"Doctor," Steven said, "she doesn't cook. Her diet is terrible."

"I'll arrange for a balanced hot meal to be delivered to her door every day. I'll also arrange for a home health nurse to make regular visits."

"Mother, what do you think?"

She spoke in a whisper. "Why bother, really?"

"You said yourself you were desperate for a good night's sleep."

"Yes, I am." She looked from Steven to the doctor. They both looked at her expectantly. "Okay. I'll take the medicine if it will help me sleep."

The following morning Steven raked and mowed the front lawn, repaired a loose step on the front stoop, cleaned out the roof gutters, replaced burned-out light bulbs throughout the house, and repaired a drippy kitchen faucet. By mid-afternoon he was exhausted. He spent the rest of the day on the phone trying to line up a home cleaning service to come in once a week. He called Glady. He asked if she would phone his mother each day and maybe take her to lunch once or twice a week. And have her hair done. Glady said she had been trying to get her out, but now that she had doctor's orders she wasn't going to take *no* for an answer.

That evening Steven asked his mother if anyone had approached her about renting out his father's office space.

"Miss Mary comes in about once a week to go through the mail and sends out bills. There's lots of folks still owe your daddy money. A few checks come in now and then."

"What about his medical records?

"There are calls for old records. Miss Mary makes copies and sends them out."

"Who keeps track of the financial records?"

"Daddy's old accountant, Ted Honeycutt, comes in every so often. He's handling all my bills and taxes, thank God."

"I'd like to look through the office. Make sure everything is okay."

"No need to ask. The key's on the wall-hook by the kitchen sink."

This was the first time he had gone through his dad's office since the week of his funeral almost two years ago. The foyer led directly into the waiting area. He flicked on the indirect lighting that ran around the perimeter of the room. The Danish-style teak furniture popular in the 1950s and the wall-to-wall carpeting gave the room a cozy feel. He checked the thermostat. It was set at 65 degrees. He checked out the two exam rooms. The wooden examination tables, whose tops were covered with real leather, worn smooth with use, were vintage 1930s. His dad had bought them used when he started practice. In a cubby-hole off a central open area were a stainless-steel sterilizer, centrifuge and refrigerator. All of them clean and unplugged. The supply room was still stocked floor-to-ceiling with boxes of gloves, diapers, disposable gowns, table paper, disposable syringes, needles and cleaning supplies. Surgical packs were labeled and stored in clear plastic bins, also labeled.

His favorite room was the consultation office. It was lighted by a floor lamp. He sat at his father's desk. He could picture his Dad sitting at the leather, high-back swivel chair, a phone cupped to his ear, charting with his gold-tipped Whitman's fountain pen. Steven was forever losing pens and wondered how his dad managed to hold onto his for so long. He slid open the desk drawer and found a box containing several fountain pens identical to the one his father used.

On one wall was a bookcase of medical texts and boxed journals. As a boy, Steven assumed his dad knew every single thing about people's bodies, diseases and medicines. Steven had seen pictures of his dad as a young boy. His favorite was one of his dad posing with his eighth-grade basketball team. He looked pretty much like the other boys in the picture. He was tall and skinny. He had his same eyes and smile.

The one-thousand-square-foot office was perfect for a solo practitioner. That breed of physician, however, was soon to be added to the endangered species category. Steven envisioned working in a small group practice. Three or four physicians at the most. It would be easier to join such a group than to attempt to build it from scratch.

The following day Steven considered offering to drive his mother to church, but decided she wasn't ready for that. He would drop the Lutheran minister a note. Ask if he'd look in on her from time to time.

Glady and Ned came over at noon. They brought a roasted chicken and all the fixings. After they left, it was time for Steven to pack and drive to the airport in Great Bend for a short hop to his connecting flight in Kansas City. And from there on to Newark airport, where he'd catch the bus to Smithfield. How much longer might his mother be able to live alone, to care for herself, he wondered. Was his sister fully aware of their mother's condition?

Chapter Twenty-Four

It was not yet light as Steven forced his weary bones to an upright position on the edge of his bed. His whirlwind trip to Kansas and back had been mentally and physically exhausting. What if his mother didn't respond to the antidepressants? And what of her hallucinations? He knew that in older persons, depression was often an early finding in dementia. As far as he knew, no one in their family had ever developed dementia. But even with modest hypertension, it was possible to suffer small strokes that can erode brain function without causing the physical impairment usually associated with stroke. He wished he could have stayed longer. But today was the day he was to start back on his pediatric rotation.

He soaked a wash-cloth in hot water and held it to his face, then soaped and lathered his beard. He was excited about his first day back on the pedes ward. He planned on getting there by six. Time to study the charts before rounds. Jerry Russo could give him a rundown on the children with the most serious problems. He might well be on call that evening. He had better be familiar with the sickest patients.

After dressing, he slipped on a fresh white jacket, affixed his name tag, dropped a couple of tongue depressors and a pen into the breast pocket, draped his stethoscope around his neck, put a stack of 3x5 index cards and a slim drug-therapy manual in his jacket pocket, and in his other, a pediatric ophthalmoscope-otoscope set, and percussion hammer. It was time to play doctor.

On the walk to the hospital, he glanced at the gnarled apple tree that had beckoned him to a near face-to-face with his maker. He suddenly remembered he hadn't taken his bee sting kit with him. Oh well, it's wasn't likely he'd be stung on hospital rounds. Not by winged creatures, at least.

He used the ER entrance to the hospital. It was the closest to the housestaff quarters, and the one place he felt most at home.

"Yo, Steve!" someone shouted.

He turned and saw Jerry Russo hurrying down the path toward him. He waited for him to catch up.

"Not going to let you beat me to the ward," Jerry said.

"Hi, Jerry. I was hoping to see you before rounds. How are things going?"

"Not bad. Busy as hell. The kids are great but the staff's uptight. How are you feeling?"

"Great. I'm on a steroid high."

"You looked like day-old puke when they dragged you into the ER."

"Were you there?"

"No. I came down as soon as I heard what happened. When I got there Jacqueline was sitting at your side, holding your hand."

"I don't remember any of that."

"You don't remember her kissing you on the mouth...running her fingers through your hair?"

Steven laughed. "Yeah. I suppose she jumped in bed with me."

"See, you didn't forget everything."

They entered the ER and walked past the nurses' station where Martha was seated, flipping through a hard-cover loose-leaf manual.

"Hi, Martha," Jerry said. "You're here early. I thought you executive types started at nine."

"JCAH will be here next week. I'm polishing my P&P's."

"Your what?" Steven asked.

"Policy and procedures," Jerry said. "They're doing the same on Pedes."

Steven glanced at the chalk board where the names of patients and their problems were listed. The board was wiped clean.

"Quiet night?" he asked.

"Sunday night often is," Martha said.

"Not when I covered the ER."

"Good luck on pedes, Dr. Steve."

"Thanks, Miss Martha. Any advice?"

"Keep your nose clean and your powder dry."

He bowed slightly. "I will do as you say, master guru."

Miss Martha waved him off and returned to her work.

"Scully's put you on call tonight," Jerry said. "Your team's admitting new patients. And you'll have to familiarize yourself with the patients on my team as well." As Jerry and Steven walked to the pediatric ward, Jerry filled him in on the patients who would require the most attention.

They took an escalator to the second floor and headed down a long corridor past the X-ray department.

Steven looked at his watch. "Ninety minutes before the start of rounds. That gives me about five minutes for each of the patients on my team."

"The medical student and resident have been doing a great job. The attending maxed-out your team at fifteen."

"And yours?"

"Yeah. We've had to pick up some. We're pushing twenty-five."

"I'm sorry."

"No sweat, man. To tell the truth, I'm enjoying it. I feel really juiced when I'm running my ass off."

They walked through the tall double doors into the pediatric ward. The bland hospital colors changed immediately to brightly colored walls festooned with cartoon characters and letter-sized paintings by former and present pediatric patients. A bulletin board next to the nurses' station was covered with photographs of smiling children.

Steven was searching for one face in particular. But she was either in a room with a patient or hadn't arrived. The second-year resident and medical student on Steven's team were standing by the door to a patient's room, a cart piled high with charts at their side. Steven's pulse quickened as he approached them. This was where he belonged. This was what he wanted to do.

Jacqueline sat on a chair in Chris's cramped office. She had just told her of Omar's unsuccessful efforts to find a home for Anna.

"There are other places he could try." Chris said. "We hadn't intended she stay with you more than a day or two."

"But no matter where she goes," Jacqueline said, "she will always live in fear. She belongs with her family in Algiers."

"Didn't Anna tell you that she called her father? That he said she had brought shame on her family and that she could not return?"

"She told me Anwar has said bad things about her, lies, to her family. If we could prove to them Anwar is lying?"

"How?" Chris asked.

"I will go to Algiers."

"Algiers?" Chris asked in disbelief. "I've already gotten you more involved than I should have. I cannot permit you to go."

"I do not ask for your permission," Jacqueline said. "I know I can convince her family that Anwar is a hypocrite, a liar. That he has done terrible things to her."

Chris could see that she was determined to go. "Why should they believe you?"

"I will bring evidence."

"You're talking about her hospital records? That's privileged information."

Jacqueline nodded. "Doesn't Anna have a right to have a copy of her records?" She took a piece of paper from her pocket and handed it to Chris. Chris recognized Anna's handwriting.

"I give Miss Jacqueline Martin permission to copy my medical record at Smithfield Hospital."

Mrs. Anna Amin

Chris looked up from the note. "Even if they accept her back, Anwar will take her baby from her."

"Her family is not without resources. With a good lawyer…"

"And what does your cousin say?

"He believes I am a crazy person. But I can tell in his heart he knows it is the right thing to do."

Chris pressed against her low-back swivel chair, looking absently at her cat-and-mouse computer screen-saver. She finally turned to face Jacqueline. "Mr. Amin is a cruel man. We have proof of that. He can hire people to do bad things to you."

"I will be there a very short time. How will he know?"

Chris chewed on the end of a pencil. "Have you spoken to Dr. Johnson about your decision to go to Algeria?"

"No."

"This is entirely your idea?"

"Yes. He knows nothing of this."

"How were you planning to get Anna's medical record?"

"I will tell the medical records secretary that we need her chart for a noon conference.

"No. The log will show it was checked out to you. I'll request it. I have reason to review it, since Mr. Amin's attorney has threatened to sue us. If someone were to slip into my office while I'm out to lunch..."

"Where might a person copy something in private?"

"The hospital library has a copy machine. The librarian goes to lunch from twelve to one."

After morning rounds, Steven decided to go to Chris's office for a few minutes before the noon conference. She usually brought a bag lunch, using the time to catch up on her e-mail and other messages. He was eager to tell her how well rounds had gone. Reviewing medical journals prior to starting back on the pediatric service had paid off. Several times he had been able to quote chapter and verse from the most recent literature.

"Obviously," Scully had said, "you've used your recent leisure time to visit the library. Let's see how well you're able to keep that up in the coming weeks."

As Steven opened the door to Chris's office, he was astonished to see Jacqueline, her hand extended as though she were reaching for the doorknob. He grabbed her extended hand and pumped it. "Missed you on rounds." She had a patient's medical record tucked under one arm. "Getting a chart for conference?"

"I'm sorry, but I must hurry."

As she brushed past him, her shoulder hit his and the chart fell to the floor. Several items dropped out. She quickly stooped, picked up the chart and tried to gather up the loose papers. Steven retrieved one, and was surprised to see Anna Amin's name on the lab slip.

"Are we talking about Anna at noon conference?"

"No. I...I have need of it for just a few minutes."

"You have need of it? What is that supposed to mean?"

"Please, Dr. Steven, do not ask. I cannot tell you."

He had never seen her flustered. What was she hiding from him? "Let's sit down and talk." He closed the door behind him. She dejectedly sank into a side chair. He sat at Chris's desk. "What's going on here, Jacqueline?"

"I promised Dr. Murphy I would not tell you anything," she said, without looking up from her lap. "I have written permission from Anna to copy her medical record," she whispered. "That is all I can tell you."

Steven placed his hand on hers. "Hey, I'm already part of this whole Amin mess. Besides, I caught you red-handed."

She looked puzzled. "It means I caught you in the act of doing something you shouldn't be doing," he said.

"You will have me arrested?"

"How did you get that note from Anna? Where is she?" Steven asked.

"She is in my apartment." She looked at her watch. "I must copy this while the library woman is out to lunch."

"Your apartment! My God! Why you? Does Omar know about this?"

"It was his idea to take Anna to a Muslim family in Hoboken. She was to be at my house only a short time."

Steven was stunned. He remained silent, hoping to coax more from her.

Jacqueline went on to tell Steven what had happened when Omar spoke with the Mullah of a Mosque in Hoboken. "Dr. Murphy was afraid to put Anna back in a shelter, for fear she would be found."

"And why copy her medical record?" Steven asked.

"I am going to Algeria to talk with Anna's family. I will prove to them what Amin has done. I will ask them to allow her to return to their home."

“My God! You can't just show up at their door. And what if Amin's there?"

"Yesterday Anna called back when she knew her father would be at the mosque. She spoke with her mother. Anna pleaded with her to let her return home. That Anwar has deceived them. She told her mother that a nurse from the hospital would come and prove to them that Anwar had lied to them."

"But what if Anna's father still doesn't believe you? If he tells Anwar."

"If, if, if," Jacqueline said. "Is it better to do nothing?"

She was right. It was only a matter of time before the INS caught up with Anna. What Jacqueline described was simple, direct and offered the best possible outcome. But it terrified him to think of her falling into some kind of trap. "What if Amin has you taken hostage? He swore he'd do anything to get his son back."

Jacqueline smiled. "You are watching too much TV. But I like that you are worried for me."

"It's pretty extraordinary that you would do this for her."

"Anna is so sweet. I was touched when I saw the way she nurses her baby, and how she cried when we talked of her family. I put myself in her place. I would want to be with my brothers and sisters and parents, not always with strangers. Always fearful they will find me and take my baby from me."

Steven reached out and grasped her hand. It was warm, her grip strong. "You amaze me. I assume Dr. Murphy knows of your plans."

"Yes."

"A last-minute flight to Algiers will cost a fortune."

"Dr. Murphy offered to pay."

"For just one way?"

Jacqueline knitted her brow. He loved the subtle change in the configuration of her nose when she grew concerned.

She smiled. "She cannot get rid of me so easily."

"I have an idea. Ask Anna if her family owns a television and VCR. If they do, you can videotape Anna. Have her tell what happened. If she shows them the scar..."

"Yes, it is a good idea. And if they do not have a VCR, I can bring Omar's camera. It has a small screen for viewing."

"What will you tell your nursing supervisor?"

"That urgent family matters demand that I be gone for four days."

"When do you leave?" Steven asked.

"At five this evening."

He glanced at his watch. "You've less than two hours to get all that done."

She nodded. "I must hurry."

He stood and put his arms around her, Anna's medical record pressed between them, their faces inches apart.

"I am sorry," she said, "to miss three days of rounds with you."

"I'll make it up to you. And when you return, you must cook me another of your fabulous Jamaican meals."

"It will be a real date this time?"

Steven recalled having told Omar that the evening she had spent in his apartment hadn't been a real date. "Yes, this time it is a real date."

"Is not kissing a custom in Kansas?"

"Yes, it's a very old custom in Kansas." He squeezed her tighter. "Kisses are like potato chips. It's hard to stop after only one." He pressed his cheek to hers. "You had better hurry, before the librarian returns," he whispered.

As he watched her disappear down the hall he realized he soon had to decide between Chris, the wholesome girl-next-door, and the exotic, intoxicating, young Jacqueline Martin. Should he follow Chris to Baltimore? Make a fresh start at another hospital where he had a chance to gain a residency position? Yet he desperately wanted to prove to Ewing, and others who had selected him from a large applicant pool, that he could meet and exceed their expectations. Breaking his contract with the hospital would rob him of that opportunity.

I must separate Chris's career choice and my decision as to where to complete my internship, from my need to choose between her and Jacqueline.

Chapter Twenty-Five

In the library copy-room, Jacqueline removed the binder from Anna's medical records. She had begun copying the chart one sheet at a time, but it was taking much longer than she had expected. She decided to use the automatic feeding tray. But after several pages passed through successfully, the machine jammed. Jacqueline read the flashing message on the panel. *Remove paper-jam from compartment three.* She looked at her watch. The librarian would soon be back from lunch. She hurriedly flipped up the lid of the copier to get at the inside compartment. She had forgotten that she had stacked a pile of copies on the top. The pages spilled down behind the machine. She removed the jammed sheet and replaced the lid. She pushed the machine from the wall to retrieve the pages that had fallen to the floor. After she had gathered them she restarted the copier. She was less than halfway through the chart when the *out-of-paper* light flashed.

She looked about frantically. Where do they keep the paper? "Blessed Mary help me," she whispered.

"I'm not blessed, but might I help, dear?"

Jacqueline jumped. She turned. Dr. Ewing's secretary smiled. Jacqueline had met her during orientation, a pleasant, soft-spoken middle-aged woman.

"I know how frustrating these machines can be," the secretary said. She opened a drawer and removed a package of paper, unwrapped it and loaded it into the copy machine. "I see you have quite a bit left to do. I have to copy a single document for Dr. Ewing. Do you mind?"

"No. Go right ahead."

"You're the student nurse from Jamaica, as I recall."

"Yes." Jacqueline noticed her glance at the sheets in the automatic feeder tray. Jacqueline's pulse quickened.

"Oh my, you can't feed sheets with glued-on lab slips! You'll jam the machine for sure." She removed them and handed the sheets to Jacqueline. "You'll have to place them one at a time on the flatbed."

The woman made her copy and left. Had she seen Anna Amin's name on the chart? It took Jacqueline another ten minutes to finish copying, and another few minutes to re-assemble the chart in its original order. As she prepared to leave, Dr. Ewing's secretary returned.

"Miss Martin, would you please come with me to Dr. Ewing's office? He would like to see you right away."

Jacqueline's thoughts raced. My God. She must have seen Anna's name and told Dr. Ewing. Why else would he want to see her? What was she to tell him? She looked at her watch. She still hadn't packed or videotaped Anna and her baby. She had to be on her way to the airport in the next ninety minutes or she'd miss her flight. What would she do if he seized the copies? She clutched them to her chest as she walked alongside Ewing's secretary. They approached his office.

"Go right on in. He's expecting you. And don't be so frightened, dear. He doesn't bite."

"Please have a seat, Miss Martin," Dr. Ewing said. "I'll get straight to the point. Would you please tell me who asked you to copy Mrs. Amin's medical records?"

Jacqueline sat upright in a chair beside his desk. Her insides shook violently, although her exterior remained calm. "Mrs. Amin. I received a note from her asking me to obtain a copy." She removed Anna's signed request from her jumper pocket and handed it to Dr. Ewing.

He slipped on reading glasses. "It's customary for such a request to go to medical records."

"She is trying to avoid deportation"

Dr. Ewing's eyes narrowed. He seemed about to explode. "I am painfully aware of that," he said. "How did you get this note? Do you know where Mrs. Amin is hiding?"

"I cannot say, Dr. Ewing."

He removed his reading glasses. "That's not an acceptable answer. How did you get her chart from medical records?"

"I cannot say."

"You're assigned to the pediatric service?"

"Yes, sir."

"It so happens Dr. Johnson is also on the pediatric service. He obviously has a strong interest in this case. Is he hiding Mrs. Amin? Did he put you up to this?"

"No. He had nothing to do with it."

Ewing walked around his desk and sat in a chair next to Jacqueline. He spoke quietly. "I called medical records. Dr. Murphy was the last person to sign out the chart. Did she give it to you?"

"No."

"You just happened to go by her office, see the chart on her desk and make off with it? Do you expect me to believe that?"

"I do not want to get other people in trouble," Jacqueline said. When she looked up there were tears in her eyes. "You must believe me. It was my idea and no one else's."

"I'm attempting to get at the truth."

"The truth is that I am trying to get a mother and her baby safely reunited with her family." Her voice shook with emotion. "I am catching a flight this evening to Algiers. I will go to Mrs. Amin's family."

Dr. Ewing stood and returned to his desk. He breathed deeply and exhaled slowly. He leaned back in his chair, studying the ceiling. "You wanted to bring a copy of her medical record to prove to them she has been physically abused?"

"Yes. I spoke with Anna's mother. They are expecting me."

"And given the remote possibility they believe you, Anna voluntarily leaves the country and is reunited with her family?" He handed her a tissue.

"Yes."

"Miss Martin, I understand that you want to help. But you are now part of a conspiracy to prevent the deportation of Mrs. Amin." He called his secretary on his office intercom. "Have Dr. Murphy and Dr. Johnson paged. Ask them to report to my office immediately."

"Why do you ask Dr. Johnson to come here? I told you he has not been involved."

He ignored her question. "You believed that all you needed was Anna's written permission authorizing you to copy her medical record?"

She nodded.

"You went to Dr. Murphy and asked her to check out the record."

"She only agreed after she saw the signed note."

"I see. Miss Martin, leave those records on my desk and wait in my outer office until the others arrive."

Jacqueline placed Anna's medical record on Ewing's desk. "Please allow me to keep the copies I made."

"No. I don't want you running off with them until we have sorted out this entire mess."

Fifteen minutes later, Steven, Chris and Jacqueline were seated before Ewing; Steven and Chris on the couch, Jacqueline in the chair beside his desk. Dr. Ewing looked from person to person, shaking his head, his expression incredulous. "Why only a single attending, an intern and a student nurse?" he said. "Hadn't you considered including someone from administration or perhaps housekeeping in your gang?" He was holding a pencil in his hand. Jacqueline recoiled when it snapped. When no one spoke, he continued. "Dr. Johnson and Dr. Murphy, my secretary found Miss Martin in the library copy-room reproducing Mrs. Amin's medical records. I brought you here to hear your version of how this came about. Dr. Murphy, you checked out that record this morning. How did it end up in Miss Martin's hands?"

"She showed me Anna's note. She told me of her intention to travel to Algiers to see Anna's family. It seemed a reasonable solution to the problem."

"And Dr. Johnson, did you have any knowledge of these actions?"

Steven looked at Jacqueline. Her eyes pleaded with him not to mention the incident. But he didn't want her to take the full brunt of Ewing's anger. "Yes, sir, I did." He went on to explain how he ran into Jacqueline as she was leaving Dr. Murphy's office.

"I've warned you that any further meddling in this matter would be a fatal error."

"Fatal?" Chris said. "A chance meeting can hardly be construed as meddling."

"He should have stopped her. He or you should have insisted Mrs. Amin get an attorney to request her records. You are highly trained professionals. You know the rules."

"Dr. Ewing," Chris said, "that process could take a week or longer. We know the INS is close to finding her. They'd return her and the baby to her husband. She had left the women's shelter just hours before the INS agents arrived with a search warrant."

"He turned toward Jacqueline. "How old are you, Miss Martin?"

"Twenty."

"Dr. Murphy, you involve a minor in a plot to keep the INS from finding Mrs. Amin? Then you allow this young woman to fly off to a foreign country, placing her in a potentially hostile situation. It's inexcusable that you or Dr. Johnson didn't stop her."

"You're right, Dr. Ewing," Steven said. "I should have."

Dr. Ewing's face reddened. "You're damn right you should have! I've gone to bat for you time and time again, Steven. But you repeatedly demonstrate remarkably poor judgment. I want your resignation on my desk tomorrow morning effective four weeks from today. That'll give pedes a chance to pull an intern from another service."

Jacqueline began to cry. Steven went to her. He knelt, taking her hand in his. "Hey, it's okay. I was about to quit anyway."

"And you, Dr. Murphy," Ewing said, "are fortunate that you have already secured another position. It saves me the distasteful process of firing a staff physician."

Chris jumped to her feet, her hands on her hips, her fists clenched. "Speaking of poor judgment, Dr. Ewing," she said, "You are an impulsive, pompous autocrat. These young people should be commended for doing what they believed was right. Even if, God forbid, it means deviating from rigid hospital protocol. And I for one can't wait to leave this place."

"Dr. Murphy and Dr. Johnson, I have nothing more to say to you. Miss Martin, you stay."

Chris left, slamming the door behind her. Steven remained seated.

"It's okay if you leave," Jacqueline said to Steven.

"No, you come with me or I stay. I'll not have him brow-beat you."

"Stay if you wish," Ewing said. He stood and went to the window staring out at the sloping lawn and distant woods. He spoke without looking at them. "An INS agent called me when they didn't find Mrs. Amin at the shelter. He said that if they discover that we're harboring her, we will be prosecuted for obstruction of justice. They are being pressured by the Algerian ambassador. I assured him I knew nothing of her whereabouts...I didn't, at the time." He walked to his desk and sat. "Miss Martin, you've given me Mrs. Amin's written request for her medical record. Unless someone tortures the truth from me I will maintain that you came to me asking permission to copy her record. That I granted you permission because your goal was to have Mrs. Amin voluntarily leave the country as soon as possible. Now take these," he pointed to the stack of loose papers on his desk, "and do what you must."

"Will you take disciplinary action against her?" Steven asked.

"At present, no. But if this messy affair comes to light, my hand may be forced."

"It is not fair to punish Dr. Johnson," Jacqueline said.

"It is both fair and unavoidable. He was already on notice that the slightest misstep would result in dismissal." He turned to Steven. "You will probably hate me for this, but I'm convinced your position here is impossible. And I hope that someday you will see that getting you out from under this situation was for your own good."

Chapter Twenty-Six

Steven and Jacqueline walked to the hospital lobby. "Where are you staying in Algiers?" he asked.

"At the Sofitel Hotel."

"Call me when you arrive. I'll be at the hospital all day tomorrow. Have me paged."

They stopped at the hospital entrance. The sidewalk was crowded with visitors and staff entering and leaving. Several cars, their engines running, lined the curb. Steven led her to a bench a short distance from the entrance.

"Steven, will you resign as Dr. Ewing asked?"

"It's that, or be fired."

She reached into her handbag and removed something wrapped in tissue. "This is for you, Steven. Carry it with you when I'm gone. It'll help you not to forget me." She brushed back several dislodged braids that fell over her forehead.

Steven removed the tissue. It was a tiny Jamaican doll. "I won't forget you so easily. But thanks." He turned it over in his hand. "It's beautifully made."

"My mother sews. She even wove the cloth. She said to give it to a special person."

"I'll treasure it." He grasped her hand. "Must you go?"

"Don't worry, Steven. It makes my heart warm to know you care."

"Do you have enough money?"

"Dr. Murphy put my plane ticket and hotel reservation on her credit card. I'll need very little money."

He removed his wallet. "You never know what might happen. Here, take my credit card." He handed it to her.

"No. I can't."

"Please. I never use it except for emergencies. There's plenty of credit available."

He watched as she hurried across the street to the hospital parking deck. She disappeared into the cavernous darkness. He knew nothing of Algiers other than what he had read in Assia Djebar's book, in which she told stories of women in Algiers in the 1950s. After the bloody, protracted war of independence with the French Colonialists, during which woman freedom fighters were among the heroes of the Algerian revolution, there was an abrupt return to conservative interpretation of Islamic law as it pertained to women. Fear of the *forbidden gaze* forced women between the ages of ten and forty to cover their bodies from head to toe whenever they ventured into the streets. And, for the most part, women remained cloistered in their apartments. A husband could renounce his wife for the slightest grievance, and in so doing, severed their marriage bonds, casting her from his household with no means of support and little chance that her own family would take her in. Had the worldwide movement over the past thirty years toward the recognition of women's rights bypassed Algeria?

What if Anwar Amin somehow had learned of Jacqueline's visit? What might he do? Steven looked at his watch. It was almost 4 P.M. There were two patients to admit before evening rounds. He hurried to the pediatric ward. On the way, he pulled the doll from his pocket. It was remarkably detailed except for one thing. The face was blank.

After arriving at her apartment, Jacqueline quickly video-taped Anna, then packed an overnight bag. She was still in her student nurses' uniform, but there was no time to change. She hugged Anna, and then hurried off in Omar's 1982 Dodge Dart. "It may not look like much, but it will get you there," Omar had told her as he handed her the keys.

As she drove, she glanced frequently at a New Jersey map spread on the seat beside her, searching for the junction with Route 518, which would take her via Route 27 to New Brunswick. From there she would look for signs to the New Jersey Turnpike.

Omar had warned her to accelerate slowly and not to exceed fifty miles an hour. He had said something about a bad clutch. She heeded his advice. She kept the Dart well under fifty; cars, like shooting stars, flashed by her on either side. Those who could not pass, honked furiously. When they managed to swing around her car, they indicated, by universal sign language, what they thought of her driving. Her mother had warned her, when she first learned to drive, that there are more crazy people on the road than there are in institutions. She admonished her to look on them kindly. They too are God's children. She would say,

"Good manners are mildly contagious, bad manners spread like the Plague."

Jacqueline fought the urge to retaliate. But she was able to control her emotions by imagining her mother sitting in her place, smiling kindly at those frustrated angry faces.

Jacqueline's eyes filled with tears, as she recalled Steven's look of disbelief when Dr. Ewing asked for his resignation. But after the initial shock, Steven had remained calm, seemingly more concerned about her welfare than losing his position at Smithfield. And he wasn't surprised when Ewing said that Dr. Murphy had already accepted a position elsewhere. He must already have known. Would he go with her? He had said he was already thinking about leaving.

She suddenly realized she had not been paying attention to her driving. Had she missed a turnoff? The route seemed simple enough on the map, but the intimidating traffic and confusing signs didn't help. Junction and exit signs were at times obscured by large trucks or overgrown bushes.

If she hadn't taken a wrong turn, she should get to the airport on time. Her 6:55 PM flight from Newark would arrive at Heathrow by 7:05 A.M. the following morning. She had about an hour and thirty minutes to make a connecting flight to Paris. An hour layover there, then a short flight to Algiers getting in around 2:00 P.M. Her travel agent had arranged a one-night stay at The Sofitel Algiers, a modern five-star hotel. She was traveling light, with only an overnight carry-on bag, the copy of Anna's medical records packed safely inside.

When Jacqueline finally reached the New Jersey Turnpike, she was astonished at the number of lanes of traffic, navigated by speeders weaving from lane to lane. She was dismayed and astonished by the clusters of grimy oil refineries, their stacks spewing obnoxious chemicals that burned her eyes and gave her an instant headache. The area was a striking contrast to the rolling hills and open pasture land in the Smithfield area.

Her heart quickened when she saw the airport tower off to her left. She watched as a procession of jet airliners roared at a steep angle toward the setting sun. She turned onto the airport exit. Soon she would be buckled into a tourist-class seat, headed northeast over the Atlantic. How she wished Steven was with her. To share this, her first trip to Europe and North Africa. She imagined a layover in Paris, visiting the Louvre, the Eiffel Tower, strolling arm-in-arm along the banks of the Seine.

Steven's afternoon was so busy he had little time to think of Jacqueline or his future. His team admitted three patients. The medical student assigned to his team, working with the second-year resident, admitted a two-year-old with bronchiolitis. Steven admitted two patients. A six-year-old boy, named Josh, who had chased after a basketball, tumbled down an embankment where a shallow creek ran below his parents' driveway. The boy's mother and a neighbor had brought Josh to the ER. While the mother comforted her child, the neighbor recounted the incident. He told Steven how he had heard the mother scream for help. When he reached her, she was struggling to carry her unconscious son up the embankment. He climbed part-way down, grabbed her extended arm and pulled her up the hill.

"How long would you estimate he was unconscious?" Steven asked the mother.

"I don't know. Ten minutes maybe?" She looked at her neighbor.

"Maybe closer to fifteen," the man said.

An X-ray showed a dislocated shoulder, but fortunately no broken bones. The dislocation was reduced in the ER. An oozing two-inch laceration over his forehead was cleansed and sutured. A head CT didn't show evidence of internal bleeding. He was admitted for observation. Steven did a thorough physical and neurological examination. It was completely negative. Scully also went over the boy. He agreed with Steven's assessment.

Steven wrote for standard neuro checks with special attention to pupil size, shape and response to light, as well as other indicators of possible focal damage or intra-cranial bleeding. He reassured the boy' mother that so far everything was looking good, but that she should report to the nurse if her son's behavior seemed in any way unusual.

Steven's other admission was a thirteen-year-old black girl with a knee injury following a fall from a skateboard. X-rays of the knee were negative. She was unable to straighten her leg. The presumptive diagnosis was a torn meniscus. She was scheduled for arthroscopy for the following day. He entered her room on the pediatric ward. Another teenager in the same room had her leg in a toe to hip cast, suspended by a contraption of weights and pulleys. The girl was asleep.

"Hi, Sharon. I'm Dr. Johnson." He spoke quietly so as not to awaken the other child. "I have to take a history and examine you. You feel up to it?"

"I guess."

Sharon was on her back. Her right knee, wrapped in an ace bandage, was supported by two pillows. She held an icepack atop her knee. Her right cheek was bruised. She wore a baseball cap with the brim toward the rear. Strands of short braided hair poked through the arched opening in the baseball cap, covering her forehead.

"You do much skateboarding?"

"No. The board's my boyfriend's. He was showing me how to jump. I'm going to kill him when I see him. The emergency doctor said I probably can’t play basketball the rest of the year. What do you think?"

"I don't know enough yet to say. If the tear is partial, they can repair it and get you back playing in a few weeks."

"Are you going to do the operation?"

"No. Dr. Quan is the surgeon who will be doing the arthroscopy." Steven had seen from the ER report that Sharon's mother had brought her to the hospital. "Your mom around?"

"She had to go. She was already late for work."

Steven's beeper went off. "Dr. Johnson, ER, stat." It was the second time they had beeped him.

"I have to run, Sharon. I'll be back."

As Steven hurried to the ER, he thought of Jacqueline. By now she should be somewhere over the vast black Atlantic. Her precious life was dependent on proper function of a complex piece of machinery, miles of wire, hydraulic lines, hundreds of computer chips, dozens of inter-connected instruments, nuts, bolts, rivets, gaskets and a million other small parts that must withstand tremendous stress as the plane's jet engines propelled tens of thousands of tons of hardware and people through space. And this miracle of technology could at any moment be swallowed by a vast, indifferent sea.

It’s a matter of luck that we get through each day, Steven thought. That the flight we take through life isn't brought down by a faulty piece of equipment, or a drunk driver in an approaching car. Emergency rooms throughout the world are crowded with the victims of accidents--his own life so recently saved by the happenstance that Chris had been standing on the ER receiving platform and had seen him stumbling down the hill, a squadron of angry yellow-jackets in hot pursuit.

Carol Conti, the medicine intern assigned to the ER, looked up as Steven approached. She was seated before a computer terminal scanning laboratory data. Steven had seen her around the hospital, but had never met her.

"Hi, I'm Steven Johnson."

"I know. The notorious Dr. Steve. I'm Carol Conti. I beeped you. I have a teen-age boy..."

"Really? You look so young."

She smiled. "It's biologically possible, I guess. Let me start over. There's a teenage boy in the ER with what looks like renal colic. Flank pain, bloody urine. A bit unusual for a seventeen-year-old. We gave him fifty of Demerol and twenty-five of Phenergan. Took the edge off, but he's still hurting."

"You leave the catheter in?"

"He didn't want to be catheterized, so I stood there until he was able to give me a specimen." She smiled. "He said he couldn't go with me watching. He placed the specimen bottle under the sheet. It still took him a while."

"X-rays show anything?"

"No. But as you know, the false negative rate with KUB films is high," Carol said.

"The attending see him?" Steven asked.

"Briefly. Thinks we should admit him for a urologic workup. He said a renal stone in someone this young, suggests a possible anatomic abnormality. Especially since the boy had a similar episode six months ago. The attending asked for a pedes evaluation."

"Was the boy treated here?"

"He said he went to the urgent care center in the Mall," Carol said.

"You check with them?" Steven asked.

"They closed at nine. I got their answering service."

"Are his parents here?" Steven asked.

"No. The boy was out riding with one of his buddies, who just got his driver's license. He gave us his phone number, but his parents weren't home. He thinks they went to a movie." She handed the boy's chart to Steven. "I've got an asthmatic lady who isn't doing well. You mind taking over this one?" Carol asked,

"Sure, but I think he should stay in the ER until we can contact his parents," Steven said. "We can hydrate him and do an IVP after we get parental permission. Sometimes the IVP even helps the stone to pass."

"Okay, but the attending isn't going to like tying up a room." She hurried off. Steven headed for the boy's room.

He checked his watch. Almost 11:00 P.M. He figured Jacqueline would be arriving at Heathrow around 2:00 A.M., 7:00 A.M. London time. Another three hours. He wished he'd asked her to call him at each stop along the way.

On entering the room, Steven introduced himself. The boy was lying on his left side in the fetal position, grimacing in pain. He either had a kidney stone or was desperately in need of a fix, Steven thought. Two months on his ER rotation had taught him to take nothing at face value. As Steven examined him, he looked for the tell-tale tracks of the IV drug user. There were none. He examined the boy's hands. He saw something on the boy's right middle finger that heightened his suspicions.

"You left handed?" Steven asked.

"Yeah. How'd you know?"

"Just a hunch."

"I swear, doc, I can't stand the pain. Whatever it was they gave me didn't help much. Last time, the pain eased off after the second shot."

"Did you pass the stone?"

"A couple of days later."

"Anyone in your family a diabetic?" he asked.

The boy looked startled. "Yes, my mother."

"Does she check her own blood sugar?"

"Yeah. Twice a day."

Steven told the boy that he had to be admitted for tests since this was his second attack, that there could be some underlying problem that shouldn't be overlooked.

“I'll come back for tests. I know my parents wouldn't agree to keep me in the hospital."

Steven's suspicions were growing rapidly. "Okay, I'll give you another shot, but first I have to put in a catheter. Don't want the stone to pass into your bladder and then get stuck in your penis."

"I didn't know that could happen."

"Not with a catheter in place." Steven headed for the door. "I'll get the medication and a cath tray."

At the nurses' station Steven drew up a syringe of sterile saline. He grabbed a catheter pack from the medication cart.

"Hey, what's up?" Carol asked.

"I'm going to slip in a catheter. I'm pretty sure we won't find any blood in his urine."

‘The specimen had 'too numerous to count RBCs."

"He probably pricked his finger, dripped a drop or two into the specimen bottle. You said it took him a while."

"I don't know about giving him a placebo," Carol said. "What if he obstructs and needs surgery?"

"Sterile saline won't cause him to obstruct. I'm betting the cath specimen will be free of blood."

"I looked for track marks."

"You're right. There were none. But did you notice the tiny gash on his right middle finger?"

"No."

"It's the kind of mark you get from a lancet. His mother's diabetic. He probably stole one of hers." Steven turned to the nurse. "Would you get his friend in a room? I want to ask him a few questions."

Chapter Twenty-Seven

Jacqueline sat in the window seat of the Boeing 767 staring into a sea of darkness. She pulled down the opaque window shade. She ratcheted her seat back another notch and covered herself with the thin blanket the flight attendant had given her. She was glad there was no one in the next seat. She pulled back the arm-rest and, moving onto her side, drew up her knees, turning her back to a woman in the aisle seat, who had talked non-stop for the first three hours of the flight.

The plane was dim except for a few reading lamps and muted aisle lighting. It had cost Jacqueline a lot to do this for Anna. She had to admit to herself that she was doing it as much for Steven. But things had all turned out wrong. At the end of the month Steven would leave Smithfield. And it was her fault he was being forced to leave. Maybe he would follow Dr. Murphy to Baltimore.

When she was with Steven she never felt like a black woman with a white man. His color made no difference to her, not consciously at least, and she sensed that he felt the same way. But Jacqueline knew her mother would not approve, even though she had raised her children to judge persons individually, not by their race or religion.

"But what of the prejudices that might be locked in Steven's heart?" her mother would ask. "Hurtful, destructive words released in an angry moment." It was testimony to her mother's constancy that Jacqueline felt she could predict her mother's response. And as she fell off to sleep, those imagined words of her mother's cycled and recycled though her head, fading eventually into the roar of the plane's engines.

She awakened to the voice of the captain announcing their approach to Heathrow. She peered out the window. Below the plane, a bed of marshmallow clouds, above, a brilliant blue sky.

"You slept right through breakfast," the woman in the aisle seat said. She pointed to a tray in the seat between them. "That's yours. Better eat it fast. We'll be landing soon."

In customs, the agent seemed concerned about her short stay. "Is this for business or pleasure?" he asked as he rummaged through her things. When he found Anna's medical record he looked puzzled. He called over another agent. Jacqueline wondered if the INS had perhaps alerted immigration agents to be on the lookout for Anna Amin.

He and the other agent chatted off to the side, and then the agent returned to where Jacqueline had remained standing. "This is obviously not your record. Who is this person?"

"It is a friend. I am bringing the record to her family. They are concerned about her care." Jacqueline reached into her purse and removed Anna's signed request. She handed it to the agent. He compared the signature to that on the hospital admission form. He nodded. He gave her back the slip of paper and continued looking through her things. He removed the video camera and examined it carefully. Then he waved her on.

Would she have to go through that same procedure at her stopover in Paris and in Algeria? Might they already be alerted to look for Anna?

At the crowded airport terminal, she hurried to the mall section where she found a store that sold luggage. She purchased a backpack several paperback books and magazines. She discarded sections of Anna's chart that didn't pertain to the history and evidence of abuse by Anna's husband. She hoped that, with a cursory look in the backpack, the immigration agents in Paris and Algiers would not give the loose sheets of paper a second thought.

It was only 3 A.M. in New Jersey, much too early to call Steven. Still, he was on call, he might even be up. She had an hour and thirty minutes before the connecting flight to Paris. She searched in her purse for the hospital number. The operator didn't have to beep him. She knew exactly where he was.

When the phone rang, Steven popped up like a submerged plastic bathtub duck. Usually the operator beeped him. He jumped down from the upper level bunk. He grabbed the handset.

"Dr. Johnson, here."

"Hi, sleepy-head. Got a lady on the phone. Calling from London. Said you were expecting her call."

"Steven?"

"Jacqueline! Hi. I'm so glad you called. Everything okay?"

"The immigration agent at Heathrow asked questions about my having Anna's medical record. It gave me a bit of a fright."

"What did you tell him?"

"I showed him the signed release and said her family in Algiers was concerned about her care. That I was bringing it to them."

"It's a wonder they'd even take notice."

"Yes. That caught me by surprise."

"What if the agents in Algiers question you?"

"I threw away most of the papers. I kept only what I absolutely needed. What's left looks pretty uninteresting mixed in with books and magazines," she said.

"Good. I still want you to call me from your hotel. Fortunately, I've been too busy for nail biting. Which airline will you take to Paris?"

"Air France." She glanced at her ticket packet. "I should arrive at De Gaulle Airport around eleven, about six your time. Then onto Air Algiers."

"I wonder if you should meet with Anna's family at the hotel. Anwar might have gotten wind of your coming. You don't want him barging in on you at Anna's home."

"But her father might refuse to come to a meeting at the hotel. It's better that I be there when he arrives home. Anna told me that Muslim people are very gracious with house guests."

"I suppose you're right."

"Steven, I must decide what to wear. I don't want to offend the Yacine family."

Steven hadn't heard Anna's maiden name before. "I would think your student nurse uniform would be okay. It would explain your access to information about Anna."

"The skirt by American standards is modest. But I would think not in Algiers."

"Many Algerian women wear western clothes."

"But would they wear such clothes in the home of a devout Muslim family?"

"What did Anna think?"

"I was in such a hurry I didn't ask."

"I'm sure the entire family will find you enchanting regardless of what you wear."

"How is your first call night going?"

"Just what I expected. A zoo. Word seems to get out when I'm on call. The lady holding up the torch in New York harbor has nothing on me."

"I will have to think about that. Get some rest, Steven. I will pray your beeper does not go off again until I call you around six."

Jacqueline's walk through Paris customs proved to be uneventful, although her stomach, the entire time, was filled with small, frantic, winged creatures. In the terminal waiting area, she removed a *Time* magazine from her backpack and pretended to read as she took in the passengers who gathered about her, awaiting the connecting flight to Algiers. She was surrounded by dark-skinned well-dressed men in western-style business suits and others in traditional Arabic robes and headpieces. There was a large contingent of young girls in identical robes and Muslim veils, accompanied by several older women dressed like nuns. Jacqueline assumed them to be students returning from a trip to Paris. They were speaking French. Jacqueline's high school encounter with French did not prepare her to understand their rapid-fire chatter.

Jacqueline felt self-conscious, dressed in her student nurses' uniform and bulky knitted cap. Was it her imagination or was everyone staring at her legs? She pressed her knees together, pulling at the hem of her skirt, but it still barely reached her knees. A dark-skinned man with a mustache and beard, clad in an expensive-looking robe and intricately wound linen turban, sat in the seat opposite her. She guessed him to be in his late forties. He glanced disapprovingly at her legs. She removed her overnight bag from the seat and placed it in front of her, pretending to be checking the nametag. She left the bag there.

"You are a nurse?" the man asked in perfect English. He spoke with a French accent.

Jacqueline looked up from her magazine. The man flashed a smile filled with gold. "American?"

"Jamaican." She looked back at her magazine.

"Ah. Your people were fortunate the English dislodged the French from your lovely country. We had to fight many years for our independence."

She checked her watch. They would be boarding passengers in five minutes. He obviously knew little of the struggles of the Jamaican people. She tucked her magazine in her backpack. She directed her attention to a wall-mounted television set across the room.

"What brings you to Algiers? Business? Pleasure?" he asked, undeterred by her obvious desire not to speak.

"I'm visiting friends."

"Is it your first visit?"

"Yes," she said, without looking at him.

The boarding light flashed above a desk where a female attendant stood. The woman spoke first in French, then in English. "First-class passengers and handicapped persons will be boarded at this time."

The man stood. "Will your friends be meeting you at the airport?"

"I'm staying at the Sofitel." Oh God. Why had she told him that? "They have a shuttle service."

"You have no need for a shuttle. I have a private car coming to pick me up. The Sofitel is on my way."

"No, thank you. I've already made arrangements," she lied.

"A pity," he said. "A pity."

He walked off toward the gate, carrying only a handsome leather briefcase. Jacqueline was relieved to be rid of him.

In less than two hours she would be in Algiers. If only Steven were with her! They could visit the Old City, the Casbah. He would fall in love with her in such a place. Her pulse quickened as she imagined someday coming to Algiers with him. They could visit Anna and see what a fine young man Anna's baby would have grown to be.

Jacqueline's tourist class seat was several rows behind the first-class section. As she entered the plane, she saw the gentleman who had spoken to her in the waiting area. She hoped to slip past without gaining his attention, but he spotted her immediately. He jumped to his feet and insisted on helping her with her bags.

He placed her luggage in an overhead compartment. She slipped her backpack beneath the seat in front of her.

"Permit me to introduce myself. I am Muhammad al-Rashid. At your service." He removed a business card from a pocket in his robe. He handed it to her.

"And I am Jacqueline. You are most kind. Thank you, sir." She settled into her aisle seat. Muhammad bowed slightly and returned to the first-class section.

As soon as the plane was airborne and the seat-belt sign went off, an attendant approached Jacqueline. "Madame," he said, "Muhammad al-Rashid invites you to dine with him in first class."

"I would really prefer not to."

"He would be most offended, Madame. In this culture, one does not decline such an invitation."

Who is this man, she wondered? She retrieved the card he had given her from the pocket of her jumper. *The Bank of Algiers. Muhammad al-Rashid, Vice President in charge of Acquisitions.* Yes, he's apparently very good at acquisitions, she thought. Was it mere chance their paths had crossed?

Chapter Twenty-Eight

Steven had been asleep barely an hour when the phone rang. The resident in the lower bunk didn't respond. Steven leaned over at a precarious angle to retrieve the hand-set from a nearby desktop.

"We're about to start a C-section. We need pedes here stat," the on-call obstetrical resident said.

A second-year pediatric resident was snoring away in the lower bunk. Steven awakened him and informed him that they had to attend an emergency C-section.

As Steven hurried to the obstetrical suite, he tried to organize his recollection of the events of the last several hours. At 7:30 A.M. he would be on rounds. He had to bring the team up to date on the various admissions and inpatient happenings, as well as give them a rundown on the status of the infants admitted to the nursery.

In the operating room, the obstetric resident quickly reviewed the patient's history. This was her first pregnancy, and all had gone well until her membranes ruptured and the umbilical cord prolapsed through her almost fully dilated cervix. The baby's head slipped into the mid-pelvis, trapping and compressing the cord. Fetal monitoring indicated marked slowing of the baby's heart rate, and changes suggesting anoxia. The C-section team was rapidly assembled.

Interns were only permitted to intubate infants under the close supervision of an experienced resident or attending physician. Steven was happy to have the second-year pediatric resident at his side.

"You ever intubate a newborn?" the pedes resident asked.

"Once, during an obstetrical rotation as a medical student, but that was over a year ago."

"Don't worry. I'll walk you through it."

Although Steven would like the experience of placing an endotracheal tube in the newborn, he knew that seconds counted if the infant was already anoxic. He was much relieved when the obstetrical resident handed him a wide-eyed, male infant with relatively good muscle tone. He did an assessment of respiratory effort, heart sounds, color, and reflexes.

"One-minute Apgar's 8!" Steven announced loud enough for the obstetrician to hear. "One off for color and one off for muscle tone."

"You hear that, Daddy?" the masked obstetrician asked.

The newborn's mother was still hadn't awakened from anesthesia. The father, who was seated next to the anesthetist, said, "Great. Can I hold him?"

Steven wrapped the infant in a flannel blanket and carried the baby to him.

After leaving the operating room, Steven wrote a note on the mother's chart. He also completed forms and wrote orders on the newborn's chart. By the time he got back to the on-call room, the second-year pedes resident was sprawled atop the covers on the lower bunk. Steven sat at a small desk, writing notes on 3x5 index cards, preparing for rounds.

The pedes resident, awakened by the phone, rolled onto his back. "You able to track down the kid with the phantom kidney stone?" he asked.

"No. He grabbed his clothes and slipped out of the ER while we were waiting for the results from the cath urine." Steven said.

"You know, he could still have a stone, even with the negative cath urine. The bleeding could have stopped."

"It's a stretch to think he'd go from too many to count to crystal clear in such a short time" Steven said. "Besides, why would he run off like that?"

"Yeah. Probably. Was all the info he gave bogus?"

"He had a phony picture ID."

"Maybe that's why he high-tailed out of here." the resident said. "You get to talk with the kid's buddy?"

"No. He wasn't in the waiting area when the nurse went to look for him."

"Better call risk management," the resident said.

"I filled out an incident report. They get a copy."

"Those have a way of getting lost. Better call. And let's hope the kid didn't take his little game someplace else. Maybe you should alert the County Medical Society. They could notify the private MDs in the area."

"And if he really had a stone," Steven said, "his family sues me for defamation of character."

"Yeah. Damned if you do and damned if you don't," the resident said. "This case would make a good noon conference. You up for it?"

"Sure. But it'll have to happen pretty soon." He was sure word of his resignation had already gotten around. The resident rolled over and was soon asleep. Steven checked his beeper to make sure Jacqueline would be able to get hold of him. The hospital operators seldom voice-paged the doctors.

Steven needed to pass his boards and complete an internship year in order to get a medical license. With that in hand, he would have the option to go into practice or into a specialty program in pediatrics or family medicine in either Baltimore or Great Bend, Kansas. He was inclining toward Great Bend, because it was only a ninety-minute drive from Zion. But then he'd be a half continent removed from Chris and Jacqueline.

He jumped when his beeper went off. The hospital operator asked if he was expecting a long-distance call.

"Yes."

"She's on line three."

"Jacqueline?"

"Steven!"

"Where are you?"

"I'm at the Sofitel. My room overlooks the Mediterranean and part of the old city. Steven, I've never been in such a luxurious hotel. There are flowers, trees and potted plants everywhere."

"It sounds nice. When do you go to see Anna's family?"

"Anna's brother, Tahar, is picking me up at four. Oh, how I wish I had planned on staying two or three days. I met an

Algerian businessman on the plane from Paris. He offered to show me the city, but of course I have no time."

"I hope you're joking."

"You needn't worry, Steven, although it pleases me that you are concerned. He says he has a daughter my age. We're having lunch at the hotel tomorrow. He's bringing his daughter. Isn't it exciting? I will have two friends in Algiers. Anna and Mohammed's daughter."

"Jacqueline, you are too trusting. Men look on a woman traveling alone as fair game."

"You are jealous of an old man?"

"I'm concerned."

"You're jealous."

"Okay. I'm jealous."

"Good. And I am not as trusting as you think. He gave me his business card. When I called the bank, the operator put me through to him only after she checked to see if he would accept the call."

"He's a teller?"

"He's vice president."

"Oh God. That's worse."

"He was very helpful in telling me what to wear and what I should and shouldn't do in a Muslim home. How I must sit, and how it is polite to refuse when food is first offered, but to accept if they repeat the offer."

"Please tell me you're making all this up."

She laughed. "Aren't you sorry you didn't drop everything and come with me?"

"If I were Superman, I would be tearing off my scrubs and be at your side before you had a chance to hang up the phone."

"I must go, Steven. There are wonderful shops nearby. I must buy a veil, a jilbab and proper shoes."

"What, no jewelry?"

"I have little time before Anna's brother is to pick me up. And don't worry, I will pay you back."

At a boutique across from the hotel, Jacqueline told the saleslady that she was visiting a Muslim family; that she wanted to dress in a way not to offend them. The woman advised her that a traditional Algerian jilbab would be too expensive for a one-time use and besides would not be in good taste. She suggested a long dress, called a khimar.

"A khimar is very acceptable here," the sales lady said. "It is stylish and modest. The fabric is elegant but unpretentious."

Jacqueline bought an ankle-length beige khimar, matching shoes, scarf and an embroidered shoulder bag that was large enough to hold Anna's records and Omar's video camera.

Jacqueline was wearing a gold charm bracelet. "Should I wear jewelry?" she asked.

"A silver necklace, perhaps. Gold is considered too ostentatious."

When Jacqueline handed the credit card to the salesperson, the woman raised her eyebrows. "This is your husband?"

"My fiancée," she lied.

"A medical doctor?"

"Yes. I'm a nurse at the hospital where he works. He said you can call him if you want to. Would you like the number?"

The woman smiled. "That won't be necessary, my dear."

Back in her room, Jacqueline dressed in her new clothes. She stood before a full-length mirror mounted on the bathroom door. Her costume was elegant. Her khimar was linen with an embossed floral design in a slightly darker beige; her shoes plain off-white pumps, and her leather handbag emerald green. Over her head and shoulders, she wore a pale beige crouched shawl.

Because of the fullness of the skirt, she could move about freely despite the length. She practiced walking, sitting and getting up from a sitting position on the floor.

Her phone rang. It was the front desk. "There is a gentleman named Tahar Yacine here, Miss Martin. He says you are expecting him."

"Yes, tell him I'll be down shortly."

Tahar had the same dark, intense eyes as Anna. He had a scant beard and sparse mustache. She guessed him to be eighteen or nineteen. He seemed somewhat taken aback by the way she was dressed. His stoic expression signaled neither approval nor disdain. His English was not as good as Anna's.

"I am Tahar. Anna's brother. I take you to my father's house." He didn't extend his hand.

"I'm Anna's friend, Jacqueline Martin. I'm pleased to meet you."

Tahar's small car, a Fiat,

was parked at the hotel entrance. He held open the passenger door for Jacqueline, and then stepped into the driver's side. Soon they were immersed in a sea of honking autos that drifted in a haphazard way across lanes and intersections. Tahar made no attempt to speak with Jacqueline. She too remained silent, not wanting to appear bold or aggressive. Eventually the traffic thinned, the streets widened into boulevards lined with beautifully landscaped homes fronted by large expanses of meticulously tended lawns. Tahar pulled onto a drive and parked in front of a two-story brick house painted white. It had black shutters and a red-tiled roof. Jacqueline wondered what Anna's father did for a living. Tahar pulled alongside a late model BMW. The winged creatures in Jacqueline's belly began to stir.

In the foyer, Tahar removed his shoes. Jacqueline did likewise. A striking middle-aged woman approached her. There was no question it was Anna's mother. The same nose and mouth and especially the large dark eyes. She was dressed in a traditional long dress but wore no veil. Her black hair hung to her shoulders. Jacqueline introduced herself. Mrs. Yacine led her to a formal living room where Anna's two sisters were seated on cushions around a low glass-top table. They jumped to their feet when she entered.

"You have already met my son, Tahar. These are Anna's sisters, Aissa and Leila," Mrs. Yacine said. The girls were wide-eyed and unsmiling. They were dressed in what looked like school uniforms. "This is Jacqueline Martin, a friend of Anna's. Please sit." She pointed to a cushion. "Do you drink tea, Miss Martin?"

"Yes, but I mustn't trouble you."

"It is already prepared. Aissa, Leila, bring the tea and cakes."

They scurried from the room.

"My husband will be arriving home in thirty minutes. I understand you have brought a videotape of Anna?"

"Yes, I have it right here." Jacqueline reached into her bag and removed the camera. Anna had told her that her family did not own a television set. She pressed the power button and flipped open the viewing screen. She handed the camera to Mrs. Yacine. "When you are ready to look at the video, just hold this button down. It will stop when you release the button."

The two girls entered carrying trays, one with a teapot, cups and saucers, the other with a platter of chocolate cookies.

Mrs. Yacine poured tea for everyone, including her two daughters. The girls watched Jacqueline's every move.

Mrs. Yacine passed the platter of cookies.

Jacqueline smiled. "How did you know these are my favorite cookies?"

"It was Aissa who suggested them."

Aissa and her sister giggled.

"Before we watch the video," Mrs. Yacine said, "tell us how you came to know Anna."

"I am a student nurse at the hospital where Anna had her baby. When the baby was ready to go home with Anna, she told one of the hospital doctors that she must leave the hospital with her baby before Anwar arrived to take her home. She told the doctor that Anwar was physically abusing her. She said she was afraid of him and afraid for her baby. She showed him a scar on her forehead. She described how Anwar would become violent when he drank too much. One time he threw a glass at her." Jacqueline paused. She knew how painful this must be for them to hear. "I am truly sorry to bring such bad news."

"It is all lies," Tahar said. "Anwar showed us American newspaper. It says she goes with a doctor. That she takes on Western ways."

"Let her finish, Tahar," Mrs. Yacine said.

"The doctor," Jacqueline said, "took Anna to the Emergency room at the hospital where she was evaluated for possible physical abuse. I brought the hospital reports with me." She reached into her bag and retrieved Anna's medical records. She handed them to Mrs. Yacine. "There are X-ray reports and descriptions of bruises and the scar on her forehead."

Mrs. Yacine's hands shook as she looked through the papers Jacqueline had given her. She took several minutes to study the papers. She handed them to Tahar. He glanced at them and tossed them on the table.

"Why do you go to all this trouble to make up lies? What do you want from us? Is it ransom money you want?"

"Hold your tongue, Tahar," Mrs. Yacine said. "Miss Martin, tell me again how do I start this thing?"

The doorbell rang. Mrs. Yacine looked startled. "Aissa, see who it is."

Aissa left. Moments later Anwar strode into the room. Jacqueline hadn't seen him before. He was dressed in traditional Muslim clothing. He had a thin mustache and full but short beard. He glared at Jacqueline from beneath his dark bushy eyebrows. Then he bowed slightly toward Mrs. Yacine.

"Mother, pardon me for this intrusion. Tahar called me and said you were expecting a visitor from America. I have come to refute her lies and demand she tell me of the whereabouts of my son."

"What we are attempting to determine," Mrs. Yacine said, "is who is not telling the truth."

"You are suggesting that I am lying?" Anwar asked, his voice shaking with anger.

"I have read the documents Miss Martin brought with her. Would you care to read them?" She picked up the papers Jacqueline had given her and handed them to Anwar.

"Documents can be falsified," Anwar said. He took them from her and threw them onto the floor. "Anna believes she can keep my son if she pretends that I have physically abused her. She lies. She ran off with a young American doctor. She walks the streets without the veil."

"Be quiet and sit down, Anwar. You have already told us those things. Now I want to hear from my daughter. Miss Martin, show us the video."

Jacqueline hands shook as she took the camera and pressed the view button. She handed it to Mrs. Yacine. Aissa and Leila stood behind their mother, looking over her shoulder at the tiny screen. Anwar sat with his chin held high. The line of his mouth stretched in anger. He stared at Jacqueline as the others watched the video. She rose and began to gather up Anna's hospital records.

Anna's voice could be heard distinctly although she spoke in barely a whisper. "Mother, father, it is me, Anna. I long to be with you. With my sisters Aissa and Leila and my brother, Tahar." She held up her baby. "Look, here is your grandchild. Isn't he beautiful?" The baby began to cry. She smiled. "He must be hungry." She placed him on her shoulder, patting his back. "Father, you must protect me from Anwar. He abuses me, mocks our Muslim faith. He has sold all the jewelry he gave me when we married. He spends his money on alcohol and other women. I live in fear for my life and that of my baby..." She set the baby on the floor. She again faced the camera. "Look, Father. See what he has done to me." The video camera zoomed in on her forehead as she pushed back her hair.

Mrs. Yacine and her daughters gasped when they saw the scar

"Lies, lies, lies," Anwar shouted. "She was forced to say those things." He stood, rushed to Jacqueline and pushed violently, sending her sprawling onto the floor.

Mrs. Yacine shouted, “Anwar, stop!”

Anwar knelt beside Jacqueline, pinning her down with one knee as he grabbed her by the hair. He yanked her head sharply back. "You are a shameless lying pig." He slapped her hard across the face. He spat at her.

"Tahar, stop him," Mrs. Yacine shouted.

Tahar moved behind Anwar and pressed his forearm tightly against Anwar's throat. "Let go of her or I will break your neck."

Anwar gasped, "Even you have turned against me, Tahar?"

Tahar pressed harder. Anwar released Jacqueline. She pushed away as Aissa helped her to her feet. Leila stood frozen at her mother’s side. Tahar let go of Anwar, who remained on one knee, coughing and rubbing his throat.

Tears ran down Tahar's cheeks. "Forgive me, Mother. I trusted Anwar. It was I who told him she was coming."

"Now none of us is deceived. Tahar, show Anwar to the door."

"Stay away from me, Tahar,” Anwar shouted. "You will hear from my lawyer for this vicious attack." He rushed from the room.

Chapter Twenty-Nine

The afternoon following Steven's first on-call night, his team wasn't admitting new patients, so he had little time to think. After the noon conference, he went to the hospital library to look up listings of internships and training programs in pediatrics and family medicine. He was especially interested in what might be offered at Great Bend General in Kansas. He found that there were several residencies available: Family Medicine, Obstetrics, Pediatrics, Internal Medicine, General Surgery and Emergency Medicine. In addition, they offered several rotating internship slots. He dialed the number of the office of the Director of Medical Education. He spoke with the DME's secretary.

He explained to her that he wanted to complete his internship in a hospital relatively close to home because of his mother's illness.

"We haven't filled all of our internship slots. I'll mail you an application packet. Hold on, I'll get Dr. McCullough on the line."

After several minutes, Dr. McCullough came back on the line. "Sorry to keep you waiting, I was on another line. Yes, we do have a Family Medicine intern position available. I'll need your medical school transcript, a dean's letter and at least two letters of recommendation. We'll also need the results of the first part of your National Boards, and a letter from the medical director at Smithfield."

Steven wondered what kind of letter Ewing would write. He knew the rest of his credentials would be strong. He also knew that hospitals did not especially like empty housestaff slots.

"Dr. McCullough, you may have known my father. Dr. Sam Johnson. He practiced in Zion for years. Sent his patients who needed hospitalization to Great Bend General."

"Why, of course. He took several CME courses here over the years. Our staff thought very highly of him. I was sorry to hear of his passing."

"Thank you, Dr. McCullough. It would take a while to get those materials from the original sources. Would you accept copies of my records from Smithfield?"

"Yes, of course. How soon would you be available?"

"By the second week in November. And how soon might you make a decision?"

"Once I have your materials assembled, the admissions committee can decide in a matter of days."

"Thank you, doctor."

"I look forward to hearing from you, Steven. Sam Johnson's son. How about that?"

Thanks, Dad, Steven thought as he hung up. His mind wasn't completely made up, but he didn't want a lot of time to pass between leaving Smithfield and starting elsewhere. That night he would meditate, clear his mind, seek direction. He left the library and headed for the pediatric procedures room. At 2:00 PM he was assisting on a bone marrow biopsy on a two-year-old girl with anemia, to be followed by a sigmoidoscopy on a seven-year-old boy with rectal bleeding. He checked his watch.

Jacqueline's meeting with Anna's family should be over by now. Why hadn't she called? Maybe she had called Chris or Omar. He started toward pedes, changed his mind and headed for Chris's office. It was the time of day she caught up on messages and paper work.

Her office door was ajar. He knocked, then entered and sat in a chair alongside her desk. She was on the phone. She smiled and gave him a high five. "Go ahead and start an IV. I'll be there in ten minutes." She hung up. "Jacqueline called. The meeting went well, but things got a little dicey when Anwar showed up"

"Damnit." He punched his thigh. "I was afraid that might happen. How did he know?"

"Anna's brother tipped him off."

"Ewing was right. I should never have let her go."

"Jacqueline told me that Anna's mother is a strong lady. She more or less told Anwar to shut up and sit down while she and her daughters watched the video Jacqueline had made of Anna."

"I can't believe he was that timid, from what I know of him."

“He wasn't exactly timid. He attacked Jacqueline."

"What?"

"He knocked her to the floor, pinned her down and started slapping her."

"My God!"

"Don't worry, she wasn't hurt. Tahar came to her rescue. He got Anwar in a half-Nelson. Mrs. Yacine ordered Anwar to leave the house."

"And he did?"

"Yes. Abusers are cowards at heart."

"What about Mr. Yacine?"

"He arrived just minutes after Anwar left. They were watching the tape. Mrs. Yacine recounted what had happened.

He was furious at first. All this had gone on behind his back. But after he read the copy of Anna's hospital record and watched the video, he cried, recalling the things he had said to his daughter. He was finally convinced that Anwar was a hypocrite and liar. He said he wanted her home as soon as possible. He said he would wire her money for the plane fare, and insisted he reimburse Jacqueline for her expenses."

"How will she get a passport for the baby without a birth certificate?" Steven asked.

"Omar will take Anna to the Registrar of Records and Deeds, first thing in the morning. They'll get a certified copy of the baby's birth certificate."

"I should have known you would have thought of that. Is Omar going to pass himself off as Mr. Amin?"

"No. She'll tell them her husband had to leave the country on an emergency. That she was going to join him. She has a valid passport. There shouldn't be a problem."

"Unless the INS has alerted customs," Steven said.

"The INS is concerned about her staying, not leaving the country

"You're right. Customs agents are looking for terrorists and smugglers, not young mothers with babies," Steven said.

"I've booked a flight for her for tomorrow evening."

"You're amazing." He reached over and squeezed her hand.

"Is that the best you can do?"

He stared at his shoes, and then looked up. "I--I need time to sort things out, Chris. I don't want to hurt you."

She tried to smile. "Someone always gets hurt." She stood. "I have to run."

"Who's taking Anna and her baby to the airport?"

"A driver from the women's shelter."

"That makes sense. Okay if I use your office phone?"

"Help yourself."

Steven sat at Chris's desk and dialed Ewing's secretary. He told her he was applying for an internship slot at Great Bend General in Kansas. He described what he needed. "I'll also need a letter from Dr. Ewing."

"You want me to fax the packet to Great Bend General?"

"That would be great. Thanks."

He looked about Chris's cozy office. He stood and examined some photographs tacked onto her bulletin board. Had they been there before? He hadn't noticed. They were snapshots taken in the ER at the send-off party the staff had given him. In one, he was standing before a layer cake, knife in hand, sporting a silly grin. In another Martha Knight was kissing him on the cheek. In a third photo, he and Chris were shaking hands. He recalled the sparks as their fingers met. The look in her eyes. He wondered who had taken the pictures. Martha would know.

Should he also apply to St. Joseph's Hospital in Baltimore? That would look to Chris as though he were following her there. But what if he didn't secure a position at Great Bend? It wasn’t a sure thing. There would still be time to explore other options.

Late that evening Steven ate a frozen ravioli dinner, showered, slipped on a fresh pair of shorts, lit some incense, disconnected his phone, and turned off his beeper. Anna Amin was on her way to Algeria. And later that evening, Jacqueline would be boarding a flight to Paris on the first leg of her journey back to Smithfield.

Steven settled into the lotus position before his miniature Buddha. With his eyes closed, he breathed slowly, rhythmically, concentrating on the movement of air in and out of his lungs. He felt his body rise and drift effortlessly through space and time through wispy puffs of clouds, the earth receding rapidly behind him. But despite his effort to journey alone, he emerged from a cloud with his arms extended, a smiling white-robed Chris in one hand and in the other Jacqueline, her braids the dust of a shooting star, her multicolored robe extending well beyond her feet. They danced, laughed and swirled, faster and faster. Soon he felt them slipping from his grasp. Both women reached for him. He looked frantically from one to the other. His grip continued to weaken. Soon they would both break away. But at the same moment each of the women grasped him by the ankle closest to them. The three cartwheeled through space, faster and faster, until he thought he would be torn in two.

Steven opened his eyes and stared at his tiny ceramic image of Buddha. Steven thought he could detect the barest hint of a sardonic smile.

Before getting into bed, he reconnected his phone and turned on his beeper. Jacqueline might call. He set his alarm for 6 AM. By mid-day tomorrow, he thought, Anna will be reunited with her family, Jacqueline will be back in Smithfield, and he will be up to his ears in admissions, discharges, newborns and trips to the ER. It would be a demanding, hectic challenging day. He was determined to endure the frustrations, to be gracious when unexpected and excessive demands were placed upon him, and above all to savor the moments of joy that made it all worthwhile.

He picked up his worn copy of *Tao Daily Meditations* by Deng Ming-Dao. He searched for a passage titled *Farewells.*

We part at the crossroads, you leave with your joys and problems, I with mine. Alone I look down the road.Each one must walk one's own path.

Chapter Thirty

The next day, Steven telephoned Chris. He got her voice mail.

"Hi, Chris. I'm going to need a letter from you concerning my performance on my ER rotation. Send to the DME at Great Bend General in Kansas. The slot is a general medicine intern position. I think it's mine for the asking. I haven't completely ruled out St. Joe's. I may apply there if I don't get the Great Bend slot. Beep me if you have any questions."

A half-hour later, Chris beeped Steven. He called her back. "Hey, I guess you got my message."

"I was shocked to say the least. I mean, after how aloof you were yesterday, I was seriously considering returning all your presents. But then I realized all you ever gave me was a bouquet of roses, and they're in no condition to travel."

Although her words were meant to be light-hearted, he noted a tight edge to her voice. Steven didn't want to get into a discussion about breaking up. He was sorry he had mentioned St. Joe's as an option. True, they had had something going. In a way, they needed each other. But compared to how he was beginning to feel about Jacqueline....

"Family Medicine appeals to me," Steven said. "But my first love is pedes, and neither Family Medicine nor a rotating internship will count for a first year of pediatric training."

"You train an extra year. No big deal," Chris said. "You'll be that much better prepared. Besides one year more or less of actual practice won't make much difference."

"True. But right now, I'm leaning toward getting my license and practicing for a while, before plunging into a specialty." A deepening relationship with Chris was also something he didn't want to plunge into.

"How about dinner tonight?" she asked.

"Sorry. I'm on call."

"You were on call the night before last. Don't tell me Scully's got you doing every other night?"

"It's the only way to make up the calls I missed."

"That's cruel and unusual punishment. You're going to need some time off before starting your next adventure."

A nurse tapped Steven on the shoulder. "They're waiting for you to do that spinal tap, Dr. Johnson."

He nodded. "I have to run, Chris. I'll call you when I get a chance."

Throughout the remainder of the day, Steven struggled to concentrate on patient care. How terrified Jacqueline must have been, bearing the brunt of Anwar's uncontrolled rage. And how had her lunch with Muhammad gone? Was polygamy still practiced in Algeria? Was Muhammad al-Rashid looking to add a Jamaican jewel to his collection? Yet it was irrational to worry about someone as wise and mature as Jacqueline. But neither his imagination nor his propensity to worry succumbed to logic. Jacqueline had described Mohammed as a mature, charming man. Such a man could turn the head of a young woman. Precocious wisdom was no substitute for experience.

Why had Jacqueline called Chris and not him? Had she decided to stay in Algiers for a few more days to take up Mohammed's offer to show her around?

Late that afternoon, Jerry Russo made check-out rounds with Steven, a second-year pedes resident, and the medical student who would be on call with Steven. After rounds, the resident and student went to the ER to evaluate a patient. Steven sat at the nurses' station, writing orders. Jerry Russo plunked down beside him.

"You okay?" Jerry asked. "You've been awful quiet today."

"Pretty much. Maybe I'm on a post-steroid low."

"Has it got something to do with a certain student nurse who happens to be AWOL?"

Steven wished he had confided in Jerry. "You up for a cup of coffee while I get a bite to eat?" Steven asked.

"Sorry. Gloria will break my neck if I don't get home soon." He checked his watch. "Our sitter is probably already there. We're going to dinner and a movie."

"You sure you wouldn't rather stay and help out your overworked buddy? I'm already sitting on three admissions."

Jerry looked concerned. "Hey, if we didn't already have plans--"

"I wasn't serious." Steven laughed. "I only have one admission, and that's just a routine pre-op."

Jerry, much relieved, broke into a broad grin. "How about dinner at our place some night this week?" Jerry asked.

"Sure. Pick a night. I'll be there."

"I'll check with Gloria. Bring a lady friend if you like. Chris or Jacqueline?" He laughed. "Or both!"

"Okay if I come alone?"

"Sure. Either way is fine."

After making late night rounds with his medical student, Steven wrote a brief note on each chart and longer notes on the more complicated patients. In the on-call room, he kicked off his shoes and stretched out on the lower bunk. The medical student was already asleep in the upper. In just two weeks he'd be packing his few belongings and heading for Zion. He wanted to spend time with his mother as he waited to hear from Great Bend General.

What if Great Bend didn't accept him? Despite what he had said to Chris, he wouldn't apply to St. Joe's. Baltimore was a package deal. As much as he liked Chris and felt comfortable with her, that spark he once felt hadn't evolved.

But Great Bend would separate him from Jacqueline. Ever since she left for Algiers he felt empty. When had he eaten last? He had to struggle to concentrate on his work. He pulled the palm-sized Jamaican doll from his pocket and looked at it closely. It had spiky braided hair, a blank face and a brightly colored shirt and knee-length pants. Its tiny bare feet had painted toenails.

"She's cast a spell on me. That's what she's done," he said quietly, forgetting there was a student in the bunk above him.

"Who did what?" the medical student asked.

"Nothing. You'd better get some sleep. I have a feeling it's going to be a long night."

He smelled the doll. It smelled like Jacqueline! It had a spicy feminine aroma. Was Jerry Russo right? Was Jacqueline working her magic on him? But isn't love a kind of magic? It fills you up. It empties you. A powerful force for both good and evil. A wonder worker that can change lives, even history. A trickster, quick-of-hand artist, master of smoke and mirrors, elusive, unseen and at times unseeing.

He slipped the doll into the rear pocket of his scrub suit and rolled onto his side. Soon he was asleep.

Miraculously, Steven slept from 2:00 AM until he received a call from the hospital operator. "Up and at 'em, Dr. Johnson."

"Thanks." He yawned and glanced at a wall clock. Six-thirty. He had an hour before rounds.

"I have a message from Dr. Murphy. She wants you to call her first thing. She said she'd be in her office by seven."

After showering and shaving, Steven called Chris. "Hi. What gets you up so early?"

"Anna called me late last night from her family's home in Algiers."

"That's great news." He wanted to ask if she had heard from Jacqueline. "How did Anna sound?"

"Thrilled. She said to thank you and everyone who helped. Steven, I brought in egg biscuits and coffee. Come by my office. We'll have a celebratory breakfast."

Steven slipped on a pair of scrubs. “I'm starved," he lied. "I'll be there in five minutes, but I haven't much time before rounds."

Chris’s office, usually ablaze from a pair of recessed ceiling fluorescents, was, instead, lighted by a desk-top lamp. “What, no incense?” Steven asked as he sat at her desk and reached for a bag on her desk, marked *Sunrise Biscuitville*.

“Whatever it takes,” Chris said.

Steven was hungrier than he had imagined. He consumed his egg biscuit in a matter of seconds.

"Hey, slow down. When the heck did you last eat?"

"Lunch, yesterday. Is there another biscuit in here?" He grabbed the oil-stained paper bag.

"I brought you a couple. Figured you'd be hungry."

They ate and sipped coffee from steaming Styrofoam cups. Chris was wearing a white turtle-neck jersey, form-fitting jeans and running shoes.

"Pretty casual dress, professor."

"I'm taking a mental health day. Need to pay a little more attention to my body."

It was an obvious invitation for him to flirt, but he wasn't biting. "You set a date for the big move to Baltimore?" he asked.

"Ewing called me. He was very nice. He said he was sorry to be losing one of his best teachers. Didn't even mention my little outburst."

"He's not a bad guy. I wouldn't want his job."

"He said they could hire a temporary ER doc until they recruit a replacement. When I leave is up to me."

Steven drained his coffee cup. He didn't want to talk about her leaving or his plans that did not include her. "You pick a date?"

"December first."

"Why so fast?"

"Why not? I don't see you hanging around." She walked around her desk, leaned forward, and lifted his chin.

He stood. "I have no choice. I'm leaving by popular demand."

"Well, at least one attending wrote you a great letter." She pulled him toward her.

"Thanks for everything. The breakfast included."

She smiled. "I don't know which cliché to believe. *Absence makes the heart grow fonder,* or *out of sight, out of mind.*"

"I guess only time will tell."

“A bird in hand is worth two in the bush," she said. They hugged without kissing.

“You saved my life, Chris.” Their faces separated but they remained in each other’s arms. “And I’m not just talking about the bee stings.”

Her eyes glistened with pent-up tears. *My God. She’s the last person on earth I want to hurt*. What should I say? *You’re wonderful...I almost fell in love with you?*

“I’ll treasure ever moment of our time together,” Steven whispered.

“Me too, Steven. That day by the river...remember?”

They had come close to making love. But he had sensed caution in her response. He had backed off...thank God, the way things between them were evolving.

“Of course, how could I forget?” he said

“I wish we had made love,” She turned and returned to her desk and sank into her chair. “Please don’t look at me like that. I know I’m being clingy.”

“That would only have complicated whatever it was...you, me, us.”

“You’re right. You’re right. Now get the hell out of here before I say something really stupid.”

****

The remainder of Steven's day was agonizingly slow. By late afternoon Jacqueline still hadn't appeared. Had she missed a connecting flight? Or had Omar's old car broken down? He checked his telephone messages. She hadn't called.

By the time he completed late afternoon rounds and signed out to the evening on-call team, it was close to 7:00 PM. He trudged up the hill toward his apartment. Night had already fallen. The winding path to the housestaff quarters was dimly lighted by a series of knee-high solar lanterns.

"Steven, wait."

He turned. It was Jacqueline. She was wearing a long dress. She had to pull it up as she hurried toward him. She carried what looked like a shopping bag in one hand. Steven retraced his steps toward her. Just before he reached her, he caught his foot on something. He tripped and fell into her. She lost her balance and they tumbled down alongside the path. The bag she was carrying flew from her hand. Two Styrofoam cartons split open, spilling Chinese food onto the grass.

"I'm such a klutz," he said.

"Men keep knocking me off my feet."

"I heard about that. The bastard." He examined her right cheek. Even in the dim light he could see a faint bruise. "Bastard," he repeated. He helped her up. "Are you okay?"

"I think so. It was a marvelous welcome, Steven. Next time we meet I'll be better prepared."

He looked at the steamy food she had been carrying. "You were bringing me dinner?"

"Yes. I know how you forget to eat."

"Can I take you to dinner?"

"Yes. And I will pay." She smiled. "I have a credit card. They are wonderful things."

They walked hand-in-hand along the path toward his apartment. "Chris told me that Anna is back with her family."

"Yes. They were so kind to me...grateful for what I had done. Tahar at first was distrustful, but he came around after he saw his sister on video. In fact, it was he who came to my rescue when Anwar attacked me."

"I wish I had been there."

"It is nothing to concern yourself with. Anwar is a sick man. He also needs help."

Steven nodded. "As usual, you're right. Tell me about your charming banker."

"Muhammad. Yes."

"You had lunch with him and his daughter?"

"His daughter could not come."

Steven stopped at the door to his apartment. "I knew it. I bet he made a pass at you."

"Not exactly."

"What does that mean?"

"He said that regretfully, polygamy is no longer legal in Algeria. Then he laughed and showed me pictures of his wife and daughter. What he had told me on the plane was very helpful."

They stepped into Steven's apartment. "Excuse the mess. There's coke in the fridge. I need to take a quick shower and change my clothes. Make yourself at home."

As he showered, Jacqueline looked through his record collection. She found a Bob Marley CD. She slipped it into his pint-sized boom-box. When he left the bathroom with a towel wrapped around his waist, he saw her dancing, slowly to the beat of the reggae music, her eyes closed. She was quietly singing along with *Is This Love*. He stood watching her, entranced. She suddenly stopped and opened her eyes. She glanced at him, then turned away. "I am so embarrassed."

"Hey, I was the one staring. I'll be out in two minutes flat. You'll have to teach me to dance like that."

She was poking through his other CDs when he returned. She looked up. He was wearing white denim slacks and a long-sleeved dark blue sport shirt. "You look fresh for one who has had such little sleep."

"You want to skip dinner? Just hang out, talk, and dance?"

"I'm already light in the head from low sugar. We can dance after we eat?"

He went to a closet and came back with a couple of helmets and two jackets. He slipped on one of the jackets. "Better put these on. Gets a little chilly in my limo."

She looked at her ankle-length dress. "But how can I?"

"You can ride side-saddle. I'll go extra slow. I don't want to lose you going around a corner. Unless you'd rather change into a set of scrubs?"

"You do not like my dress?"

"I love your dress. Maybe I should call a cab."

Jacqueline slipped on the helmet and jacket. "No. Let's go. I will ride side-saddle."

"You'll have to hold on extra tight," he said as he cinched the helmet strap under her chin. Their faces were inches apart. Her perfume reminded him of the small doll she had given him.

"You will be surprised," she whispered, "how strong I can hold onto you."

Chapter Thirty-One

During the week following Jacqueline's return from Algiers, Steven waited anxiously for word from Great Bend General. He also spent almost all his free time, what little there was, with Jacqueline. She rounded with him each morning. They had lunch together when they could, went for long walks and bike rides, and on his only weekend day off, took in a Princeton home football game.

The subject of his leaving never came up. He was sure it was as much on her mind as his. Three days before Steven was due to leave Smithfield, Dr. McCullough called, confirming that Great Bend General had decided to offer him a rotating internship. A contract was in the mail.

That evening he took Jacqueline to dinner at the Silver Bullet. Now that his plans were definite, they had to talk.

It was a cool night. Jacqueline had worn her navy- blue cape. She slipped it off as she slid into the booth opposite him. A waitress handed them menus and placed a basket of warm dinner rolls on the table.

"What is on your mind tonight, Steven? You are looking very serious."

"I'm relieved you can't actually read my mind."

"I can read your face. It tells me things."

"You mean my expression?"

"No. Expression reveals only what the person intends. It's what the face attempts to hide that is more interesting."

"As you like to say, 'I'll have to think on that.'"

She sipped her water as she studied the menu. "Tell me what is on your mind."

Steven buttered a roll. He took a bite. "I heard from the hospital in Kansas. They offered me an internship."

"Isn't that what you wanted?"

"Kansas is a long way from New Jersey."

She smiled. "What will you miss? The hospital food? The New Jersey Turnpike?"

Steven buttered another roll. "Jacqueline, when will you be twenty-one?

"That is a different subject."

"I'm considering abducting you. The penalties are more severe when you abduct a minor."

"Even if the minor desires to be abducted?"

"It's assumed that a minor is too easily led astray by one who is more experienced in the affairs of life."

She laughed. "A debaucher? You?"

"Exactly."

Jacqueline squeezed a lemon slice and dropped it into her water. "Yes, you are more experienced. But you are none of those other things."

"You see," he said. "The face doesn't always show what's on the mind."

"You must also look at a person's life." She looked about the crowded diner and spoke in almost a whisper. "Your kindness to others, what you choose to do, what you value most. Those things tell me what is in the heart."

"Can you see into mine?" he asked.

"We've made rounds together. I know how you talk with the children. How much you care to help them. How you risked so much to help Anna."

The waitress approached their table. "You folks need more time?"

Steven ordered chicken pot-pie and a side order of fries. Jacqueline ordered a bowl of chili and coffee.

"Anything to drink, Dr. Johnson?" the waitress asked as she gathered up the menus.

"Coffee please." Steven was surprised she knew his name. "Have we met?"

"I brought my daughter to the ER a couple of months ago."

He looked at her more closely. "Yes, of course. Your child was the little girl with the nasty spider bite. How is she?"

"Fine. She loves the tongue thingies you gave her. She plays doctor with her dolls."

After the waitress left, Jacqueline said, "I am dining with a famous pediatrician." She sipped her water. "When will you start to work at the hospital in Kansas?"

"Two weeks after I finish here. I want to spend some time with my mother."

"Is her condition not better?"

"I spoke with her doctor a couple of days ago. The medicine's helping some."

"You are the medicine she needs. Will you ride your motorcycle to Kansas?

"Yes."

"What of your things?"

"I don't have much. Mostly books, my stereo and television. I'm going to buy a small two-wheeled trailer to drag along behind my bike."

Jacqueline added hot sauce to her chili. "I will be twenty-one in six months."

He realized she was telling him that at twenty-one she would be in control of her life. Not her cousin Omar or even her mother. “You were born in the spring. I should have known."

She looked up. There were tears in her eyes. "I guess I added too much hot sauce."

He reached out and held onto her hand. "I promise to write every day."

She intertwined her fingers with his. "I do not want letters. I want to be with you."

"Jacqueline, there is nothing I would like more. But you must think this through. You're here on a student visa."

"Is there a nursing program at the hospital in Great Bend?"

"A hospital that size...yes I suppose there is. I'll check first thing tomorrow."

The following day, Steven and Jacqueline walked to a pay phone in the hospital lobby.

"Since they've already offered me a position," Steven said, "I believe it might help if I called Dr. McCullough."

He dialed Great Bend Hospital.

"Yes, we do have student nurses," Dr. McCullough said, "but just the two clinical years. They spend the first two years at the medical school in Kansas City."

"I have a very close lady-friend here at Smithfield." He winked at Jacqueline. "She just started her third year as a student nurse. Is there any chance she could transfer to your program?"

"I see. Hmm. Well, I certainly don't want a love-sick intern on my hands. I'll connect you to the director of nursing. Hold on."

Steven waited for her to come on the line. He covered the telephone mouthpiece. "Hopefully Dr. McCullough's doing a little arm-twisting."

"Hello, this is Miss Greene. Dr. McCullough just told me of your inquiry concerning our nurses' training program. Where did your friend receive the first two years of training?"

"In Jamaica."

“Was she in a degree program?” Miss Greene asked.

“I believe so. Would you like to speak to her? She's right here."

Steven put Jacqueline on the line. He checked his beeper. There were two messages. One was from the nurses' station on the pedes ward. He walked to a bank of in-house telephones and dialed the number.

"Dr. Johnson, did you forget you're supposed to be assisting Dr. Scully in the procedure room?"

"Thanks for the reminder. I'll be right there."

When he turned, Jacqueline was standing behind him, smiling radiantly. "What did she say?" he asked.

"That if I meet their entrance requirements, there is an excellent chance they will accept me. She needs a copy of my

Smithfield record and a letter from my nursing supervisor. She also needs a transcript from the nursing program I attended in Jamaica. She said even with the materials from Smithfield, she can't offer me a position until they receive my transcript.”

"That will take a couple of weeks or longer."

"If I don't get the hospital position, I can find a job in Great Bend. I am a good cook. I can type. I will not starve."

"But you have a student visa."

"Will you report me?"

He grabbed her hand and drew her close to him. He didn't care who might be looking. "You might want to fly to Kansas. I can drop you off at the airport. A direct flight will get you there in about four hours. On my bike, it'll take two days."

"You do not want me to go with you?"

"You'll have to travel light."

"Will one suitcase and a backpack be too much?"

"Give your suitcase to Omar. Bring your things in a plastic bag."

"Why?"

"A suitcase won't fit in my caboose. You'll need long pants, a warm jacket, boots and gloves. If we run into bad weather, the trip may take an extra day or two."

They embraced, oblivious of the glances of visitors, doctors and hospital personnel who streamed past them. They kissed.

"In just three days we will fly away to Zion," Steven whispered.

"Yes," Jacqueline said, paraphrasing, "*one bright morning, when our work is over, man and woman will fly away home*."

Made in the USA
Columbia, SC
15 September 2017